Relentless

REBECCA DEEL

ISBN-13: 9781791720049

DEDICATION

To my amazing husband. You make the journey fun. I love you.

ACKNOWLEDGMENTS

Cover design by Melody Simmons.

CHAPTER ONE

Piper Reece threw open the back door of Wicks, the candle shop where she worked, and rushed into the alley. She pawed through her favorite pink purse for shop keys that had slipped to the bottom and disappeared. She had to hurry.

A heavy footstep sounded nearby. Piper froze, hand still buried in her bag. She glanced around the darkened alley, looking for the source of the noise. She frowned. The light over the shop's door was burned out, leaving the area bathed in shadows and pools of deepest midnight. She had changed the bulb herself last week.

Later. She didn't have time now. Gavin, a man she'd hadn't spoken to for three years, had called and begged for help. Piper grimaced. Gavin wanted something from her. She almost refused to meet him. His voice, though, conveyed an emotion she never expected to hear from her former boyfriend. Bone-deep fear.

Another footstep, closer this time, caused goosebumps to surge across Piper's skin. Otter Creek, Tennessee, wasn't a major metropolitan city. It was safe. Not only did Otter Creek have great police officers, the town was also the home of Personal Security International, a training school for bodyguards. Bad things didn't happen here.

Right. So why did she feel like someone stalked her in the darkness? Not for the first time, she wished Liam McCoy was here. Unfortunately, he was out of town with his teammates, return date and mission location unknown to her. Liam guarded information about the details of his work.

Piper wanted to know everything. The operative fascinated her. Building a lasting relationship with Liam was a challenge when he kept disappearing for weeks at a stretch because of his job. Good thing she enjoyed challenges.

Uneasiness grew in her gut. She needed to leave the alley and go to the lighted street. Next time she closed the shop alone, Piper promised herself to leave by the front door where the area was well lit. She usually did. Today, however, the parking spaces near the shop were full and she had parked further away. Leaving by the back door saved her a few steps. No more being lazy, though.

Piper's fingers wrapped around her shop keys. She yanked them out, found the right key, and reached for the knob to close the door.

A hard hand clamped over her mouth and a rock-hard arm encircled her waist, plucking Piper off her feet. Her purse and keys fell to the ground.

She kicked and thrashed, desperate to free herself. Who was this creep?

"Stop fighting or I'll hurt you," the man growled. "Cooperate and you might live to see tomorrow."

Piper didn't believe that for a minute. She couldn't let him take her away from the shop. Redoubling her efforts to escape, Piper dislodged Rock's hand enough to scream.

The thug swore, slapped his hand over her mouth again, and raced toward the street.

Hope bloomed inside Piper. Maybe a passerby would help her. Rock reached the mouth of the alley with Piper still fighting him and ran to a black van idling on the street, side door open.

No! Piper gave a muffled scream. Rock's hand pressed harder against her mouth, cutting the inside of her lip.

"Shut up!" He covered the remaining few feet to the vehicle in long-legged strides and threw Piper into the back of the van.

She righted herself and dived toward the opening. Houses were on the next block. One of Wicks's Otter Creek neighbors would offer her sanctuary until the police arrived. Assistance was two minutes away.

With a furious curse, Rock backhanded Piper and shoved her back inside, this time climbing in after her and slamming the door. "Go!" he yelled at the driver.

Rock turned a glare her direction. "You're more trouble than you're worth, Ms. Reece." He loomed over Piper. "You better hope we find you useful for a long time."

Piper cradled her aching cheek with her palm. "What do you want?"

"We're going on a treasure hunt."

Treasure hunt? She stared. "I don't understand."

"You will retrieve information for us."

What was he talking about? "And if I don't?"

"I call my associate and your boyfriend dies."

Blood drained from Piper's cheeks. Rock and his friends had Liam? No way. Liam was with his teammates. She didn't know what Bravo did on their mysterious missions, but she'd heard the members of a second black ops team assigned to PSI talk about them with great respect and that was saying something. The other team had served together in the military and were some kind of elite Special Forces unit. If Bravo was in the same league as Durango, Rock and his friends couldn't defeat them and take Liam.

But what if they had? What if these men had ambushed Bravo and captured Liam? Her breath caught at the possibility that Liam could be hurt. These men might also be lying to her.

Her friend and boss, Delilah Rainer, shared minimal information about her husband, Matt, a teammate of Liam's. Their work involved dangerous tasks and a great deal of secrecy. Saying the wrong thing now would endanger Liam and his team. "I don't know what information you're talking about."

Rock wrapped his meaty hand around her throat and squeezed. "Rethink that, Ms. Reece, or you'll be dead along with your boyfriend."

CHAPTER TWO

Liam McCoy turned right on Poplar Avenue and drove toward Wicks. Piper should be working, and he couldn't wait to see her. He'd spent three weeks in a backwater cesspool country with his black ops team tracking and rescuing a diplomat's daughter, a hostage of terrorists. On the way home, Fortress had sent his unit into Venezuela to assist another team.

He'd gone too long without seeing Piper Reece's beautiful eyes. Liam had planned to ask if Piper was interested in an exclusive relationship with him. Bravo had deployed unexpectedly in the middle of the night and he wasn't able to broach the topic before his team left the country.

If Piper agreed to exclusivity, he would give her the secured cell phone he'd obtained for her to use. He'd missed her like crazy while deployed this last time. At least with a secured cell phone, Liam would be able to talk to her when he was on a mission.

He snorted. For a man who prided himself on operating in the field without support for weeks at a time, the fast attachment to Piper puzzled him. Somehow, she had slipped under his skin.

Liam parked in front of the candle shop. The lights were off. He glanced at his watch. Thirty minutes before the shop was due to close and the place appeared deserted. Maybe Piper was in the office.

He exited the SUV and walked around the side of the shop toward the rear of the building. Since he didn't want to scare her by banging on the back door, Liam grabbed his phone and called Piper's cell.

He heard the ring tone she'd chosen for him and frowned. Was she in the dark alley? Why wasn't the security light on over the back door?

Liam ended the call, slid his phone away, and palmed his weapon. Something was wrong. Worry for Piper's safety gnawed at him.

When he reached the mouth of the alley, Liam peered around the corner of the building and froze. The door to Wicks stood open, and Piper's purse and keys lay on the ground outside the door.

On silent booted feet, Liam approached the doorway, weapon up and tracking. If nothing was wrong and he scared Piper, he'd apologize profusely and convince her he'd been worried about her safety. But he wasn't wrong. The woman haunting his dreams at night adored that ridiculous pink purse. She'd never leave the handbag and shop keys on the ground in an alley.

He paused at the door and listened. No sounds coming from the interior of the building. Liam moved into the candle shop. Still no sign of life.

Urgency beating at him, he walked toward the office, senses on alert. Where was Piper? Within two minutes, he'd determined the woman he sought wasn't in the building.

Liam returned to the alley, leaving everything as he'd found it, and ran to his SUV.

He called Josh Cahill, an instructor at PSI and a cop on the Otter Creek police force. "It's Liam. Piper's missing."

"Sit rep." Josh's clipped tone and military jargon forced Liam to focus.

"I'm at Wicks. The shop's rear door is standing open and Piper's purse and the shop keys are lying in the alley. She's not inside Wicks."

"Did you touch anything?"

"No, sir."

"I'll call it in and be at the shop in ten minutes."

"I won't be here. I'm calling Zane to see what he can tell me." Zane Murphy was the tech guru at Fortress Security, the parent company of Personal Security International. "If Zane gives me a direction, I'm going after Piper."

"Understood. Keep me in the loop. Remember, you're not a cop."

"You remember the same. I'll do whatever is necessary to protect Piper." No matter what it took. Liam ended the call to Josh and contacted Zane.

"You just returned to Otter Creek, Liam. I thought you'd be too busy with a certain woman to call me," Zane Murphy teased.

"I need help."

"Talk to me."

"Piper is missing." He gave Zane the address of the shop. "I need you to hack into traffic cams in the area."

"Time frame?"

"I arrived at Wicks at 5:30 p.m. The back door was open with Piper's purse and keys on the ground."

"I'll contact you the minute I find anything."

"Hurry, Z." Gut instinct told him Piper was in deep trouble.

"Copy that." Zane ended the call.

Liam punched in the number for his teammate, Matt. He hated to interrupt the newlyweds' reunion, but Delilah needed to know about Piper.

"What's up?" Matt asked.

He summarized what he'd found. "Z's checking the traffic cams."

"Call the cops?"

"Josh will be here soon. If Z gives me a direction, I'm going after Piper."

"Delilah wants to come to the shop to see if anything is missing. Do you want help with the search for Piper?"

Liam appreciated the offer, but his friend needed to be with his wife who must be shaken by the news. "Stay with Delilah. I'll call if I need you."

"I'll alert the rest of the team. We'll be on standby."

"Thanks."

"Watch your back, Liam."

A moment later, Liam's phone rang. He glanced at the screen. Zane. "Tell me you found something."

"Late model black van with tinted windows racing away from the alley behind Wicks." He paused.

"Talk to me, Z." Liam's hand clenched around the cell phone.

"I'll send you the footage so you can see for yourself. She's alive but her abductors aren't afraid to hurt her."

Cold fury swept through Liam. "Which direction did they drive?"

"I tracked them to Highway 18. They're still moving."

Liam cranked his engine and sped away from Wicks. "Tag number?" He memorized the license plate number Zane rattled off.

"It's a rental from the Knoxville airport."

He frowned. Highway 18 intersected with Interstate 40, the main thoroughfare through Knoxville. If Liam didn't stop them, the kidnappers could force Piper onto a private plane, making it almost impossible to track her.

Liam pressed the accelerator to the floor as soon as he merged onto the highway. "How many kidnappers?"

"I saw two, the driver and the thug who grabbed your woman."

His woman. Liam's heart skipped a beat at that description of Piper. "I don't want to pull over and look at the footage. Tell me what happened."

Zane complied.

Liam's hands clenched around the steering wheel as his friend described Piper fighting against the thug who hit her.

"The kidnapper backhanded Piper. I don't think he wanted to seriously injure her."

"Yet. He's not afraid to use force to get what he wants." But what did he want? Uppermost in Liam's mind was the possibility of rape. Then again, if that was his intent, the kidnapper would probably go after Piper alone.

Information? Liam scowled. What information? Piper worked in a candle shop. She didn't have access to sensitive government secrets.

Nausea boiled in Liam's stomach. But he did. Had his enemies tracked him down and targeted the only woman to capture his interest since he joined Fortress? Liam prayed he was wrong because his enemies were ruthless and wouldn't blink at hurting an innocent woman to draw him out. "One of the kidnappers had to present ID to rent the van."

"John Brown. I checked the address. A vacant lot in Philadelphia."

He growled. "Van still on course?"

"Yeah. Just passed Cherry Hill."

Liam glanced at the speedometer. He'd be lucky if one of the county cops or Highway Patrol didn't pull him over. "Call Ethan Blackhawk. Have him contact law enforcement agencies in the area. Explain what's happening because I'm not stopping, Z. If these clowns reach the airport and force Piper onto a plane, I may never find her."

"The cops will want to handle this on their own."

"They are backup only. They can have the collar but we're doing this my way."

Zane was silent for a moment. "You think this is connected to you?"

"I have to assume as much until I talk to Piper."

"Hold." The phone was silent while Zane called Otter Creek's police chief.

Weaving in and out of traffic, Liam used his combat driving skills to keep his reinforced SUV on the road and avoid civilian drivers.

Two minutes later, Zane's voice filled the cabin again. "Done. The Highway Patrol is setting up a road block at the entrance ramp to Interstate 40. I'm monitoring their transmissions. They won't be in place for another twenty minutes."

"Too late. The kidnappers will be halfway to Knoxville by then. Do the cops know not to stop me?"

"They do. Whether they'll cooperate is unknown."

Frustration swamped Liam. If the cops were trigger happy, he could end up on the receiving end of a bullet. "Any change in the van's direction?"

"Negative. Still on course for the interstate."

Liam coaxed a little more speed from his vehicle. "How far away is Piper?"

The clicking of keys on the keyboard filled the cabin. "Seven miles. Interstate entrance ramp is sixteen miles ahead."

"Copy that."

"Want me to contact your team?"

"Call Matt. He'll inform the others."

"Hold." Zane returned a moment later. "Matt's on his way with Simon. He said for you to shut up and deal."

He gave a short huff of laughter. Matt told the members of Bravo what they needed to hear. Liam wouldn't need backup to handle two kidnappers. However, if they had friends waiting along the route, things would be more challenging. Besides, he wanted Matt to check Piper for injuries.

"You should see the van in the next mile. Want me to stay with you?"

"No. Keep monitoring their movements. Let me know if they pull off the highway."

"Copy that. Contact me when your woman is safe."

"Thanks, Z." Liam ended the call and floored the accelerator. The SUV leaped ahead.

Thirty seconds later, he saw a black van racing toward the interstate entrance ramp.

CHAPTER THREE

Liam confirmed the van in front of him was the target vehicle and scanned ahead for a suitable place to force the kidnappers off the road. The trick was to stop them without endangering Piper.

Nothing but ditches, trees, rocks and rock faces lay between the van and the interstate. That left one option. He passed the van on the left and whipped in front of the vehicle.

Hoping his ride was as reinforced as Bear, the favored Fortress mechanic, had promised, Liam braced himself for impact and hit his brakes. At the speed with which the van was traveling, the driver didn't have time to react. He slammed into the back of the SUV.

Liam fought to control the slide as the van's momentum shoved his SUV forward. As soon as both vehicles stopped, Liam scrambled out the passenger side door and rolled to a crouch, Sig drawn and ready.

He moved to the rear fender well, the section in the deepest shadow. He saw the driver but not the thug in the back. He also didn't see the woman who was sunshine to his darkness.

"Get out of the vehicle with your hands up," Liam ordered. "Now."

The driver stirred, glanced back into the cargo area, leaned to the side for a second, then opened the door.

He had a gun. Liam scowled. Idiot. He hated that Piper might have to see him kill someone, but her safety was paramount even if he lost her because of it.

The driver raised one hand in the air. "Hey, man, sorry about the accident. Couldn't stop fast enough."

"Raise both hands."

"Can't. I, uh, think I cracked a rib or something. Hurts too bad to reach with my right hand."

Keeping the passenger side door in his peripheral vision, Liam waited for the driver to make his move. "Walk toward me."

The driver shuffled toward the front of the van. At the last second, he raised his right hand and pointed a weapon at Liam and fired.

Liam squeezed the trigger of his Sig. His bullet pierced the driver's forehead. The body dropped to the ground. Liam dove into the ditch as the van's side door opened and the second thug fired multiple shots at him.

"Back off or I kill the woman," the kidnapper shouted.

"Not going to happen."

"You think I'm kidding?"

"I think you want to walk away in one piece. If you harm her, you're a dead man."

A harsh laugh. "Want to negotiate?"

"Terms."

"Safe passage out of this wilderness."

"Let her go and you walk away."

"Just like that?" Skepticism rang in the stranger's voice. "How do I know you'll keep your word?"

"You don't."

"Not much of a bargain."

"I want the woman. You want to save your own skin. Guess it comes down to which one you value more." He silently urged the thug to make up his mind. Liam needed to check on Piper.

"Yeah, all right. We're coming out. Don't shoot." Seconds later, a big bruiser appeared, using Piper as a human shield. His arm was wrapped around her neck to hold her in place, a weapon held by his side.

Liam's lip curled. Piper wasn't a good human shield. Although the thug kept her in the center of his chest to protect his heart and hunched enough to obscure most of his head, Liam had been trained by the best snipers in the business. He didn't need a large target to do a lot of damage.

"Put down your gun," demanded the kidnapper.

"And if I don't?"

An ugly smile curved the other man's mouth. "I'll shoot her, then kill you. In fact, I kind of like that idea. Get rid of the broad and you at the same time." His hand tensed around the stock of an HK, forefinger stroking the trigger.

Although Liam longed to assess Piper's injuries, he didn't dare. He had to remain focused on the target.

Liam saw the exact moment the kidnapper made his decision. The choice had just been taken from Liam's hands. "Piper, do you trust me?"

"Yes." No hesitation.

Thank God. "Close your eyes and drop."

Piper lifted her feet and slipped from the man's grip.

Liam pulled the trigger. The kidnapper's body went limp as part of his head disappeared in a pink mist.

"Liam." Piper remained stock still on her knees, eyes still closed, her expression one of terror.

He scrambled from the ditch, shoved his weapon into his thigh holster, and whipped off his black t-shirt. "Keep your eyes closed for another minute. You're safe now."

"Are you hurt?"

That made him pause for a second before he raised his cloth-covered hand to wipe Piper's face. "I'm fine." Aside from his mother and sister, no woman had ever worried about his safety. When he'd been active-duty military, women had seen the uniform, not the man. As a result, he hadn't dated much.

The situation hadn't been much different in Otter Creek. The women in town knew he worked for PSI and they were fascinated with his job, not him.

Piper was the exception. She never asked about his work other than wanting to know if he or his teammates were injured each time he returned from deployment. Other than that, she seemed content to let him share what he wanted about his work, concentrating on getting to know him when they were together.

After making sure her face was cleared of blood and brain matter, he did what he could with her hair and shirt.

"Is it safe to open my eyes?"

"Another minute." Liam crouched beside her and laid his hand on her shoulder. "I'm going to carry you to my SUV. It's safer than standing at the roadside."

"Isn't the danger over now?"

His gaze swept the area. "Not sure." Liam lifted her hands to his shoulders and helped her stand. "Wrap your arms around my neck. My SUV is reinforced and has bullet-resistant glass."

As soon as her arms encircled his neck, Liam bent and slid an arm behind her knees and lifted Piper against his chest. "Keep your eyes closed another minute." He didn't want her to see the men he killed.

He placed her on the passenger seat of his SUV. "You can open your eyes now."

Piper blinked, then her gaze focused on Liam's face. She launched herself into his arms.

Liam gathered her tight against his chest, grateful to have her in his arms once again. "I've got you."

She shuddered. "Thank you, Liam."

"I'm glad I was close enough to help." He eased back and studied her face, focusing on the bruised and swollen cheekbone. Liam's fingers brushed over her skin. "Are you okay?"

She nodded. "He didn't have a chance to do anything other than threaten to hurt me."

He heard sirens in the distance and knew time was running out to get answers before he was separated from her. That thought didn't sit well with him. He wanted someone he trusted with her at all times until he could take over her security. "What did the men want?"

Piper frowned. "Information and they threatened to kill my boyfriend if I didn't cooperate."

"Your boyfriend?" Was her abduction connected to him? Or were they referring to another man? Liam's eyes narrowed. "Did they mention your boyfriend by name?"

She shook her head. "When can we leave?"

"Not for a while. The police will have many questions and you should be checked by medical personnel."

"I'm fine. I want to get out of here."

He frowned. Liam understood her need to separate herself from the crime scene, but she seemed almost desperate to leave.

The cops would be here any minute. Both of them would be tied up for hours. Liam sent Josh a text to tell him what happened, then sent another text to Matt, asking him and Simon to watch over Piper.

That done, he handed his cell phone to Piper and told her the code to unlock it.

"Why are you giving me your phone?"

"I want you to have access to help. My teammates and Durango are programmed into the contact list. Matt and Simon will be here in a few minutes. Don't allow the cops or ambulance to take you to the hospital until Matt's with you."

"Where will you be?"

He cupped her jaw and stroked her velvety skin with his thumb. "In police custody."

Piper's eyes widened. "Why?"

"Two reasons. When the cops roll up, they won't know if I'm one of the kidnappers. Until they determine my role, I'll be handcuffed and taken to a local police station for questioning. They'll get it sorted out eventually."

"And the second reason you'll be in custody?"

He wondered if this was the last time he would see Piper. "I killed both men. They didn't leave me another option, Piper."

When she started to turn, Liam caught her chin in a gentle hold. "Don't. You'll have nightmares without seeing the evidence yourself."

Instead of backing away in disgust as Liam had expected, Piper once again wrapped her arms around him. "You could have been shot saving me."

"Better me than you."

"Not in my book. I'll never be able to repay you."

He squeezed her tight, marveling that she allowed him to touch her. "I don't want repayment." He just wanted her in his life.

Two police cruisers skidded to a stop and four officers bailed from the vehicles with weapons drawn.

Piper held on when he would have eased away from her.

"I'll be all right. I promise," he murmured against her ear. Piper shivered and tightened her grip.

"Get on your knees, hands locked behind your head," one officer ordered.

"Liam." Piper's eyes glittered with unshed tears.

"Trust me." He straightened, clasped his hands behind his head, and backed away from Piper, his gaze locked with hers. When he was far enough away, Liam knelt on the asphalt.

Tears trickled down Piper's cheeks as law enforcement rushed Liam and forced him to the ground. Man, he hated this, hated her tears.

One of the cops yanked Liam's arms down and cuffed his wrists as another headed for Piper.

"You'll need my Sig from my thigh holster." Hated to give up his Sig, too. He doubted the weapon would be released anytime soon.

"You carrying more weapons?" another officer asked.

"Backup piece on my right calf, boot knife, and Ka-Bar."

The air grew thick with tension. One of the officers swore softly. "Why are you carrying that much hardware?"

"I'm with Personal Security International."

A snort. "That mercenary outfit out of Otter Creek? Bunch of good old boys with peashooters."

"Shut up, Vince. I did some training at PSI," said another. "They're a legitimate outfit, the training arm of Fortress Security."

"Ma'am, you need to come with me." The fourth cop reached for Piper. "You'll be safer in the squad car."

"I'm not moving from this vehicle."

"You don't have a choice."

Liam's hands fisted. He turned his face toward the man familiar with PSI. "Tell your buddy to back off. Piper is waiting for one of the PSI medics to arrive to check her."

"He'll keep her safe in the squad car."

"My ride is more reinforced than your state-issued vehicle. What will it hurt to leave her inside for another five minutes?"

A slight nod. "Al, leave her alone. She's fine."

Al scowled. "How can you say that? This guy is dangerous."

"Never to her," Liam insisted. "Piper and I are dating."

A blinding smile lit her face at his statement.

Wow. His heart turned over in his chest. Beautiful.

"Is that true, ma'am?" the cop at Piper's side asked.

"Yes, it is."

"Help me get him up," the cop by Liam said.

A moment later, he leaned back against his SUV a few feet from Piper. At least he could better protect her from this position. "Thanks," he murmured. "I'm Liam McCoy."

"You're with Bravo?"

He glanced at the man's name tag. "That's right, Colton. I don't remember training you."

"Your team was deployed the week I was there. Want to tell me what happened here? We got a call from Otter Creek's police chief to assist with road blocks to stop a black van involved in a kidnapping."

"That's correct." He explained what he'd found at Wicks.

"How did you know where the van was headed? Did you see the men take her?"

"A friend checked the traffic cams."

"What happened when you caught up with the van?"

Liam gave him the short version, ending with, "I didn't have a choice. The kidnapper threatened to kill Piper. He'd already made the decision in his mind."

"You a mind reader?" Vince snapped.

"I've been in this business a long time. Body language and eyes telegraph a wealth of information."

"What's your specialty?" Colton asked.

"Sniper."

A soft whistle greeted his statement. "Guess you've seen enough action to know the truth when you see it."

More than he wanted.

An ambulance screeched to a halt in front of the SUV. The EMTs grabbed their gear. One checked on the status of the two kidnappers. The other approached the officers.

"What do we have?"

Al motioned to Piper. "Kidnapping victim."

"Let's have a look."

Piper glanced at Liam. He gave her a nod. As long as the EMT didn't try to take her to a hospital without one of Bravo to keep watch over her, he didn't see the harm in on-site first aid.

Five minutes later, a familiar black SUV parked at the side of the road.

Relief flooded Liam. He looked at Colton. "Two of my teammates just arrived. One of them is a medic. I want Matt to check Piper."

"You don't have a say in what happens here, McCoy." Vince scowled at him. "You'll be transported to the station as soon as the detectives arrive."

Liam remained focused on Colton. "I'm not sure Piper is out of danger. I want someone I trust with her."

Matt climbed from the SUV with his mike bag in hand followed by Simon.

"No harm in that, I guess." Colton motioned for his partner to let the operatives through.

The medic scanned Liam. "No injuries?"

He shook his head. "One of the kidnappers backhanded Piper."

A scowl from his friend.

Piper pushed aside the EMTs hand. "I'd rather have my friend check me," she told him.

"I'm a trained EMT, ma'am. I can help you."

"I want Matt to do it."

"Whatever," the man muttered. He got up and moved to make room for Matt.

The medic spoke softly to Piper and checked her for injuries. Two minutes later, he reached into his mike bag and pulled out a chemically-activated ice pack. He shook the pack and laid it against Piper's cheek. He said something to Simon who trotted toward their SUV and returned with a blanket.

Matt shook out the cover and wrapped it around her shoulders. He glanced at Liam. "A few bruises. I think she'll be fine, but she needs to be checked out at the hospital."

"We'll transport her," the EMT said, a smirk on his face.

"No." Liam stared at the man until he dropped his gaze and looked away. "Matt and Simon will take her to Memorial Hospital in Otter Creek."

Colton frowned. "That's out of our jurisdiction."

"I want her on our home turf and the original crime happened in Otter Creek. Blackhawk will have a say in the jurisdiction. Your detectives can ask her questions after she's been cleared by a doctor." Liam trusted Matt's opinion more than any doctor's. The extra time, however, would give Piper a chance to settle.

A nondescript car rolled up and parked. Unmarked police unit. The detectives had arrived. Let the circus begin.

CHAPTER FOUR

"What aren't you telling me, Ms. Reece?" Kevin Ralston asked. Anger simmered in the Cherry Hill detective's eyes. "I'll charge you with obstruction of justice if I find out you withheld pertinent case information."

"I can't tell you what I don't know." Piper's patience ran thin. Her face hurt, Liam was still being detained, and Piper wanted out of this hospital.

"But you suspect something else. I need every bit of information I can get."

"Why?" She refused to apologize for her cross tone. "The kidnappers are dead. I'm safe." Except Liam wasn't convinced that was true. Remembering his concern made goosebumps surge up her spine.

The man wasn't one to overreact to anything. After hearing his comment to the county cop, Piper understood why nothing rattled Liam. Snipers had legendary icy control in order to do their jobs under extreme conditions.

Although excellent at his job, Liam's feelings ran deep beneath the surface. But Piper had caught a tantalizing glimpse of them on the roadside tonight. For an instant, his control slipped as he held her in his arms. One revealing statement. I've got you. A possessive tone, the relief, the almost desperate hold all added up to a man more emotionally invested in their relationship than he'd let on. The little sneak. She wished he'd let on that he felt more than mere friendship. Would have saved her several sleepless nights.

"I have loose ends to tie up," Ralston insisted. "I need to be sure your boyfriend wasn't behind the kidnapping attempt."

Piper froze. Did the detective know about Gavin? No way. She hadn't seen Gavin in years. Why had he called her? That question plagued her during the abduction, rescue, and subsequent medical care. She and Gavin hadn't parted on amicable terms. Why turn to her now?

Matt stirred. He'd remained quiet during the police questioning. "You're accusing Liam of setting up Piper's kidnapping?"

Piper stared at the small-town cop.

"He has the skills to pull it off." Ralston glared at Matt.

"Why would he do that? He and Piper have been dating for months."

A shrug. "Impress the girl."

Piper rolled her eyes. "He already impresses me by being who he is. He doesn't need to set up a fake abduction and ride to the rescue. Liam has been out of town. How would he have arranged a kidnapping when he didn't know the day or time of his return to the area?"

"Men have egos. Maybe he felt the need to prove himself."

"No." Matt's eyes were filled with anger. "He didn't need to do that. Piper knows what he does for a living. Those men used weapons. One of them hit Piper. Liam would never endanger someone he cares about. We have lethal skills, Ralston. We're trained by the best military and black ops people in the business. We're not teenagers out to impress a gullible woman. We don't play games with people's lives."

"How well do you know McCoy, Rainer?"

"I've spent five years in the trenches with him. You get to know the people at your back in a firefight. I trust him with my life and have on more than one occasion."

"A lot of loyalty is built in foxholes," Ralston said. "That doesn't mean he's the man you think he is in a more personal arena." He turned his attention back to Piper. "How well do you know McCoy?"

"Liam isn't behind the kidnapping. I trust him."

"He used lethal force on the highway, shooting a man pressed against your back. The man you trusted with your life could have had faulty aim and shot you instead of the alleged kidnapper."

Matt shook his head. "Liam doesn't miss his shots. He wouldn't have pulled the trigger unless he knew he could make it."

Fury flared inside Piper. "He did what was necessary to save my life."

A snort. "You don't know that. McCoy is a killer for hire, Ms. Reece. I hope you wise up before you end up dead." Ralston reached into his pocket and pulled out a business card. He pressed it into her hand. "Call me if you think of anything else or if you need help." His intense stare left Piper in no doubt as to what kind of help he expected her to need.

The detective paused with his hand on the door knob and glanced over his shoulder. "Don't wait too late, Ms. Reece. I'd hate to investigate your murder." With those parting words, he left.

Piper sank further into the pillow, suddenly exhausted. Man, all she wanted to do was sleep. If Liam was in this hospital room, she would probably take a nap.

A moment later, Simon peered inside. "Nick Santana is here."

Matt turned to Piper. "You ready for another round of interrogations?"

"Interviews," came the correction in a familiar voice accented by the detective's Hispanic heritage. "I leave interrogations for the criminals." The dark-haired detective eased into the room behind Simon and walked to the bedside. "How are you feeling, Piper?"

She smiled. "Not bad considering I was kidnapped, tossed into a van, and ended up in an accident within one hour's time."

Nick moved a chair close and sat. "I know you talked to Detective Ralston. Go through the same information. Don't leave anything out, even something minor. If you need a break, tell me and we'll talk about my beautiful nieces and nephew or my drop-dead-gorgeous wife for a few minutes."

His brown eyes were kind as he took in her appearance. She had no idea what she looked like in the aftermath of the past few hours, but she wasn't at her best.

How much should she tell him? Piper trusted Nick and Josh Cahill but she'd promised Gavin to keep silent. He'd stressed that no one could know where he was.

Gavin might not be involved in what happened. Knowing the type of work he did, her kidnapping could be connected to Liam's job.

She froze. If her kidnapping was related to his work, Liam was in danger. Did he know or suspect the root cause of his troubles might lie in his background instead of hers?

"Piper?" Matt touched her hand. "Are you okay?"

"Sorry. I zoned out for a minute."

He didn't look convinced. A lame excuse and Matt knew her well enough to recognize she wasn't telling him everything. The medic was observant.

Piper turned her attention to Nick and walked him through the events. "Matt and Simon brought me here to see Dr. Anderson." She wrinkled her nose. "The doctor admitted me for observation."

"You should be released tomorrow morning," Matt said.

"Why were you closing the shop early?" Nick's pen hovered over his notepad.

Piper's heart sank. She was a terrible liar. The other policemen hadn't asked her that question because they didn't know the shop's hours. Nick did.

"Who are you protecting?" Nick asked, his voice soft.

Matt stiffened. "You're protecting someone?"

"A former friend." Piper focused on the detective as her cheeks heated.

"Name?"

"Gavin James."

"Was he involved in your kidnapping?"

"I don't know. I haven't heard from him in three years, but he called me a little after five tonight, begging me to meet him. Nick, I have to get out of here. Please talk to Dr. Anderson and convince him to let me leave."

"In my line of work, we don't believe in coincidence. Gavin called you for the first time in three years, then two men kidnapped you, demanding that you give them information or they would hurt your boyfriend. Obviously, they didn't have Liam. Who is Gavin James to you?"

Piper felt Matt's gaze on her, but she hadn't acted without honor. "I told you the truth. We used to be friends."

The detective raised an eyebrow and waited.

"We used to be more than friends," she finally admitted. "We dated for a year, but I haven't seen him."

"What did he want?"

"For me to meet him. He sounded scared and made me promise I wouldn't tell anyone. I broke my word to him."

He shrugged, not looking the least apologetic. "No secrets in a police investigation. You parted ways amicably?"

Piper flinched. "Not exactly. I found out he was having an affair with my best friend. I confronted him in a restaurant." Her cheeks heated at the memory. "Not my finest moment."

"Did he want to continue your relationship?"

She nodded. "Gavin said he made a mistake and begged me to take him back."

"Did you?"

"No. I couldn't trust him after that. If he slept with another woman while we were dating, what would stop him from continuing that behavior? I told him to take a hike. I deserved better treatment from a man who was supposed to be on his best behavior while trying to win my heart."

"How did he take the news?"

"Not well. He yelled at me and said that if I gave him what he wanted, he wouldn't have to find another woman to take care of his needs."

Matt stared. "Let me get this straight. Gavin was angry because you wouldn't sleep with him?"

She nodded. "You know what's worse? He was enjoying a late, intimate dinner with yet another woman in a secluded corner of a restaurant I'd been wanting to go to for months. She had no idea Gavin was dating me and my best friend."

Nick's eyebrows rose. "How do you know?"

"Anita came to see me at work the next day. She convinced me to go to lunch and we talked. Anita thought she was the only woman in Gavin's life. Anyway, Gavin tried for months to get me to take him back. He finally must have gotten the message because I didn't hear from him again until tonight."

"After what he did to you, you were going to meet him anyway?" Matt asked.

"He was terrified. Gavin wouldn't tell me much, but I know his voice when he's afraid. I heard that exact tone a handful of times when he encountered a spider. Eight-legged creatures are his kryptonite. I need to get out of here. Please, Matt. Help me."

The medic scowled. "First, Liam would have my hide if I convinced Dr. Anderson to spring you before he thought you were ready. Second, I have no intention of being in my friend's crosshairs for letting you waltz into a meeting with the man who may be responsible for your kidnapping."

"It's not Gavin. He wouldn't do that to me."

"Yeah? Bet you said the same thing before you found out old Gavin was cheating on you."

Hurt and anger spiraled through Piper. He was right. Didn't mean she liked having the truth thrown in her face.

"Stay in the hospital until Dr. Anderson says you're ready to leave," Nick said. "Where and when were you supposed to meet your ex-boyfriend?"

"At Wilmington Resort off Highway 18 outside of town. He rented a small cabin." She gave the detective the necessary information. "Did someone find my purse?"

"Delilah has it." Matt patted her forearm. "She'll bring it to you tomorrow along with a change of clothes."

"Thanks." She looked at Nick. "What are you going to do?"

"Have a chat with your friend."

"Hurry, Nick. Gavin said it wasn't safe for him to stay in one place for long. He might have been spooked when I didn't show up."

Nick stood. "I'll let you know if I find him. I'll be in touch soon. In the meantime, when you leave the hospital, drop by the station and sign your statement."

He handed his business card to Piper. "If you need me, call." His lips curved. "I think you'll have plenty of people looking out for your safety. Just the same, I want to know when something else happens."

Piper's breath caught. When something else happened, not if. Liam wasn't the only one who thought the danger wasn't over.

CHAPTER FIVE

Liam stepped outside the Cherry Hill police station a few minutes after midnight and scanned the parking area. A tall, broad-shouldered man dressed in black camouflage pants and a black t-shirt leaned against the hood of a PSI SUV.

He headed toward his team leader. "Thanks for picking me up, Trent. How is Piper?"

"Confined to the hospital for observation until tomorrow morning. Grace said she will be fine."

Liam took his first free breath in hours. Grace St. Claire worked in Memorial Hospital's ER. "I want to see Piper," he said when Trent set the SUV in motion toward Otter Creek.

"It's late."

He stiffened. "Your point?"

"Visiting hours are long over and I hope Piper is sleeping."

Anger simmered in his blood. No one was keeping him from Piper, not even a big, bad Navy SEAL. "I don't plan on having a long, in-depth discussion with her. I need to be with Piper, Trent. She's...." He paused, afraid to even voice out loud the first word that popped into his head.

Everything. She was everything to him. Liam shrugged. "Mine. She's mine."

Bravo's leader slid him a speculative look. "Like that, is it?"

"Who's with her?"

"Simon's at the door. Matt is in the room with her."

"Any problems?"

"Aside from repeated questioning by the police, no."

He scowled. "Why are they badgering her? I'm the one who pulled the trigger and dropped those two clowns in their tracks." The Cherry Hill detectives had grilled him for hours.

"Have you been cleared?"

"Not yet. The detectives who questioned me said it looked like the shootings were justified but the final call on whether or not to file charges would come from the district attorney." Their attitude, though, said they both thought he should be tossed in jail.

"The Fortress lawyer is on standby. Zane has been forwarding all the information about your case so she'll be up to speed if she's needed."

"Let's hope I don't need her." Liam didn't want Piper to see him in a bad light. The prospect of the man she was dating being brought up on charges for killing two men might end their relationship before it had a chance to flourish.

Pain gripped his heart. He prayed that didn't happen. "I had no choice, Trent."

"Tell me what happened."

Liam spent the rest of the drive to Otter Creek recounting the events of the night.

"You did what was necessary to protect Piper," Trent said when he shut off the engine near the emergency entrance at Memorial Hospital. He turned to Liam. "If faced with the same circumstances, would you make the same choice?"

"Absolutely."

A nod. "We have your back. Focus on Piper. The rest will sort itself out."

Liam followed his team leader to the bank of elevators inside the hospital. On the fifth floor, they walked the corridor to Room 5235 where Simon kept watch. His best friend glanced up as they approached.

Simon clapped Liam on the shoulder. "About time the cops sprung you. How much hardware did you lose?"

"The Sig, the Beretta, Ka-Bar, and boot knife."

He flinched. "Sorry, man."

"I'll get the Beretta and knives back eventually. Don't know about the Sig." Liam inclined his head toward the closed door. "How is she?"

"Piper has been asking for you."

Was that good or bad? Depended on whether or not she wanted to cut him loose. Trent laid a hand on his shoulder and squeezed. Yeah, time to man up. If she wanted to stop dating, he'd do everything possible to change her mind because he was crazy about Piper Reece.

Liam tapped on the door to warn Matt he was coming inside. He didn't want to add another bullet wound to his collection.

He pushed the door open and slipped into the darkened room. Rounding the corner, his gaze locked on the woman huddled under a sheet and blanket. Even with the dim lighting, Liam could see the bruise forming on one side of her face.

Matt crossed to his side. "She's been restless," he murmured. "Wakes every hour to ask about you." A slow smile curved the medic's lips. "I tried to tell her you could take care of yourself. For some reason, she insists on seeing your ugly mug before she'll believe that."

Maybe he had a chance with Piper. "Go home to Delilah. I'll take over the watch. Take Simon with you. Trent will keep watch in the hall."

"I'll be back in the morning with Delilah. We'll bring clothes for Piper and a loaner SUV from PSI."

"Thanks."

With a nod, the medic left.

Liam sat in the chair Matt had vacated and settled in to watch over Piper while she slept. Now that he was in a quiet place, he allowed his mind to replay the events of the night, processing and cataloging everything. Once again, he analyzed his options to defuse the situation and came up with nothing. He'd had no choice but to pull the trigger both times.

Life was precious, and he never took one lightly. Still, if faced with the same situation, Liam would make the same decision to pull the trigger. If he'd hesitated, he could have been killed, leaving Piper in the hands of two killers. That was unacceptable on every level. He wouldn't have a problem accepting the deaths and moving on. Would Piper?

She stirred and moaned softly. "Liam," she whispered.

He stood and sat on the side of her bed. "I'm here, Piper. Sleep now."

The woman stilled for a moment, then relaxed into deep sleep.

Liam remained in place until he was sure she was out again, then returned to his chair. They repeated the same sequence twice more. The last round, Liam scooted his chair against the side of her bed and threaded his fingers with Pipers. This time, she settled into a dreamless sleep.

He allowed himself to fall into a light doze, knowing his team leader would prevent anyone from sneaking into the room.

At five o'clock, Piper stirred again. Liam sat up and squeezed her hand. "Piper?"

Her eyelids flew up. "You're here."

Liam went motionless. Was this it? Was she going to dump him? "Do you want me to leave?"

"No! I thought I was dreaming. I'm happy to see you."

Thank God. "How do you feel?"

"Better now that you're here. Did the police clear you?"

"Not exactly. The detectives will complete the investigation and send their findings to the district attorney. He'll decide whether or not to file charges against me."

Piper scowled. "You were protecting me and yourself."

"Everything will be fine."

"How can you say that? The police want to put you in jail."

"Hey." Liam sat on the side of the bed and cupped her cheek with his palm. "The Fortress lawyer is in the loop. She's a sharp lady, a real shark in a courtroom. If I end up in court, I'll have the best legal defense money can buy. My boss and my teammates have my back."

Piper nuzzled her face against his hand. "I'm sorry, Liam."

"For?"

"Maybe ruining your life."

"You didn't ruin my life, Piper. In fact, you're the best thing to happen to me in a very long time."

Her trademark sunny smile appeared. "Flatterer."

"Nope. Honest. I hear Dr. Anderson is springing you this morning."

"I hope so. I need to get out of here."

Liam tilted his head. "Don't like hospitals?"

"Who does? No, I need to check on a..." She stopped.

"Check on what?" he prompted when she remained silent.

"A former boyfriend."

His eyebrows soared. "Why?"

"He's the reason I closed the shop early. Gavin called and begged me for help yesterday."

"What kind of help?" And why did Liam want to find Gavin and punch him in the face?

"He's in trouble and doesn't trust anyone but me to help him." Piper recounted her phone conversation with her former boyfriend, ending with, "Gavin sounded terrified."

"You think this is a legitimate crisis on his part?"

"We dated for a little more than a year, Liam. I know every nuance of his voice. He was scared."

What kind of man called a woman he used to date for help? Liam figured he wouldn't elevate his own standing with Piper if he pointed that out to her. "Did he say what he wanted?"

She shook her head.

"While we wait for the doc to arrive, tell me about Gavin. Start at the beginning. Where did you meet?"

"We met at a friend's birthday party. Gavin works for a gaming company. He's creates video games." Her gaze skated away from his.

What was she hiding from him? "He any good?"

She named a couple war games and three strategy games that Liam enjoyed playing. "He created those, huh?" Might have to find himself new video games from a different company.

Liam kissed the back of her hand. "Piper, look at me." He waited in silence for Piper to turn her face toward him. "I'll find out why you were kidnapped and who is desperate enough to take the risk. I won't stop until I know everything. It's the only way I can protect you. You'll make my job easier if you're honest with me."

"You think I'm lying?"

"I think you're hiding a secret. I need you to trust me."

"How can you say that? I trusted you with my life on the highway last night. I just don't want to talk about this anymore."

"Why not?"

"It's not something I'm proud of, okay? Can we just drop it?"

"Your life is at stake. Tell me. Please."

CHAPTER SIX

Liam waited for Piper to spill the secret tearing her apart inside, a secret that might cost her life if she didn't tell him what he needed to know.

Her beautiful eyes shifted away from his gaze again, tension in every line of her body. "I'm afraid to tell you."

Not what he'd expected from her lips. Was her reluctance to share the information related to him killing two men? "Why?"

"Once you know the truth, you'd be wise to walk away from me and never look back." Pain and resignation filled her voice.

He stared. "You know what I do for a living. You saw a prime example on the highway last night and I've done many more things in the gray zone, edging toward black. Nothing you tell me will change my opinion of you."

"You say that now."

"I'll always say that." Liam squeezed her hand. "We have time to talk without an audience now. Once we leave the hospital, we'll be hard pressed to find a time to talk this out alone."

Piper frowned. "Why do you say that?"

"Until I'm sure there's no more danger, you'll have at least one member of Bravo by your side." As long as Fortress didn't deploy his unit again until this was resolved, Liam would be by Piper's side or have someone in place that he trusted. If his boss, Brent Maddox, needed Bravo, Liam would arrange for members of Durango, the Delta team assigned to PSI, to watch over Piper.

"But you killed the kidnappers."

"Someone may have sent them to grab you. If that's true, the instigator will find someone else to complete the job. Hit men are easy to find if you pay the right price."

"That doesn't make me feel better."

"It's not meant to. Talk to me, Sunshine."

Her gaze flew to his. "You've never called me that before."

"Do you mind?"

"Are you kidding? I love it. Why Sunshine instead of sweetheart or honey?"

"I might call you those, too. To me, you're as bright as a ray of sunshine."

"Liam." Tears glimmered in her eyes.

"You light up a room just by walking inside. You cheer me up every time I'm around you. Trust me to handle your secrets."

"The story's not pretty."

He shrugged. "I'm not going anywhere. May I hold you while you tell me the story?"

Her lips curved. "I'd like that." Piper scooted close to the opposite edge of the bed, making room for him to sit beside her.

Excellent. Liam eased down beside Piper and gathered her against his side. Her head rested on his shoulder. "Comfortable?" When she nodded, he pressed a light kiss to her temple. She might feel more comfortable baring her soul when he wasn't looking at her.

He relaxed against the upraised mattress and pillow and waited for her to begin.

"I told you I met Gavin at a friend's birthday party and that's true. What I didn't mention to Nick Santana is that Gavin works for my uncle." She fell silent again.

Rather than rush her, Liam stroked her arm with a gentle touch, reminding her of his presence and support without pushing her to say more until she was ready.

"My uncle is my only living relative. I lost my parents in a plane crash when I was three years old. Uncle Gino took me in and raised me. We were close when I was growing up. At least, I thought we were." She sighed. "Anyway, Uncle Gino wanted me to settle down and raise a family."

"Let me guess. Gavin was his choice of mate for you."

Piper nodded again. "It took me a long time to figure out my uncle had set up the first meeting between me and Gavin." Wry laughter escaped her. "I should have known something was up when Brandy planned a birthday celebration for herself. She'd never done that before and hadn't mentioned it in the weeks prior to the party. I found out after I broke up with Gavin that my uncle had arranged to pay off Brandy's school loans if she had the party."

Gino had paid a steep price to set up the meeting. Liam frowned. Was something else besides seeing Piper settled behind the planned meeting? "So, you and Gavin met at the party. I guess you hit it off." His gut twisted at the thought of Piper dating another man. He pulled her tighter against his side, unable to fight the possessiveness riding him hard.

"We did. He seemed perfect. In retrospect, that was another thing that should have triggered an alarm."

"Why?"

"Gavin was engaging, handsome, tall, dark, and I believed he was honorable, exactly the characteristics I'd mentioned to Uncle Gino for the type of man I'd be interested in. Those characteristics are what drew me to you."

Pleased, he gave her a gentle squeeze. "Why is he in a hurry to see you settled?"

Piper wrinkled her nose. "It wasn't because he longed for great-nephews or nieces to rock to sleep if that's what you're thinking. Gino's ulterior motives weren't that honorable. He owns Galactic Games, but he borrowed the money to start the business from his best friend, Matteo Barone."

Oh, man. Liam already knew where her story would lead. "The crime boss?"

"You've heard of him."

He snorted. "All you have to do is turn on the news. His name pops up in relation to drugs, prostitution, and murders. No law enforcement agency has managed to pin the crimes on Barone, just his lackeys."

"They happily take the fall for Barone. For some reason, his employees are intensely loyal to him."

"Money and fear buy their silence. What does Barone have to do with Gavin?"

"Gavin is Barone's son. I didn't know about that connection until two weeks before I broke up with Gavin. I never liked Barone. I avoided any contact with him or his family. There's something slimy about him. Anyway, Barone divorced his first wife, Lauren, and two days later, married his mistress, Anne James, Gavin's mother."

"Barone asked your uncle to hire Gavin?"

"A favor between friends, especially since he'd loaned Gino the money to start his company. My uncle was happy to hire him because Gavin is in the top five percent of programmers. Having him work for Galactic was a real coup and hiring Gavin meant his good buddy Matteo owed him a favor."

"Gino groomed Gavin to be the perfect match for you."

She nodded. "I dated Gavin for more than a year and never knew about the connection to Matteo." A wry laugh escaped Piper. "I also didn't know about his multiple affairs until the day I broke up with him."

Oh, yeah. He definitely needed to punch Gavin James in the face. "He's an idiot."

"I won't argue."

"I'm sorry he hurt you." But he wasn't sorry Gavin screwed up and gave Liam a chance with Piper.

"You know what the worst part is?"

"Tell me."

"He had an affair with my best friend, Brandy, and blamed me."

Liam scowled. "Why was it your fault?"

Her face flamed and she went silent.

"Hey, no fair holding out now. Why did he blame you?"

Piper sighed. "He turned to Brandy because I wouldn't sleep with him. What she didn't know was he was also seeing another woman, too."

Liam pressed a kissed to the top of her head. "Still haven't changed my mind about him. He's a fool, Sunshine. I'm grateful, though."

"For what?"

"If he hadn't been stupid, I would never have met you. His loss is my gain."

"How do you always know the perfect thing to say to me?"

"It's a gift." He smiled at her soft laughter. "Knowing what he did and his connection to Gino and Matteo, why would you rush to Gavin's aid? You can't have parted on good terms."

"Not even close. I confronted him in a restaurant full of people. I know it doesn't make sense, but he was a friend before he became more. He doesn't scare easily. Something is wrong."

"Does it have anything to do with your uncle or Matteo?" Liam could see all kinds of trouble coming if Gavin's fear was connected to either of those two men.

"I don't know. He talked fast, begging me to come to his Wilmington Resort cabin. He said he'd tell me more when I arrived. The kidnappers derailed my plans. I have to go see him. If he's in trouble with my uncle, I may be able to help." She sighed. "Probably not, though. Uncle Gino was furious when I refused to go along with his plan and moved away from our hometown to get away from him, Matteo, and Gavin."

"Is it possible Gavin pretended to be afraid to have a chance to win you back?"

Piper was silent a moment, then shook her head. "The fear was genuine. Looking back, Gavin loved himself more than he did me. I can't see him crawling back three years later to beg forgiveness. He has to have moved on with his life by now."

Maybe not. Some women haunted you, grabbing a piece of your heart and never letting go. Liam had a feeling Piper was one of those women. "All right. We'll go together."

"That's not necessary."

"Yeah, it is. I'm not convinced you're safe. I won't take chances with your life. We also don't know if Gavin was involved in your kidnapping attempt."

"He wasn't."

"Hear me out. If Gavin knows you at all, he understands convincing you to take him back will require more than a pretty apology. Maybe he wanted to be the hero and rescue you."

She eased back to look Liam in the eyes. "That's what the Cherry Hill detective said about you."

He'd been afraid of that. "Do you believe him?"

"Why would I?"

Despite the dim lighting in the room, Liam saw the hint of color staining her cheeks. "It's no secret that I'm crazy about you and have been for a while. Maybe Gavin had a friend who scouted around town, heard the scuttlebutt, and decided to capitalize on it by painting himself in a good light."

"It's possible although I'm not convinced. He wouldn't go to that much trouble to get me back. He would simply find another woman. He never had problems lining them up. Liam, I know you didn't set up the kidnapping to ride to my rescue. You already impress me by being who you are."

He stared. "How can you say that? I killed two men last night."

"To protect me. You keep forgetting that part. How can I not be impressed with a man who does the right thing even though taking those actions might cost him his own life? I'm sorry you were forced into that position, but I'm grateful you didn't hesitate. You're an amazing man, Liam McCoy. Thank you for what you did."

He laid a finger gently across her lips. "Enough. I don't need your thanks. I just want you safe."

A light knock on the door brought Liam to his feet, weapon in his hand.

His team leader slipped into the room and smiled when he saw Piper was awake. "You look good. How do you feel?"

"Like I ran into Rocky's fist. I want out of here."

"Grace told me Dr. Anderson usually starts his rounds at seven o'clock. You have another hour to wait. Nick Santana is here. You up to talking to him again?"

Piper sighed. "Send him in."

The Otter Creek detective strode inside the hospital room a moment later, fatigue evident. Looked like he'd been awake all night. He shook Liam's hand. "Glad you're back safely from your mission."

"Thanks."

"Got a copy of the initial report on the shooting from the Cherry Hill PD. Looks like justifiable homicide."

Liam shrugged. "We'll see if the DA agrees."

"Ethan knows the DA. He'll do what he can to turn the tide in your favor." Nick turned toward Piper. "How are you?"

"Ready to break out of this joint."

He smiled. "I'm not surprised."

"Did you talk to Gavin?"

Nick's smile faded. "By the time I arrived at the cabin, Gavin was gone."

CHAPTER SEVEN

Piper's heart sank. Had Rock been telling the truth about having captured Gavin? If so, how would she find him? Rock and his buddy were dead. She shuddered to think what would happen if Gavin was bound in a place only the two dead kidnappers knew. "Did you talk to the resort owner?"

Nick sat in the chair at the side of her hospital bed. "He said Gavin paid in cash for two days. Doesn't matter to him if Gavin left early or not, as long as he left the key card in the room. I checked the resort records for his vehicle registration. Do you know what Gavin drives?"

"Last time I saw him, Gavin drove a fully-loaded Escalade. His father is generous with money, though. I don't know what he drives now."

"He still drives an Escalade and his vehicle isn't in the parking lot. Do you know where he might be?"

She shook her head. "I don't have my phone. If he called to set a meeting in a different place, I wouldn't know. Delilah is bringing my phone to the hospital along with clothes for me."

"When you have the phone, check for a message from Gavin. I need to know if he contacted you. I'm not sure what's going on, but his life might depend on me locating Gavin and bringing him in."

Worry formed a knot in her stomach. "I'll let you know if I hear from him."

Nick turned to Liam. "I talked to Piper about last night's events. It's your turn."

Piper hated for Liam to endure another police interrogation. Although he hadn't said, she suspected the Cherry Hill detectives grilled Liam over the highway incident. Otherwise, he would have been at the hospital sooner.

This time he wasn't alone. She captured his hand and tugged him down beside her again. Although he looked surprised at her silent demand, he didn't protest as he settled against her side.

Nick's eyes glinted with amusement as he retrieved his notebook and pen. "Start at the beginning."

Liam summarized what happened, his words terse and unemotional.

The almost robotic recitation made Piper's heart hurt. He buried emotional baggage in order to do his job with logic instead of emotion.

"What do the detectives think?"

A snort. "That I set up Piper's kidnapping to play hero."

"Are you surprised?"

"Wouldn't be the first time law enforcement accused an operative of grand standing."

"He didn't do it," Piper insisted. "Don't waste your time going down that rabbit hole, Nick."

"You're sure?"

"Yes." No hesitation or doubt.

"Anything else either of you want to tell me?"

Liam cupped Piper's chin and turned her face toward his. "Tell him about Gino and his buddy."

Her cheeks burned. "Is it necessary?" Admitting how gullible she'd been about her uncle was embarrassing.

"If Gavin isn't guilty, then his father might be. For his own safety, we can't allow Nick to walk into this blind."

Liam was right. Nick needed to be prepared for the dangerous players he might face. "All right."

When Liam released her, Piper told Nick what she'd told Liam. The longer she talked, the grimmer the detective's expression grew.

Nick dragged a hand down his face. "I'm familiar with Matteo Barone's work. I didn't know you were connected to him and his minions."

"I'm not." Her hand fisted on the blanket. "That's why I left Alabama. I didn't want anything to do with my uncle's association with Matteo. I thought Matteo made his money with his casino. I didn't know about the rest of his money-making schemes or that Gavin was Matteo's son because I made it a point never to be around him. I freely admit to being the most gullible woman on the planet."

Liam pressed a soft kiss to her temple. "You look for the best in people. That's your nature, Sunshine. When you discovered Gavin's deceit and his connection to Matteo, you did the only thing you could. You walked away."

"Leaving took courage." Nick slid the notebook and pen into his pocket. "Call me if you hear from Gavin. If he's on the run from Matteo, law enforcement may be his only hope to survive. Matteo's people don't mess around. If they believe he's a weak link, Gavin won't survive on his own."

Ice water poured through Piper's veins. Gavin wanting to get back together was a better alternative than him running from his crime-boss father. "I promise to keep you updated."

He rose. "Call if you need me. Watch your back, Liam. Barone's crew is ruthless. They don't quit until they achieve their objective and their talent roster is several layers deep.

Might be wise to bring Fortress into the loop. They aren't restricted by the same rules I have to follow."

Wordless communication passed between the two men before Liam said, "I'll talk to Zane and Brent Maddox."

"If I were in you, I'd be ready to leave town at a moment's notice with a series of prepared safe houses."

Piper shuddered. "Nick, you're scaring me."

"I'm trying to keep you both alive," he countered. "Liam will put himself in front of any bullet headed your direction. Keep that in mind when you consider your options. His life is at stake, too. Stop by the station when you're released. Stella will have your statements." With those words, he left.

"You have to stay away from me, Liam." Just saying the words pierced her heart with pain. Separating from him was the last thing she wanted, but Piper feared for his safety. "I don't want anything to happen to you."

"Not happening, Piper. I'll take care of myself and you." He cupped her cheek, a fierce light in his eyes. "I won't leave you to deal with this mess alone. I'm in this with you and that's where I plan to stay."

"Why put yourself at risk?"

"You matter to me."

Another knock sounded on the door. Trent peered inside the room. "Dr. Anderson is here. So are Matt and Delilah."

Thank God. Maybe she would be out of here soon. "Send Dr. Anderson in."

A moment later, Otter Creek's favorite doctor walked in. He smiled at Liam. "Glad you're back, Liam."

"Thank you, sir."

"Have you been keeping an eye on my patient?"

Liam chuckled. "I have."

"What's your opinion on how she's doing?"

"I think she's perfect."

Piper stared, surprised. Liam's gaze met hers and he winked.

"Let me examine her and see if my assessment matches yours. Wait in the hall and I'll let you know when I'm finished."

Liam leaned down and brushed a feather-light kiss over Piper's lips. "I'll be outside the door if you need me." He left.

Piper touched her lips. To this point, Liam had been careful to buss her cheek, the corner of her mouth, or her forehead after their dates. His platonic kisses coupled with the proprietary touches frustrated her enough that she had planned to initiate a real kiss herself. When she finally worked up the courage to act, Liam had been deployed with his teammates for almost a month.

Her shock at Liam's kiss must have been apparent because the doctor's blue eyes twinkled at her. "Well, that's news for the town gossip mill."

"If you spread the word, I might have to drop hints all over Otter Creek that the town's favorite single doctor is looking for companionship."

Anderson chuckled. "Not that, please. I have no interest in delivering extra casseroles to the women's shelter. My freezer is still filled to the brim with more food than I can eat if I want to stay a healthy weight. I give the shelter two or three casseroles a week. The single women in Otter Creek don't need more incentive to cook and bake for me."

"If you're interested in one of the ladies, ask her out. It would stop the others from bombarding you with food bribes."

His smile grew wistful. "I loved and lost the woman of my dreams. I'm not interested in anyone else." He squared his shoulders. "Now, enough about me. Let's have a look at you." Ten minutes later, Anderson declared her fit to leave.

"The bruising should fade soon. Wouldn't hurt to apply ice packs every few hours."

She grinned. "You're back at the top of my list of favorite doctors. Thank you."

He patted her hand. "Glad you weren't hurt worse. You're very lucky Liam was home to come to your aid. I'll send the nurse in with your discharge papers and you'll be free to go home."

Home sounded great. Would Liam think her home was safe now?

As soon as the doctor left, Delilah tapped on the door and walked inside the room with a bag in her hand. She hugged Piper. "You look good considering what you went through last night."

"Thanks for bringing a change of clothes."

"No problem. Do you want to shower before you go home or after?"

"Now. I still feel Rock's hands on me."

"Rock?"

"The kidnapper who grabbed me and threw me in the van." She scowled. "He was the creep who hit me."

Delilah gave her a sympathetic look. "I understand. I'll wait here in case you need anything. I put your favorite toiletries in the bag along with the clothes."

"You're an angel."

Her boss laughed. "I keep telling Matt that. He doesn't believe me. Get moving, Piper. A certain operative's pacing the hallway like a caged tiger, anxious to be at your side again."

Holy cow. Liam was more invested in their relationship than he'd let on. Piper hurried into the bathroom and started the shower. While the water heated, she pawed through the bag's contents, thrilled with the supplies Delilah included. Shampoo, conditioner, brush, shower gel and body lotion in her favorite orange blossom and vanilla scent, toothbrush and toothpaste, deodorant plus a change of clothes.

Her fingers brushed against her purse, nestled at the bottom of the bag. The urge to check her cell phone rode her. After the shower. If she checked before she showered, and Gavin had left a fear-laced message, Piper would want to meet him immediately. She longed to wash the feel of Rock off her skin.

Piper raced through her shower and the rest of her after-bath routine, then dragged on clothes in under ten minutes. She sighed, grateful to be wearing something besides a drafty blue and white hospital gown. She finished tying her tennis shoes before checking her cell phone.

Piper scanned six messages from Gavin, each one more frantic. Anxiety increasing by the second, she listened to two messages on her voice mail, both from Gavin.

A brisk knock on the bathroom door. "Piper, the nurse is here with your discharge papers."

Piper swept toiletries and the clothes she wore yesterday into the bag, grabbed her purse, and opened the door.

Delilah frowned. "You look pale. Are you okay?"

"Not really." As Delilah left the room, Piper listened in silence to the nurse's spiel, her mind half on the signs for potential problems and half on the danger her former boyfriend could be facing.

"Come back to the emergency room if you have any of the symptoms I mentioned," the nurse instructed.

She forced a smile to her lips. "Got it. Thanks."

After the nurse left, Liam returned, concern in his eyes. He wrapped his arms around Piper and held her close. "Delilah said you're upset. What's wrong?"

"Gavin's on the run. He says he has information to prove Matteo's dirty."

CHAPTER EIGHT

Liam's mind filled with ugly possibilities wrapped in those few words. He didn't have a problem taking on Barone's crime syndicate but didn't want Piper caught in the crossfire. "Did he set up another meet?"

"Gavin said he left information for me at our ski lodge. About twenty of us stayed at the Copper Ridge Ski Resort a month after Gavin and I became a couple. He called it our resort."

Liam frowned, not liking the thought of Piper dating Gavin. "Isn't that near Gatlinburg?"

She nodded. "It's two hours outside of Knoxville."

Still too close to Barone's stronghold to suit Liam, especially considering he'd killed two of Barone's henchmen. Were the two men in the morgue the only ones the syndicate boss sent after Gavin and Piper? "Gavin left the information and bolted?"

"That's what his voice-mail message said."

"Do you mind playing it for me?"

Piper tapped her phone screen and a man's voice came from the speaker.

"Piper, why didn't you meet me? Look, I know we didn't part on good terms, but I need to get this information into the hands of someone I trust to do the right thing. I'm leaving everything I have on M in the crevice at the ski resort. You know the one. Do what you want with it. If you're smart, you'll burn it and run. Disappear and take on a new identity. I'm going underground to do that. I stashed money in a Swiss bank account. I'll be fine. I won't be breathing if I don't disappear. I found out too much and now I'm a liability. I will always love you, Piper. Don't forget me."

Liam tightened his hold on Piper. "Do you know what he meant about leaving the information in the crevice at the resort?"

She nodded. "On one of the hikes we took around the resort, Gavin and I found a cave in the mountainside. Inside the cave was a deep crevice. He joked about it being deep enough to hide a body inside." Piper shivered. "I told him that was a ghoulish thought. He just laughed and called me melodramatic. That cave was dank and creepy."

"I'm not a fan of dank and creepy myself." He eased her away enough to look into her eyes. "Can you describe where you found the cave?"

"Why?"

"Could be dangerous going to retrieve this information. I don't want you exposed to more danger. Tell me where it is and I'll go after it myself."

"I appreciate you trying to protect me, Liam, but I have to go with you. I don't remember enough details to describe where the cave is. There was more than one in the area. I have to do this. If there's any chance to take down Barone and my uncle, I have to try."

He'd been afraid of that. "We'll find another way, one that doesn't involve putting you at risk again. Fortress is in the information business. People owe us favors and I know two men who can hack into any database and mine for information. I want you safe."

Piper cupped his face between her soft palms. "I'm already involved. Rock and his buddy came after me because they thought I had the information. If you're right and Matteo sent them to retrieve it, the minions won't quit until they have the information in their hands."

He pressed his forehead against hers. "The only way to stop them is turn the information over to law enforcement." He needed to talk to Maddox about going after Matteo's organization.

"It won't be enough."

"I know." If Matteo sent goons after Piper, he assumed she knew too much. Even if she gave the information to Barone, thugs would come after Piper until she was dead. Liam wouldn't let that happen. If he had to take on the mob by himself, so be it. "I won't let them hurt you again, Sunshine."

He trailed the backs of his fingers down her unbruised cheek. "Are we driving to Copper Ridge Ski Resort today?"

"I'm going. I'm sure you have a ton of work waiting for you at PSI."

Piper Reece was a stubborn woman. Despite her fear, she was still trying to protect him. "My teammates will cover the workload for me."

"What if your team is deployed?"

Liam shook his head. "We're off rotation for a month unless there's an emergency. Besides, we'll only be an hour away from Otter Creek." He tapped her nose. "Give up. You aren't doing this on your own. I'm trained to handle dangerous situations like this one. Trust me."

Piper laid her hand over his heart, her touch possessive. Liam liked that. A lot. "All right. When do we leave?"

"Two hours. We need to stop at the police station first, then pack overnight bags."

"The resort isn't that far. We'll be gone a few hours at most."

"That's the best-case scenario. In my line of work, we expect the worst. Pack enough for a couple of days."

Liam escorted her from the hospital, Matt and Trent flanking them.

The medic tossed Liam a set of keys and indicated the black SUV to his right. "That's your replacement ride. Bear had this one ready to go. When he heard what happened on the highway, he and his wife brought this SUV to Otter Creek for you."

"Great." He helped Piper into the passenger seat and stashed her bag in the cargo area. His Go bag and equipment bag were already in the back.

He looked at Trent, eyebrows raised. "How did you get my gear? I thought the Cherry Hill cops would confiscate it."

His team leader shrugged. "Ethan's handiwork."

Wow. The Otter Creek police chief had serious pull.

"Need backup?"

"Doubtful but I won't rule it out."

"We'll be ready."

"Forget going by yourself," Matt said. "Simon has his bag packed. He's waiting for a direction to drive. Call him, Liam. Otherwise, he'll have Zane track you down."

Yeah, he would. Liam would do the same if Simon was in danger. "I'll talk to him."

"Where are you headed?" Trent asked.

"Copper Ridge Ski Resort."

"We'll study schematics and maps of the area in case you need a hand. Watch your back." He turned to Piper. "Be careful. Do exactly what Liam and Simon tell you to do. They'll keep you safe."

"I don't want Liam in trouble for skipping work."

Liam wrapped his hand around hers. "I'll talk to my boss. I'll be fine."

"Brent Maddox is fiercely protective of women who are in trouble," Matt agreed. "He won't have a problem with Liam protecting the woman he's dating."

Trent clapped Liam on the shoulder. "Check in every two hours. If you run into trouble, I want to know."

"Yes, sir."

He shut Piper's door, circled the hood, and slid behind the steering wheel. On the drive to the police station, Liam called Simon.

After his detailed explanation, Simon said, "I'll drive to the resort and do reconnaissance. Want me to see if two rooms are available?"

Liam glanced at Piper. Would she like to spend time at the resort? He didn't think Delilah would protest Piper taking another day off. "A suite." After almost losing her to thugs, Liam preferred having Piper close.

"Let me know when you arrive."

"Copy that." He ended the call and glanced at the silent woman by his side. "Are you hungry?"

Piper twisted in her seat. "I'm starving. The food at Memorial is less than stellar."

Liam chuckled. "Not surprising."

"Have you been admitted to a hospital?" She rolled her eyes and held up a hand to stop him from answering. "Never mind. Of course you have. Perhaps a better question is how long were you admitted?"

"A few months. I was injured on a mission with my Marine unit."

"How long were you enlisted?"

"Ten years."

"Good experience?"

"Aside from the sand, heat, and terrorists, joining the Marines was the best decision I ever made. Those men and women became my family."

"Did you do the same job in the military that you do now?"

His grip tightened around the steering wheel. "Yes."

"Tough job. Thank you for your service, Liam."

"Serving was an honor," he said, throat tight. Thank God Piper hadn't turned away from him after learning of his specialty. "My job doesn't bother you?"

"You protect your teammates."

"More than one person called me a murderer for hire."

Her jaw dropped. "That's ridiculous. You're do a job most people can't or won't do. You're one of the bravest men I've ever met. You don't shrink from gut-wrenching work and find a way to get the job done."

Liam didn't say anything until he parked in the lot beside the Otter Creek police department. He turned off the engine and came around to open Piper's door. Instead of giving her room to exit the vehicle, he cupped her cheek. "Are you sure you want to be with me, Sunshine?"

"Positive." She twined her arms around his neck. "I haven't been interested in dating anyone in a long time. I count myself lucky you noticed me among the scores of women who flock around you in town."

The ice flowing through his veins from the moment he'd discovered her missing melted away. "What other women? The only one I've noticed in years is you. I'm the one who is lucky. Thank you for giving me a chance."

She smiled, her eyes twinkling. "Will you kiss me now?"

Liam's lips curved. "Do you want me to?"

"Very much. I almost initiated a real kiss last month, but Fortress sent you to unknown parts of the world for weeks."

His gaze dipped to her mouth. "You don't know how hard it's been to hold off and let you learn to trust me. I'd love to kiss you."

"But?"

"I don't want to be concerned about your safety when I kiss you. You're too exposed out here and I guarantee I'll be distracted. Much as it pains me to say this, we have to wait a little longer."

"Today, though?"

"Oh, yeah. Today." He'd been wanting to kiss Piper from the first moment he saw her. Years of discipline drilled into him by the Corp and Fortress kept his lips from hers at this moment.

Liam found the grit somewhere to step back. Watching for anything suspicious, he escorted her into the police station, hand pressed to her lower back.

The desk sergeant nodded at Liam. "McCoy. Glad you're back. How can I help you?"

"Detective Santana left statements for us to sign."

"You'll need to see Detective Armstrong. Santana is off shift. He went to breakfast with his wife." He picked up the handset. "I'll tell Armstrong you're here."

Two minutes later, Stella Armstrong opened the double doors and motioned for Liam and Piper to follow her. They walked through the bullpen and into an office where Stella closed the door and shut out the noise of ringing phones and raised voices.

"Sorry. It's crazy out there today." The dark-haired detective motioned to the seats in front of the desk. "I heard what happened last night. How are you, Piper?"

"I'm fine. Liam rescued me before the kidnappers did too much damage." She covered the bruised cheek with her palm. "This is the worst of the injuries."

Liam frowned. "You have more?" Why hadn't he heard about them?

"A scraped knee. It's nothing."

"I read the police report." Stella crossed her arms over her chest. "Nice work, Liam. No repercussions from Fortress?"

"Haven't had time to call Maddox yet. Trent talked to him. I have to report in soon." He tilted his head, studying the detective's solemn expression. He'd spent time with

Stella and her husband, Nate, a fellow Fortress operative, enough to know she was worried. "What's wrong?"

"We got an ID on the two men you shot. They're connected to organized crime, Liam."

CHAPTER NINE

Liam's stomach tightened into a knot at Stella's news. He'd hoped for a different answer. Liam exchanged glances with Piper. Seeing her distressed expression, he wrapped an arm around her shoulders. "We'll handle it."

"Why do I have the feeling you're not surprised?" Stella's eyes narrowed as she looked from Liam to Piper and back. "I want to know everything you know or suspect. Nick and I are working this case together."

He told her everything and played the voice mail message from Gavin.

Stella recorded the message on her phone. "Barone and his minions play for keeps, Liam. Don't underestimate them."

"I have too much at stake to be careless."

"I can't give you as much information as you want and need. Zane would be helpful."

Liam analyzed what she said and what she didn't. She was obliged to keep quiet about the case. However, Stella had learned something he and Piper needed to know. "I'll contact him as soon as we leave."

The detective's muscles loosened. "What are your next steps?"

"Grabbing a meal, packing an overnight bag, and heading to the Copper Ridge Ski Resort."

A frown. "You're leaving town in the middle of an investigation. Did the Cherry Hill detectives tell you to stay in the area?"

"I'll be an hour outside of town. If they need to talk to us, contact me."

"Why shouldn't I call Piper?"

"Her phone isn't secure." A stop by his house would solve the problem.

"When you solve the problem, I need the number."

He inclined his head without comment.

Stella rolled her eyes. "Stubborn operative. I noticed you didn't agree to give me her contact information. I have one of those encrypted phones, buddy. No one breaks Z's encryption program. Her contact information will be safe with me."

"You can't keep the information from the Cherry Hill detectives. You, I trust. I don't trust them to keep the information secure."

At that moment, Piper's stomach growled.

With a grin, Stella twisted and grabbed a file from the desktop. "I need to get you out of here so you can eat." She handed them the statements to read and sign.

Ten minutes later, Liam and Piper were on the sidewalk in front of the station with Stella's warning to be careful ringing in their ears. "Would you like to go to That's A Wrap?" Liam asked.

"That sounds great."

They walked to the deli owned by a fellow operative's wife. As soon as they entered the shop, Darcy beamed at them and hurried around the counter. She threw her arms around Piper.

"I'm glad you're safe." She pulled back, scanned Piper's face, and winced. "That bruise looks like it hurts."

"A little," Piper admitted.

"Come on." Darcy tugged her toward the back of the shop. "The deli is a madhouse this time of morning." She led them to a small break room. "Tell me what you want to eat and drink and I'll bring your meals." Within five minutes, she returned with a tray loaded with breakfast wraps, coffee for Liam, and hot tea for Piper.

After Darcy returned to the front of the shop, Piper sipped her tea and sighed. "Chamomile mint."

Liam set Piper's plate in front of her. "At least it's quiet enough to talk back here." He waited until she finished her wrap before capturing her hand and kissing her knuckles. "How are you?"

"Better now that I have food in my stomach."

"Are you ready to pack your overnight bag?"

She nodded. "I want this over with."

"Worried?"

"Aren't you?"

"Yeah, I am." Not for himself. For her. He didn't want Piper near the resort and knew insisting she stay in Otter Creek wouldn't do him any good. Piper could drive herself to the resort. Worse, she wouldn't have protection and would be vulnerable to attack along the road. He'd rather she remained with him than attempt the drive to the resort alone.

"What will we do?"

"Hope for the best and plan for the worst."

"Was that what you did in the military?"

He nodded. "Still do the same with my work now. We make plans and several backups."

"Why?"

"Missions never go like we plan. Things happen we can't anticipate even though we plan for every contingency we can think of."

"What if you run through all your contingency plans?"

"We develop new ones on the fly. Don't worry, Piper. I won't let anything happen to you. Nothing matters more to me than your safety."

"Your safety is just as important as mine. I don't want you hurt because of me."

An invisible band tightened around Liam's chest. "We'll watch out for each other." He drew Piper to her feet. "We need to get going. The longer we wait, the more time we give Barone to prepare a counterattack. I'd rather keep him off balance."

He escorted Piper to his SUV and tucked her inside. Minutes later, he parked in her driveway and turned off the engine.

"Do you want to go to your place while I pack a bag? I'm sure it will take me longer."

Liam shook his head. "I'm not leaving you alone."

"You took care of the kidnappers."

"Your uncle or Barone could have sent more men."

He walked with Piper to her front door and held out his hand for the key. "Let me make sure it's safe before you go too far inside the house."

"Overprotective much?"

"I care about you, Sunshine. Let me do this for you."

She thrust her hand into her purse, grabbed her house key, and handed it to him. "Where should I wait?"

"Inside the front door. Don't move until I tell you it's safe." When she nodded, Liam unlocked the front door and eased his weapon from his holster. Motioning for Piper to stay behind him, he turned the knob.

As soon as he crossed the threshold, Liam froze. Oh, man. Piper wouldn't be happy when she saw the state of her house.

"What's wrong?" She gasped when she saw the chaos. "What are the odds of a burglary hours after being kidnapped?"

"Zip."

Piper stared. "Did the kidnappers trash my house before they threw me in the van?"

"It's possible. Stay here while I check the rest of the house. I want to be sure you don't have a visitor waiting for you and I need to know where you are while I search."

She nodded.

Liam went from room to room, searching for a lingering intruder. He didn't think he'd find one of Barone's flunkies. Nine hours was a long time to wait for Piper to return home.

His frown deepened as he continued the search. Every room was trashed. Organizing her house again would take long hours.

When he'd cleared the house, Liam returned to the living room to find Piper in the same place, her gaze locked on the broken picture frames and glass, books scattered everywhere, DVDs tossed on the ground, their covers flung to various parts of the room. The desk drawers were upended, the contents dumped into a pile. Pictures had been ripped from the walls.

"Piper."

She blinked and looked at him. "No unwanted visitors?"

He shook his head. "We have to call the police. Maybe they'll find some prints." He eyed her. "You don't have an alarm system."

Piper shrugged. "Couldn't afford one. Delilah pays me what she can, but it's not enough to install a state-of-the-art alarm system and keep up with the monthly monitoring fee."

"I'll call Fortress and see what they can work out. You need better protection, especially now that we're together."

"We'll see."

Yeah, they would. He didn't want her life at risk because of money. If nothing else, he'd have Fortress take money from his pay and charge Piper a cut rate. He wanted her safe. Although he was careful, and Fortress scanned for mention of his name or work aliases, his identity could leak and provide a target for enemies. Piper would now be a prime target for anyone wanting revenge.

He grabbed his cell phone. "Pack your bag. Once the police arrive, you won't be allowed to remain in the house. Touch as little as possible. We don't want to contaminate evidence more than we already have. Cops will be here in a few minutes."

"I'll be quick." Piper hurried down the hall to her bedroom as Liam tapped in the number for the police department.

When the dispatcher answered, he requested police assistance for a break in. Liam gave her what information he could. By the time the sirens sounded close, Piper returned with her bag packed.

He walked her to the SUV and placed her bag in the cargo area. At least now she'd have her own clothes and toiletries without worrying about when the police would release her house.

A prowl car arrived with lights and sirens, followed closely by a department SUV. Stella hopped out and headed for them. "What happened?"

"Someone trashed my house."

"Let's take a look." Stella followed them into the bungalow and whistled low when she stepped inside the living room. "Does the whole house look like this?"

"Afraid so." Piper scowled. "This will take forever to clean up. I'd love to get my hands on the person who did this and make them help me straighten the place."

Stella trailed Liam and Piper throughout the house. When they returned to the living room, she asked, "Is anything missing, Piper?"

"My electronics are still here as well as my jewelry. I didn't check for anything else."

"The burglars were looking for something." The detective waved a hand at the chaos in the living room. "No destruction of property. Everything is still intact, just dumped on the ground and rifled through. Do you know what they were looking for?"

Piper's fists clenched. "Maybe the same thing the kidnappers wanted."

"Did Gavin give you any indication in the previous texts what kind of information he had on Barone?"

"I wish. I don't know what Gavin might have learned. He creates video games."

"His father assumed he'd be loyal because of the blood tie." Stella looked at Liam. "Have you talked to Zane yet?"

"Not yet."

"Soon, okay?"

Liam blew out a breath. That didn't sound good. "I'll contact Z while we're driving." He was careful not to say too much. He hadn't had time to search Piper's house for bugs. No need to announce they were driving to Copper Ridge in case the burglars had left a bug behind. "Do you need us to stay?"

Stella shook her head. "I'll contact you when the crime scene team finishes with Piper's house. Take the day and enjoy yourselves. Let me worry about this."

"Yes, ma'am." In other words, get his woman out of here.

Liam threaded his fingers through Piper's and led her to his SUV. On the way to his house, he called Zane.

"Yeah, Murphy."

"It's Liam. Need a favor."

"Shoot."

He explained what had been happening and said, "I need you to dig into Gino Romano, Matteo Barone, Gavin James, and Piper Reece."

Piper's head whipped his direction, her eyes wide.

"Piper? Isn't that the woman you're interested in?"

"Definitely. She's in the SUV with me, Z. Say hello."

A pause, then, "Piper, I'm Zane. It's nice to talk to you."

"Hello, Zane. The PSI teams mention your name with a great deal of respect in their voices."

A deep chuckle filled the cabin of the SUV. "That's because I have mad research skills and can make a computer do all kinds of neat tricks. Liam, what am I looking for?"

"Not sure. Stella Armstrong knows something about this situation that she can't tell us. She encouraged me to contact you."

"Huh. I'll see what I can find out and get back to you. Anything else I can do?"

Liam slid Piper a look. "I need the accessories with trackers for Piper."

"Where do I send them?"

"Copper Ridge Ski Resort. Piper and I will be there at least until tomorrow."

"I'll have the package to you in a few hours. Talk to you soon." He ended the call.

"What accessories?" Piper asked.

"Jewelry with embedded GPS trackers. The men who took you from Wicks may have friends who want to do the same thing. If you have trackers on you, I don't have to worry about areas with no surveillance or traffic cameras. For my peace of mind, will you wear the jewelry?"

"All right. What about you?"

"What about me?"

"Do you have jewelry with GPS trackers in case you're kidnapped?"

He reached over and squeezed her hand. "Fortress operatives have trackers embedded under their skin. It's not foolproof, but the trackers at least give reconnaissance units a starting point."

Liam turned into the driveway of his ranch-style house located on a quiet street. "Come on. I won't be long. Why don't you grab a couple bottles of water and a few snacks for the road." Although they wouldn't be driving that long, the task would occupy Piper's mind.

He unlocked the front door and turned to disable the alarm. His eyes narrowed. He'd set the alarm before he left Otter Creek for South America with his team. His alarm had been disabled.

CHAPTER TEN

Piper noticed the change in Liam's demeanor. "What's wrong?" She didn't see anything amiss, unlike the disaster at her place.

"My security system if off." Liam pulled a gun from his holster. "Stay here while I check the house."

"Same song, second verse," she murmured. "At least they left your house intact."

As he searched for signs of intruders, Piper studied Liam's living room. Big, masculine furniture covered with a rich brown leather. Couch, loveseat, and recliner, heavy wood coffee table and matching end tables. Paintings and drawings, all outdoor scenes, decorated his walls. His choice of artwork wasn't surprising given his job. Piper couldn't see Liam behind a desk for hours at a time. His rugged physique wasn't developed in a gym.

Liam returned with a duffel bag, his expression grim. "I need to take you out of here."

"But..."

He placed his forefinger on her lips. "Wait," he murmured.

Why didn't he want her to talk? A moment later, she sat inside his SUV, his gear stored in the cargo area.

Liam climbed into the driver's seat and grabbed his cell phone. He called his team leader. "Trent, you're on speaker with Piper. I need a tech team at my place."

"What happened?" Despite standing watch in the hospital hallway all night, Trent sounded alert.

"Someone disabled my alarm system in a way that didn't alert Fortress to the breach in security. Piper's house was also broken into, but her place was tossed. Stella is processing that scene."

"Different intruders."

"The ones in Piper's place were amateurs. The intruder in my home was professionally trained."

"Black ops?"

"That's my guess."

"Ask Z to run a deeper check for new threats against you."

Threats? Piper gripped Liam's hand. Having a crime boss and his best friend targeting her was bad enough. Someone else could be after Liam.

He entwined their fingers. "As soon as I end this call."

"Take extra measures to protect Piper."

"I have her covered. Alert the others in Bravo and Durango. If a terrorist located me, he might go after the rest of you and your families."

"Want me to notify the cops about your B & E?"

"I'd rather our tech team handled it, but we need the break-in on record."

"I'll call Stella and convince her that the tech team needs to go in with the crime scene team. Otherwise, we could have a leak."

Piper frowned. A leak? What did that mean?

"I'll let you know what we find at your house. In the meantime, watch your six. Hopefully, we'll catch the break-in artists before they up their game."

When Liam ended the call, he turned to look at Piper, regret in his eyes. "I'm sorry, Sunshine."

"For what?" She prayed he wouldn't walk away from her. Liam had already burrowed his way into her heart.

"Looks like I should have waited to start a relationship with you."

"Why?"

"My job is dangerous. There's always the possibility my identity and location will leak to my enemies. Looks like that's what happened here. The MOs are different, Piper." He glanced toward his house. "The people who broke in here have training similar to mine."

"How do you know?"

"This is the best Fortress security system. The people who burglarized your place would have tripped the alarm system in mine. The same people are not responsible for my home invasion."

"Could you break into your own place?"

A slow smile spread across his mouth. "What do you think?"

That's what she thought. "You have skills, Mr. McCoy."

He chuckled. "Come on. We should go before the police delay us again. I want to leave town as soon as possible."

"How will they get inside?"

"Trent has a key. We have keys to each other's homes in case we need emergency access."

"Why did Trent say you might have a leak if the tech team didn't accompany the crime scene team?"

"The tech team will look for surveillance equipment planted in my house."

She stared. "Surveillance equipment?"

"Bugs and cameras. The intruders had plenty of time inside the house and we don't know how long ago they broke in."

Oh, man. Being under that kind of scrutiny made Piper's stomach twist. "You were gone almost a month."

He frowned. "Someone could have been targeting me the entire time." Liam glanced at her. "Did you notice anything odd while I was gone?"

Other than missing him until she could barely breathe most days? Piper shook her head.

"Did anything strike you as weird while you were at Wicks?"

She thought about the weeks when Liam and his teammates were gone. She and Delilah spoke frequently of the men in their lives in those long days. At least her boss talked to Matt every day or so. With her phone unsecured, Piper understood why she received a handful of texts from Liam but no conversations. He'd been concerned about her safety.

That's when she remembered the stranger who visited the shop soon after Bravo left town.

Liam glanced Piper's direction at her continued silence. "Tell me."

"This may be nothing. We have visitors from out of town in Wicks all the time."

"But someone stood out."

"One man," she confirmed.

"When did he visit Wicks?"

"Three days after Bravo left town. Otter Creek Community College had family day so the shop was crazy busy. The man I'm thinking of came in near the end of the day."

"Why did he stand out?"

"He came alone. The rest of our customers came in with other family members and friends."

"And?"

"He asked me to go to dinner with him."

Liam's eyes narrowed. "What did he say when you turned him down?"

Satisfaction bloomed inside Piper. Liam assumed she turned the man down without asking for confirmation. "He acted disappointed, but his eyes were filled with irritation."

"Have you seen him since?"

"Not in the store. I thought I saw him a time or two from the corner of my eye. When I turned to look, no one was there."

"Did he tell you his name?"

"Jerome. No last name." Why was Liam tense?

"Did he leave when you refused to go out with him?"

She snorted. "I wish. He stuck around a few minutes, pressuring me to change my mind. I finally told him I was dating someone. About that time, Delilah finished helping the last of the other customers and informed Jerome that Wicks was closing for the night."

"What did he do?"

"Bought seven lavender candles and left."

"Did he use a credit or debit card?"

"He was the only person who paid with cash that day. Everyone else used plastic."

"Describe him."

"Taller than you by a couple inches at least, thin salt-and-pepper hair, black-rimmed glasses. He was in shape. Powerful build."

"Was his hair long, short, in between?"

"Short. Reminds me of yours."

"What about his eyes? Do you remember the color?"

Piper shook her head. "Sorry."

"What about his clothing?"

"That's another thing that made him stand out. The visitors in Wicks for family day wore jeans, long-sleeved shirts, and tennis shoes. Jerome wore camouflage pants, black t-shirt, and boots similar to yours."

"Did he ask about the man you were dating?"

"He was more interested in persuading me to go on a date than finding out about his competition. Do you think you know him?"

"I don't know. He seems to be an average guy with average coloring who takes care of himself." Liam activated his Bluetooth system.

After one ring, Matt's voice filled the SUV's cabin. "How is Piper?"

The question brought a smile to her face. "I'm fine, Matt. Thanks for watching over me until Liam came to the hospital."

"No problem. What do you need, Liam?"

"Two things. Can Delilah handle Wicks a few days without Piper?"

"She'll work out something. If she needs help, I'll see if a PSI trainee will assist her."

"And serve as her bodyguard."

"You're sworn to secrecy, Piper. I don't want her to know I might assign someone to protect her."

She laughed. "Your wife is one smart lady. She'll know. To keep you from worrying, she'll allow it."

The medic chuckled. "What's the second thing you need, Liam?"

"Did Fortress install the alarm system in Wicks?"

"Two PSI trainees installed it under my supervision."

"Cameras inside?"

"One facing the front door, another facing the cash register. I'm installing another camera at the back door tomorrow to deter a repeat of last night. Why?"

"I want your permission for Z to access the security footage from three weeks ago." Liam explained about the break-ins at both houses and the man at Wicks.

"You think he's the one who broke into your house?"

"Maybe. If we can identify him, I'll be able to clear him if he's not involved."

"And if he is?"

A grim smile curved Liam's mouth. "I'll have a starting point, won't I? If he wants me bad enough to try for Piper while I'm on a mission, he won't go far."

"Tell Zane to check the security feeds. I want to know what he learns."

"Copy that. Thanks, Matt."

"Yep. I have to go. My trainee class is waiting. Don't be a hero, Liam. If you need us, we're there."

"I hear you." He ended the call.

"You think Jerome broke into your house?"

"I'll find out." He made another call, this time to Zane at Fortress. "It's Liam. Need another favor."

"Before you tell me what you need, I have information for you. Is Piper with you?"

Piper straightened at his grim tone. "I'm here."

"What's wrong, Z?" Liam asked as he wrapped his hand around Piper's.

"Gino Romano and Matteo Barone are more than childhood friends."

Piper's stomach lurched. "What are you saying?"

"I'm sorry, Piper, but law enforcement suspects your uncle is laundering money for Barone."

CHAPTER ELEVEN

Piper felt as though she'd taken a punch to the gut. "That can't be true. Uncle Gino didn't approve of Matteo's activities. You said law enforcement suspected money laundering. They don't have proof."

"The feds are close to having what they need to file charges against him."

No. Just no. Pain speared her heart. "Uncle Gino knows how I feel about Matteo. He admitted his old friend had changed and not in a good way."

"Be prepared, Piper. If your uncle is involved with Barone, he's going to prison."

She dropped her head against Liam's shoulder, too stunned and hurt to reply. She prayed the feds cleared her uncle.

"Keep digging, Zane." Liam rubbed his cheek against the crown of her head, offering silent comfort. "We have to know for sure."

"Copy that. Now, what do you need?"

"Access the security footage for Wicks, Delilah Rainer's candle shop in Otter Creek." He gave Zane the date. "Start at noon and make a copy of the feed until seven o'clock that night."

"What am I looking for?"

"A man with salt-and-pepper hair, black-framed glasses, built, dressed in camouflage pants and black shirt." He frowned. "He'll be the one asking Piper for a date."

Zane laughed. "Are you serious?"

Liam growled. "Just do it."

"You can't convince me you're checking this guy because of jealousy. I doubt she looked twice at him. What's behind the sudden interest?"

He explained about the break-ins at Piper's house and his. "Can't prove it, but I think this man is involved in the security breach at my place."

Zane gave a low whistle. "Are the break-ins connected?"

"Doubt it. Piper's place was tossed. Mine was searched but nothing is out of place. Whoever broke into my house was trained. In addition, run a deeper search for interest in me or Piper."

"Your teammates report security breaches?"

"No. This feels personal."

"I'll see what I can find. Expect the security feeds in your email within the hour."

"Transfer me to the boss. I haven't reported to him yet."

"Roger that. Later."

In seconds, another deep voice filled the cabin. "You're home from deployment less than a day and you ran into trouble. What's going on?"

"You're on speaker with Piper Reece."

"Ah. Nice to talk to you, Piper. I'm Brent Maddox, owner of Fortress Security. What's happening, Liam."

He gave a rapid-fire report. "Zane is running a deep check to see if someone is inquiring about us."

"I assume you haven't taken out an ad or fired up a social media presence in recent days. Has your family or Piper mentioned you online?"

"Not me." Piper was aware of the extra lengths the operatives' wives went to in order to protect their mates. No one mentioned a spouse on any social media platform and said almost nothing about their work with the townspeople, much to the annoyance of Otter Creek's gossips.

"I'll talk to my mother and sister, but they're used to a media blackout from when I was in Special Forces. They don't view my current job in a different light."

"Is it possible Barone is targeting Piper through you?"

"The MO is different for both break-ins, Brent."

"He might have hired a trained professional since you work for Fortress."

"How would he know?" Piper asked. "I haven't talked to my uncle since I left Alabama. Gino doesn't know I'm involved with Liam."

"People pass through Otter Creek all the time, especially since the community college is so large. Who would notice another stranger in town? A little reconnaissance and Barone would have the information. People talk. Go to Delaney's Diner, mention Wicks, and I'd bet the waitress would talk about the staff at Wicks and their significant others. The whole town's been watching your relationship with Liam slowly come to life."

"It's my fault Liam is a target." The knowledge she might be to blame for another threat to Liam made her insides knot.

Liam pressed a kiss to her temple. "We don't know that. When we identify the culprit, we'll track him down and find out why he chose my house. Brent, the security cameras at my house might have caught an image. Given the professional nature of the search, I'm not holding my breath on that."

"I'll have Zane check anyway. If the security breach is connected to you, which direction we should look?"

He was silent a moment. "I was involved in an incident six months before I mustered out of the Marines."

"Spencer?"

Liam chuckled. "My file is supposed to be classified."

"Nothing is out of Zane's reach."

"Yeah, I'm beginning to see that. Start with Spencer and Major Conrad Graham."

A soft whistle. "You don't mess around when you tick someone off, do you? I'll get back to you."

After the call ended, Liam glanced at Piper. "Ask."

"Do I have a neon sign on my forehead?"

"It's natural to be curious. I'd be surprised if you weren't."

"Who are Spencer and Graham?"

"Spencer was in my unit and Conrad Graham was our CO."

"Why do they have a grudge against you?"

"I turned Spencer in to our CO for stealing artifacts and selling them for profit. Turned out Graham was in on the scheme and I almost died in my effort to keep the Marine Corp's name clean. Spencer and the CO were sentenced to prison for antiquities theft. They were dishonorably discharged and will forfeit their pension."

"What happened to you?"

"Our unit was sent on a mission in Afghanistan to retrieve an HVT."

"Wait. HVT?"

"Sorry. High-value target. Anyway, we walked into an ambush. I lost three good friends that night."

"I'm sorry, Liam. Were your other teammates hurt?"

"Two had minor injuries."

"And you?"

He remained silent.

"You were shot, weren't you?"

Liam nodded. "Once in the chest, once in the abdomen."

Piper sucked in a breath. "Is this the incident that landed you in a hospital for months?"

"Yeah, it is. I had a lot of time to think while recuperating. A few buddies visited or called. Didn't take long to figure out my CO was responsible for leaking my unit's location to the area insurgents."

Horrified that she might have lost her chance to know Liam because of greed, Piper couldn't stop herself from planting a kiss on his jaw. So close.

Liam wrapped his hand around hers. "Me, too. I feel guilty, though."

"Because you survived and your friends didn't."

"They're dead because the CO targeted me. Graham knew I suspected someone else helped Spencer. He was afraid if I kept digging, I'd track the leads to him. He used insurgents to do his dirty work."

"Would you have stopped your investigation before you found the partner?"

He slid her a look, his expression grim. "Never."

Once Liam locked on, he wouldn't let go. "How serious were your injuries?"

"The doctors weren't sure I would pull through." He shrugged. "They were wrong."

"No matter what happens with us, my life is better for having known you."

Liam didn't say anything, just squeezed her hand. The miles passed with him watching the mirrors and the surrounding area. Over an hour after leaving Otter Creek, Liam parked in the lot beside the ski resort's main lodge. He met Piper at the front of the SUV. "It's beautiful here."

"This resort used to be one of my favorite places to retreat from the real world."

He tilted his head. "What happened?"

"Gavin brought Brandy here."

Liam tugged her into his arms. "I hate that he hurt you, Sunshine."

"I'm over it and, looking back, I'm grateful."

"Why?"

"Gavin showed me his true self before I fell too hard for him. He was pushing for more, but something held me back. Now I'm glad I hesitated to make a deeper commitment. If he cheated on me with Brandy and Anita, he would have done the same throughout our relationship and marriage."

He cupped the side of her face. "You don't have to worry about that with me. I wouldn't cheat on you."

Piper tightened her grip around his waist. "I know." When Liam gave his word, he kept it.

After pressing a kiss to her forehead, he released Piper. "Let's store our gear in the suite and meet Simon."

"Maybe he found Gavin and confronted him."

A somber glance from the man at her side. "Nothing is ever that easy."

They registered at the front desk and obtained a key card. Liam escorted Piper to the suite and returned to the SUV for their gear. When she offered to help him, he waved her offer aside. "Explore the suite. I'll be back in a minute."

Piper freshened up, then wandered onto the balcony. She breathed deep, dragging in pine-scented air and shivering as a cool breeze blew across her skin. She'd forgotten how cold the temperature could be at the resort in December. She wouldn't be surprised if snow fell in the next few days.

Liam returned to the suite with Simon on his heels. Both men carried bags inside.

Piper left the balcony and locked the French doors. "What do you think of the resort, Simon?"

"It's nice. I might return the next time Bravo is on a break and do some skiing."

Liam's eyebrows soared. "You interested in a date with a ski bunny?"

A quick smile. "Maybe. Depends on whether or not the woman I have my eye on in Otter Creek is interested in going out with me."

Piper grinned. "Who is she, Simon?"

He shook his head. "I'm not saying."

"Aww, come on."

"Forget it, Piper. If she turns me down, I don't want pitying looks from my friends."

"Fine. Have it your way. Have you chosen a bedroom yet?"

"It's ladies' choice. I don't care which room I sleep in."

"I'll take the room on the right, then."

Liam carried her bags to her room and returned to sit on the couch with Piper. "What have you discovered?" he asked Simon.

"I flashed Gavin's picture around the resort. A waitress and a ski instructor remember him being here yesterday." He slanted a look at Piper.

"Let me guess. He hit on them?"

"Yes, ma'am."

"He hasn't changed since I broke up with him." Once again, she was grateful she'd seen the truth before it was too late.

"Is he still at the resort?" Liam asked.

"I chatted up one of the housekeepers. His bags are here but no one's seen him in hours."

They would find Gavin and get some answers. "What about his vehicle?"

"I located a late-model black Escalade with Alabama tags in the parking lot. According to Zane, the tags are registered to Gavin James. He's at the resort somewhere."

"He's waiting for Piper to arrive," Liam said.

Piper's eyes narrowed. "I want to talk to him."

Liam slid her a look. "So do I."

Oh, boy. That look said Liam wanted to do more than talk. Great. She might have to enlist Simon's help to keep the two men separated. "What should we do first?"

Liam glanced at his black watch. "We have about four hours of daylight left. Do you want to eat first or try to find the cave?"

"Cave."

"If we can't find it within two hours, we'll try again tomorrow."

"I'll grab my pack," Simon said.

Minutes later, they left the lodge. Liam and Simon each carried packs on their back.

"Why are you carrying equipment into the forest?" Piper asked Liam. Simon walked about twenty feet in front of them, his gait covering the terrain with ground-eating strides.

Man, the Fortress operatives were in fantastic shape. Liam and Simon weren't even breaking a sweat while Piper was breathing hard and they were only fifteen minutes into this hike.

"We don't go anywhere without survival gear."

"Even in Otter Creek?"

Liam threaded his fingers through hers. "I keep a bag packed in my SUV at all times."

"What's in the bag?"

"Enough supplies to keep us comfortable for a couple days and basic camping gear."

"That's part of expecting the best but being prepared for the worst?"

He nodded as Simon stopped and looked back at them.

"The path forks. Which way, Piper?"

"Left toward the rock face."

The other operative surged ahead.

Liam pulled a sleek black phone with a metallic pink cover from his pocket. He handed it to Piper. "Your new phone. It's encrypted. No one will intercept your calls or texts. I'll also be able to talk to you while I'm deployed now."

She took the phone from him and grinned in delight at the cover. "Thank you, Liam. I miss hearing your voice while you and your teammates are gone."

"I planned to give you the phone before we deployed last month but Fortress only gave us an hour's notice at two in the morning. I didn't have the heart to wake you to deliver the phone."

Piper gave him a sideways glance. "I wouldn't have minded. I hated that I didn't have a chance to say goodbye."

"Me, too. I missed you like crazy."

"Same here. You were gone a long time."

"Longer than we anticipated. We had to assist another team." He was silent a moment. "There will be times I'll be gone for several weeks. It's part of my job, Piper."

"I understand."

"I don't have control over when the deployments occur. We go when and where we're needed. That means I will miss some birthdays, holidays, and anniversaries."

Anniversaries? "I'll handle the absences like the other women involved with Fortress operatives. I'll stay busy until you return." She nudged his shoulder with her own. "I expect you to spoil me when you return from deployment."

"I'll do my best to make up for my absences. Most women can't handle what we do and the unpredictable schedule."

"I'm not most women. Give me a chance to prove I can handle it, Liam. You're worth the learning curve."

The subtle tension in his body eased. "I'll do anything I can to help you adjust. I don't want to lose you."

She squeezed his hand.

They walked in silence until Piper recognized a large split rock. "Simon, head for that rock formation to the left."

With a wave to acknowledge her instructions, he veered to the left. Ten minutes later, Simon stopped at the foot of a mountain with multiple caves dotting the rocky surface. As he waited for them to catch up, he studied the terrain. "I hope you remember which cave your friend referred to, Piper," he said when she and Liam stopped beside him. "There must be a dozen caves up here."

Piper studied the hillside. She pointed to one of two caves near the center of the mountain. "I think it's the one on the right."

"We'll find out soon enough." Liam slid his pack off his shoulders, grabbed a bottle of water, and gave it to Piper. While she drank, he scanned the area.

"I feel it, too," Simon murmured.

Piper looked from one man to the other. "Feel what?"

"Someone is watching us." Liam wrapped his arms around Piper and turned so her back was to the mountainside and his body stood between her and the observer.

She pushed at his chest to look for herself.

Liam didn't loosen his hold. "We don't want to let on that we're aware of his presence. Act as though we're on an outing with a friend."

Although the idea of someone watching them from the shadows creeped her out, she snuggled into his embrace, her head resting over his heart. "I hate that you have to protect me."

"I will always stand between you and danger, Sunshine." Liam held her for a couple minutes before easing her away from him, still keeping his body between her and the unseen threat. "You ready?"

"Let's get this over with."

"Simon will take the lead. You go up after him. I'll be right behind you."

Covering her back and protecting her with his own body. Almost sick with worry for his safety, Piper hurried after Simon. The sooner they were inside the cave, the quicker Liam would be out of the crosshairs.

After fifteen minutes of climbing, Simon skirted the large outcropping of rocks near the cave entrance. He walked to the mouth of the cave and came to a sudden stop. He looked at Liam, expression grim.

"What's wrong?" Piper asked, her heart rate accelerating.

"Don't go into the cave."

"Why not?"

"Stay with her." Liam pressed a light kiss to Piper's lips and disappeared inside the cave. He returned two minutes later. "Describe Gavin."

No. Oh, no. "Black hair, brown eyes, about six foot two, maybe two hundred pounds."

"Any distinguishing characteristics?"

"He has a mole near the outside corner of his right eye. Liam, what's going on?"

He pulled her against his chest. "I'm sorry, Piper, but Gavin is dead."

CHAPTER TWELVE

"I want to see. You might be mistaken."

Liam shook his head, holding Piper tight as her body reacted to his news about Gavin's death. Tremors wracked her frame. "You don't want your last memory of Gavin to be of him like this." He'd seen plenty of death in his years in black ops. Piper didn't need the sight of her former boyfriend with a bullet through his heart burned into her brain.

She buried her face against his neck.

"I'm sorry, baby." He held Piper while she wept. When the tears slowed, Liam bent until his mouth was beside her ear. "You aren't safe here."

When she gave a slight nod, he started them down the mountainside.

"We can't allow Barone to find the information and destroy it or Gavin's death will be in vain."

"We'll talk later." When they couldn't be overheard and Liam wouldn't worry about bullets flying toward them.

He tightened his arm around her waist and lengthened his stride. Urgency gripped him. He needed to get Piper under cover. This whole thing felt like a setup.

On the other side of Piper, Simon scanned the area as he pulled out his phone and made a call. "Z, we've got trouble." In terse words, he gave updated the tech guru. "We need everything you can find on Gavin James." Simon glanced at Liam. "And tell the lawyer to stay on standby."

Piper wiped tears from her face. "What will we do, Liam?"

"Whatever we have to do." Despite the pitfalls of reporting Gavin's death, Liam didn't have the heart to leave the man's body for a hiker to stumble upon or for the wild animals to devour.

His only hope of staying out of jail lay in the time of death and the fact Gavin hadn't been seen for hours before he and Piper registered at the resort. Definitely not an air-tight alibi, though. Liam hadn't stopped on the way to the resort to minimize the risk to Piper, a problem now that he needed proof he wasn't in the area prior to registering at the resort.

He hoped Zane could hack into the traffic cams on their route and get the time-stamped footage of their SUV passing various points along the way. Liam's gut tightened into a knot. That would take time and meant being separated from Piper again. At least Simon was here to protect her if the cops hauled Liam in for intensive questioning. Unfortunately, they might question Simon as well, which would leave piper without a bodyguard. Liam had to be sure she was covered. "Everything will work out, Piper."

"How can you say that? These people killed Gavin. I don't want to lose you."

Something startled wildlife to their left.

He tightened his hold on Piper's waist and propelled her faster through the woods. Simon dropped back to cover them.

Liam scanned to his left and noticed a bright reflection. His gut knotted. "Gun!" He shoved Piper behind a large boulder and dragged her to the forest floor as shots rang out. He covered her body with his. Shards of rock flew in every direction, some peppering him and Piper. "Stay down," he murmured, getting into a crouch beside her.

He glanced at Simon. "Get a bead on his location?"

"Ten o'clock. Stay with Piper. I'll circle around and take him down."

Although he longed to go after the thug himself, Liam nodded. Keeping Piper safe was his priority. "We need him alive."

"That's up to him."

"Watch your back, Simon. He might have a friend."

He was gone with a whisper of movement.

"Where's he going?" Piper started to get up.

Liam laid a hand on her shoulder. "Not yet. Simon is hunting for the shooter."

Her eyes widened. "Go with him. He shouldn't go alone."

"Simon knows what he's doing. One of us needs to stay with you in case the shooter has a friend using the shots as a distraction to capture you."

More shots rang out, this time from a different location. On alert, Liam maneuvered to the right side of the rock and surveyed the dense brush and trees, wishing he had his M107 sniper rifle instead of a Sig. Would have looked odd striding into the forest with his sniper rifle strapped to his back, though. He'd have to make do with the shorter-range weapon.

A single shot was followed by a loud yelp from the left. Then there was silence.

Piper gripped Liam's forearm. "Simon?"

"Not the one who yelled." He hoped his friend had winged the shooter.

Ten minutes later, Simon strode into view with his hand gripping a big bruiser by the arm. The thug's hands were restrained behind his back and his mouth moved continuously in a string of inventive curses.

Simon shoved him to the ground in front of the rock formation. "Watch your mouth. There's a lady present."

The man glared at the operative and glanced around with cold eyes. Looking for an escape route, a partner, or Piper?

Liam reached down and helped Piper stand. "Did he have friends?" he asked Simon.

"One. He won't be a problem."

"It's your fault," the stranger growled, his gaze fixed on Piper. "You're the reason he's dead."

Who was he referring to? The second shooter or Gavin? Liam stepped in front of Piper, blocking her from the shooter's view. "He's dead because of his own choices." He pulled out his cell phone.

The shooter smirked. "No signal out here, dude."

He ignored the verbal jab. "Get his prints," he told Simon. Zane could run them while he and the others waited for the local cops to arrive.

More cursing filled the air as Simon shoved the stranger onto his stomach, jarring the shoulder with a bullet wound, and proceeded to press the man's fingers and thumbs to the screen of his phone, one at a time. When he was finished, Simon slapped the back the man's head. "Shut up or I'll gag you."

Another hate-filled glare Simon's direction but the man subsided.

With Piper at his side, Liam reported the murder and attempted murder to the police. He gave the dispatcher their coordinates and promised to wait for law enforcement to arrive. Although he'd rather get Piper out of here, he couldn't leave Simon to deal with the cops alone. He'd defended himself when the two thugs shot at him. Liam had been inside the cave with Gavin's body as he was sure the remaining shooter would be happy to inform the police. Anything to muddy the waters and separate Liam from Piper.

He caught Simon's eye. "You okay here for a minute? I need to talk to my woman alone."

"Yeah." He gave a slow smile. "Our new friend and I will get better acquainted."

For the first time, the thug looked uneasy. He should. Simon was a top-notch interrogator. Whatever this guy knew, Simon would find out before the cops arrived on the scene.

Liam ushered Piper deeper into the trees. He stopped far enough away that they wouldn't be observed but close enough to aid Simon if he needed help. A muffled yell sounded behind them.

Piper turned back. "Something's wrong."

"Simon's asking the shooter a few questions."

She stared a moment. "Doesn't sound like a friendly question-and-answer session."

"Don't ask me anything about that. Take this." He dragged an envelope from his pocket and held it out to Piper. "Don't open or read it right now."

She frowned. "What is this?"

"Gavin left it for you. Hide it."

Piper sat on a nearby fallen tree and unlaced her hiking boot. She arranged the envelope inside, slid her foot in, and tied her laces. "Why give the envelope to me?"

"There's an excellent chance the police will take me into custody and transport me to the station for interrogation. I don't want them to get their hands on this."

"Liam." Piper's voice sounded choked. "Not again. This isn't your fault. You didn't kill him."

He cupped her jaw and leaned in to brush a soft kiss over her lips. "I'll be their primary suspect."

"You didn't know Gavin."

"I'm involved with you. They'll assume I'm a jealous, insecure boyfriend who felt threatened when Gavin contacted you and asked you to meet him."

"You aren't jealous or insecure."

"Not insecure, no. Jealous?" He cupped her nape. "Don't kid yourself, Sunshine. If I thought another man was a rival for your affection, I'd have a hard time with it. Any man would."

"You don't have any reason for that. I haven't looked at another man since I arrived in Otter Creek. The only man I want is you."

Liam drew in a shuddering breath. "You don't have any idea how badly I want to kiss you right now."

"Why don't you?" Her lips curved into a smile. "I won't tell."

He gave a rough laugh. "No way. I want to be where I won't worry about your safety. The woods where we were shot at a few minutes ago is not the place and this isn't the time. Soon, though. I promise."

A siren sounded in the distance.

"We need to go back." Liam reluctantly moved away from her. "The police will separate us. I want Simon to stay with you but that won't happen. Use your new phone to call Trent. The numbers for each of my teammates, Zane Murphy, and Brent Maddox are programmed into the phone already. Lock yourself inside the suite and stay there until one of my teammates arrives."

He moved toward Simon and the prisoner despite his driving need to drag Piper against his chest and kiss her until they both forgot about anything but each other. Liam had never wanted to shirk his duty as much as he did at that moment.

He couldn't. Piper's life was at stake. The best thing to do for both of them was discover what Gavin had dragged them into and find a way to get them out.

Bravo had a month in Otter Creek before they were up for deployment again. Liam would rather spend his time courting the beautiful woman by his side than hunting for a killer. Worse, if he didn't unmask the killer before their leave time was up, he'd be forced to leave Piper's safety to Durango or one of the PSI trainees. He didn't think he could do it. He'd have to wrap this up before his leave ended. There was no other option that he could live with.

When they returned to the small clearing, Simon stood near their prisoner. The thug's face was pasty white.

Liam stopped Piper before she moved too close. "What did you find out?" he asked Simon.

"Dude's name is Mark Oberfeld. According to our tech friend, Mark has a record a mile long. He likes to play with guns and knives and doesn't think twice about hurting people. Takes pride in his free-lance work and is well-paid for his efforts. His boss won't be happy with him."

"Who sent him?"

"He's a gun for hire. He doesn't know who put money in his account to shoot you."

Liam stiffened. That's not what he'd expected to hear. "Me? Not my woman?"

"Somebody doesn't want you near the lady."

Leaving her vulnerable to attack. Barone's handiwork? Her uncle's? "What about our friend in the cave?"

"He doesn't know anything about that."

"You believe him?"

Simon snorted. "He told me everything in less than two minutes."

Liam's gaze shifted to Oberfeld. "What about your friend? Did he know anything about the body in the cave?"

"Never saw him before today," he muttered. "The person who hired me said to expect another person to take the woman. My job was you."

"Loused that up, didn't you?" That crack earned Liam a glare.

"Cops will be here in less than five," Simon murmured. "Get what you need now."

He grabbed his phone, checked the email Zane sent, and brought up the picture of Gavin. Liam turned his phone around so the thug could see the picture. "Know this guy?"

Oberfeld glanced at the picture and shook his head. "Never seen him before."

Liam showed him the picture of Barone and Piper's uncle. "What about these two?"

Another head shake. "Told you. I don't know who hired me. It's part of my protection."

Terse voices and running feet heralded the arrival of the police. Liam pressed a kiss to the top of Piper's head. Now the real fun would begin.

CHAPTER THIRTEEN

"Hands in the air," shouted the first officer in the clearing. "Get on the ground. Now."

"Everything will work out," Liam murmured to Piper. "Do exactly as they tell you and don't volunteer information. Answer questions they ask and nothing more."

Liam wished he had time for more coaching but he didn't want to be shot by a twitchy cop because he didn't obey the commands. They didn't know the circumstances and, until they did, would have to treat everyone as guilty of a crime.

He released her and backed away, hands in the air. He lowered himself to the ground and spread his arms and legs as did Simon. Piper was slower to react but complied as well. Liam hated to see the fear on her face. He kept his gaze locked with hers as law enforcement rushed to their sides and searched them for weapons. Their tension ratcheted up several notches when they found multiple weapons on him and Simon.

Once all three of them had been cuffed, the senior officer separated Liam, Simon, and Piper from each other and called in to dispatch to request an ambulance for the thug with the shoulder wound. That done, the officer turned to Liam. "What's the story here?"

He gave a brief account of discovering Gavin's body in the cave, the shots fired at them as they left the mountainside, and the hunt for the shooters.

"Why didn't you run for help? You should have called us," the policeman insisted.

"I was in the Marines and my friend was in the Army. We don't run from trouble and my girlfriend's life was in danger." He inclined his head toward the pile of weapons confiscated from him and Simon. "Obviously, we're well armed. If your girlfriend or wife's life was in danger, would you run for help?"

The man grunted. "I'm the one with the badge. What about the man with the gunshot wound?"

Liam shrugged. "He was shooting at us. We defended ourselves."

A shout went up a moment later. "Got a body here."

The cop's eyes narrowed as he rounded on Liam. "A second body?"

"Second shooter. He fired first."

"Did you kill him?"

Liam shook his head. The cops would test his Sig and find he hadn't fired his weapon. Since Piper wasn't armed, that left Simon. "I stayed with Piper in case a third shooter was in the woods."

"How long have you been at the resort?"

A small smile curved his lips. "Less than two hours."

The other man shook his head. "The homicide detectives will be here soon." He waved one of the other officers over to watch Liam and walked to Piper.

Liam kept his attention focused on the other man, watching for signs of aggression. Having his hands cuffed behind his back wouldn't prevent him from protecting Piper should there be need. The odds were against him with this many cops in the clearing but between him and Simon, they would get to her if these cops were dirty.

From the body language Liam observed, the policeman treated Piper with respect and gentleness. Within a couple minutes, he waved another officer over to stay with Piper and moved on to Simon.

Liam knew the exact moment the cop learned Simon had killed one thug and wounded the other. The man's body stiffened and his focus intensified. After a few minutes, he rose and signaled two officers to stay with Simon.

Yeah, this was going to be a mess. Liam angled his body to keep Piper in view at all times. He wanted to go to her and was frustrated that he couldn't. She didn't deserve to be cuffed, sitting on the cold ground.

Thirty minutes later, a man and woman strode into the clearing and met with the senior officer in the center of the open space. After a short discussion, the two newcomers approached Liam.

The man held out his badge as did the woman. "Detectives Barrett and Kerrigan," he said. "Officer Rothchild says you found a body in a cave up the mountain."

"That's right."

"We need you to show us where you found the body."

"Either uncuff me or restrain my hands in the front."

Barrett's eyebrows rose. "Why should I?'

Liam inclined his head toward the mountain. "The climb is steep. I'm unarmed. The trek will be less hazardous for all of us if I have better balance." A slight prevarication. He'd make the climb whether or not his hands were restrained in the front or back. He stood a better chance of defending himself with the change. He was still unsure if another shooter lingered in the area.

Barrett help Liam to his feet. A moment later, he was restrained with his hands in front.

Liam glanced at Simon who gave a slight chin lift in acknowledgment of his silent order to keep Piper safe. His attention shifted to Piper who watched him with wide eyes, worry in her gaze. He winked at her and allowed the detectives to lead him from the clearing.

He guided the two officers to the cave. He inclined his head toward the entrance. "Gavin's about fifty feet from the entrance."

Barrett frowned. "How do you know his name?"

Here's where things would become dicey. "Piper knew him well. He called her and said he was leaving something for her in this cave."

"How well did she know him?"

"They used to date. She hasn't seen him in three years."

"He wanted to see her and she came running?" Barrett looked skeptical. "Sounds like their relationship wasn't over."

Liam sighed. Just what he'd figured the cops would say. "Look, I didn't know about Gavin James until a few hours ago and I've never seen him until I found him in the cave."

"You expect us to believe that?" Kerrigan shook her head. "You had the motive to kill this poor sap. Your girlfriend was going back to her former lover, leaving you in the dust. You decided to take him out and end the competition for her affection once and for all."

"My weapon hasn't been fired which you'll find out when you test it. Gavin's been dead longer than I've been in Copper Ridge."

"We only have your word for when you arrived."

"You'll investigate and confirm my arrival time."

Barrett glanced at his partner. "Wait with McCoy. I'll check inside and see what we have."

Kerrigan stepped a few paces away from Liam and, with her hand on her weapon, motioned for him to move further from the cave entrance.

Barrett returned a moment later. "One shot through the heart. Small-caliber weapon. We need the crime scene team and the coroner." He glanced at Liam. "Let's go. We need to be closer to the resort to get a cell signal."

Liam retraced his steps to the clearing and crouched by Piper's side. "You okay?" He didn't like the pallor of her face.

She nodded.

"Get away from her, McCoy," Kerrigan snapped, weapon in her hand.

Simon snorted.

Liam's lips twitched. "Just making sure Piper was all right."

"You can't talk to her. Sit on that rock." The detective indicated the large rock fifteen feet away from Piper.

He knew things moved slower in law enforcement than he was used to with Fortress, but by the time the coroner pronounced Gavin and the other shooter dead and the crime scene team moved in to do their job, Liam was fed up with watching Piper shiver in the cold night air. Part of the trembling was from shock.

Liam clenched his teeth, wishing yet again he had Matt here to help Piper. "Barrett."

The detective walked over. "What is it?"

"Have one of the officers take Piper to the resort or the station. She's cold and in shock."

Barrett glanced at the woman who visibly trembled. He turned back. "What about you? Aren't you going to demand I send you to a more hospitable environment?"

"Doesn't matter about me. Take care of Piper."

The detective crossed the open space and spoke to the officer with Piper. A moment later, she stumbled from the clearing with the officer's hand around her arm to steady her.

Although Liam didn't want her out of his sight, she needed to get warm. When Barrett returned, Liam asked, "Where did he take her?"

"The station. That's where I'm taking you and your buddy. On your feet, McCoy."

The ball of ice in his stomach melted. At least he would be in the same building with Piper. He hoped she'd be released soon and would call Matt or another member of Bravo to stay with her until Liam returned to her side.

He and Simon walked to the resort parking lot where the law enforcement vehicles waited. They rode in the backseat of Barrett's SUV after a stern warning not to talk to each other on the drive.

Inside the station, Liam and Simon were taken to two interrogation rooms. Liam noted the camera, two-sided mirror, and the one exit. Some enterprising soul had defaced the table with a variety of curse words and racial slurs while he or she waited for the interview process to begin.

Instead of giving away his agitation, Liam remained still and used the wait time to review everything he knew about what was happening to Piper, sifting the facts into different order, hunting for a solution.

Too many pieces were missing to make much headway. He wasn't sure whether the kidnapping and shooting this evening were connected to Piper's past or his own. If it was hers, Liam knew where the intimidation and danger dogging her heels originated. If the events were connected to him, the list of people who wanted him dead was a long one. As soon as the cops sprung him, he would find Piper and call Zane. If anyone could nail this down, it would be the tech guru.

The door opened. Barrett and Kerrigan walked in and sat down on the other side of the table, a file between them. "Let's talk," Barrett said.

CHAPTER FOURTEEN

"What is taking so long?" Piper pivoted and walked the other direction. She'd been pacing the length of the suite's living room for the past two hours and the clock had just ticked past midnight. She was ready to demand a member of Bravo drive her to the police station and insist the police release Liam and Simon. "This is ridiculous. Simon defended himself and Liam protected me. They didn't do anything wrong."

Trent St. Claire stretched his legs out in front of him. "Police investigations take time. Don't waste your energy."

"Those are your teammates. You should be raising a ruckus to get them released."

"First, Liam would have my hide if I ended up tossed in jail because he's more concerned with your protection than his own comfort. Second, Matt and Cade are searching Gavin's room before it's cordoned off. Third, the lawyer will do more for Liam and Simon than I can. She knows the ins and outs of the law far better than I ever will. That woman is a shark and Fortress pays her a large retainer fee to be available 24/7 for their operatives. You can trust her to vigorously defend Liam and Simon."

Piper scowled. "Did the Fortress lawyer have to be a woman?"

Bravo's leader chuckled. "She's happily married with two kids under five. She's a threat to police plans for Liam and Simon, but no threat to you."

Feeling catty, Piper held up her hands in surrender. "How soon will Matt and Cade return?"

"Anytime."

Someone inserted a key card into the lock and opened the door. When Liam and Simon walked in, Piper breathed a sigh of relief.

She threw herself into Liam's open arms and the tension riding her for the past seven hours disappeared. "Liam."

"Are you okay, Sunshine?" he murmured against her ear.

"I am now. What about you? Did they hurt you or Simon?"

Liam shook his head. "Barrett and Kerrigan are slow but they're good cops. We're fine." He cupped her face between his callused palms. "Thank you for doing as I asked and calling in my team." He glanced at Trent. "Thanks for watching over Piper."

"No problem. Matt and Cade are searching Gavin's room."

"Barrett and Kerrigan are returning to the resort soon to search his room."

"Catch up later." Simon frowned. "Piper, is the kitchen open this late?"

"No, but we ordered food from room service before they closed. The plates are in the oven." She set the plates on the small table and retrieved the canned drinks and bottles of water the other operatives had purchased for them.

Liam seated Piper before seating himself and uncovering the meal. A large serving of lasagna filled the plate along with two foil-wrapped breadsticks. "This looks terrific. Thanks."

The two men scarfed down the food and polished off a soft drink by the time Cade and Matt returned to the suite.

"Did you show them the dessert you ordered?" Matt asked Piper.

Simon's eyes brightened. "Dessert?"

"One piece of strawberry cheesecake and one of chocolate cake."

"I call dibs on the cheesecake." He rubbed his hands together, anticipation on his face.

Liam laid a hand on Piper's shoulder when she started to stand. "I'll get them. Did you find anything we can use, Matt?"

The medic settled on a barstool at the breakfast bar. "Not me. Cade did, though."

The EOD man's gaze flickered to Piper then back to Liam. "Two passports. One a male with Gavin's picture on it with a different name. The second one belonged to a woman with the name Sienna Chambers. Looks like old Gavin was planning to skip the country with a woman."

Piper stiffened, her hand fisting on top of the table. She shouldn't be surprised. Three years had passed since Piper had last seen him and Gavin always had a woman on his arm. "What does she look like?"

Maybe she knew the woman. If so, she may be able to answer questions. At the very least, Piper planned to warn her that her life was in danger. If Barone was protecting himself, he wouldn't balk at hurting an innocent woman who had the misfortune of dating Gavin.

Cade pulled out his phone, tapped the screen, and turned it around. "Do you recognize this woman?"

She glanced at the screen and froze. Piper thought Gavin would have moved on by now. Three years and he was still with her. Was it possible Gavin had found true love at last?

Her brows knitted. If he had, why jeopardize the relationship by pursuing other women while he was still dating her?

"Piper?" Liam covered her fist with his hand. "Do you know her?"

"It's Brandy Strickland."

"The friend Gavin cheated on you with?"

She nodded.

Matt gave a low whistle. "Cold."

Piper flashed him a quick smile. "Frigid."

"You haven't seen Gavin in years." Liam squeezed her hand. "Have you talked to Brandy since you broke up with Gavin?"

"No. While I still lived in my hometown, I stayed away from anyone I knew except for the people from my job. I deliberately kept my personal and work life separate. With my uncle's questionable friendships, I didn't want to chance a co-worker coming into contact with Hartman's criminal element. Soon after breaking up with Gavin, I moved away from Alabama and started fresh in Knoxville. Two years later, I moved to Otter Creek."

He pressed a soft kiss to her temple, then retrieved the desserts.

"How did the interrogation go with the cops?" Trent asked.

A snort from Simon. "About like you expected. Local law enforcement pulled our service records and learned enough to convince them we're hired assassins out to make a name for ourselves. They think we used our military training to make bank and prove our prowess with weapons."

"Do we need to call in a favor to throw them off your backs?"

Piper's eyebrows rose. What kind of favor would convince the police that Liam and Simon weren't murderers for hire?

Liam waved that suggestion aside as he swallowed his first bite of cake. "Not yet. Barrett and Kerrigan figured out we have high-powered friends and influence in the military and Washington, D.C."

Okay, she couldn't keep silent any longer. Curiosity was eating her up inside. "High-powered friends?"

Liam glanced at Trent and received a nod of approval before turning back to Piper. "Our unit rescued a state department official's son from a terrorist group at the request of the president."

Piper's mouth gaped.

Cade sat on Piper's other side. "The terrorists threatened to kill him if four extremely dangerous men weren't released from a US prison and flown to Mexico. The men were responsible for multiple attacks against American civilians and troops abroad. The president would have refused the demand. He sent us to free the hostage before the terrorists carried out their threat. President Martin and the boy's father are long-time friends. Since he couldn't officially sanction a military mission, he contacted our boss at Fortress and requested Bravo."

"Because of that mission, several high-powered politicians and government leaders basically gave us a blank marker to use when we need it," Liam added.

Not if. When. "Why did your service records cause a stir? Did the detectives see mission details?" Civilian access to military files seemed to be a disaster in the making, especially since she suspected Liam and Simon weren't simple grunts on the front lines.

"Our missions are classified because we were Special Forces." Simon stuffed a bite of cheesecake into his mouth and sighed as he chewed. "Barrett and Kerrigan saw enough to realize we have elite training."

"The detectives know Simon and I are comfortable with weapons and excellent shots. We have the training and experience to commit the shootings and murder."

Simon flashed Liam a look. "You're not on the hook for shooting the thugs."

"Maybe not, but they're looking at me in connection to Gavin's death." When Trent scowled, Liam held up his hand. "We asked Zane to provide security and traffic cam footage to prove I wasn't near Gavin when he died."

"You could have hired a shooter," Piper pointed out.

"Why involve someone else in a job I could easily do myself?"

"Alibi?"

"Lousy alibi. I didn't stop anywhere along the route between Copper Ridge and Otter Creek. I can't prove where I was with a neutral witness. Although you rode with me, you're personally involved with me. They'll want proof. With security and traffic cam footage, Zane will provide irrefutable proof of our journey."

"He can't send the footage to the detectives. Wouldn't that look suspicious?"

"He's sending it to Stella. She's former FBI with law enforcement credentials a mile long. Stella will share the information with the detectives."

Trent nodded. "Smart."

"We need to find Brandy." Talking to Brandy again was not appealing on any level. If she knew something about Gavin's situation, though, Piper would handle the awkward situation to obtain answers.

What if something had happened to Brandy, too? Although their friendship had fallen apart, Piper didn't want Brandy hurt by the person who killed Gavin.

"Would Gavin hit on more women if Brandy was with him?" Liam asked.

Piper frowned. "Not if she was staying here at the resort. She could catch him in the act."

"Brandy might be staying somewhere else," Matt said. "Doesn't make sense, though. If they planned to flee the country, wouldn't she stay in the room with him so they could leave as soon as he hid the information?"

Piper straightened and glanced at Liam. How could she have forgotten? "The envelope. I forgot about it while I waited for you."

He swallowed the last bite of cake and crouched by Piper's side. "Let's take a look."

Liam unlaced her boot, slid it from her foot, and grabbed the white envelope. He handed her the envelope.

This was the moment where her belief in her uncle was confirmed or her foundation was torn away. With growing dread, Piper pulled out the piece of paper stuffed inside and unfolded the last message from Gavin.

As she scanned the contents, her heart sank. How could Gavin do this? Liam was right. Problems like these never had an easy solution. Now, instead of handing off the information to the feds, she would have to go into the lion's den. Worse, Liam would never let her do this alone which meant he'd be in more danger than ever.

CHAPTER FIFTEEN

Liam laid his hand on Piper's knee, concern knotting his gut. Distress had filled her eyes the longer she read Gavin's last letter. "What is it, Piper?"

"Gavin is sending us on a scavenger hunt."

He frowned. "This isn't the information on Barone?"

She shook her head. "He was afraid to leave the evidence where anyone could find it. This is a clue to the next location."

Simon stared. "A deep crevice in a cave is not exactly on the main tourist route."

"You have to understand how his mind worked. Gavin created quests for video games for a living. He loved the hunt."

"Do you like them?" Matt asked.

Another head shake. "I guess he forgot."

Gavin was more attuned to his interests than hers. Unable to vocalize his certainty without hurting Piper, Liam squeezed her knee and rose. "Where are we going, Sunshine?"

She locked a somber gaze on him. "Hartman, Alabama."

Stunned, Liam dropped into his chair. Gavin left the next puzzle piece in their hometown where Barone and Piper's uncle lived? Unbelievable.

Simon dragged a hand down his face. "We can't leave town, Liam."

"I'm not letting Piper go to Hartman alone."

Matt's eyes narrowed. "What's wrong with going to Hartman?"

"It's my hometown," Piper said. "My uncle and Matteo Barone live there along with Barone's network of thugs and spies." She turned to Liam. "Brandy also lives there. If we can't find her in Copper Ridge, we might be able to trace her from Hartman."

Cade groaned. "Going to Hartman is a bad idea, Liam. You'll be in the center of Barone's stronghold."

"Tell me something I don't know." Wouldn't change his mind. He refused to let Piper return home without him. Even if her uncle wasn't laundering money, that still left Barone desperate to destroy the information Piper sought.

"You aren't going alone."

Liam shook his head. "I can't ask you to go with us. I don't want Bravo on Barone's radar. He's too dangerous and you have wives to protect."

"I don't have a wife." Simon glowered. "Don't even think about telling me to stay in Otter Creek, man. You need backup."

"You need the team," Trent said. "You can't tackle this alone."

"This discussion is moot if we don't have permission for Liam and Simon to leave," Matt said. "The last thing Liam needs is a warrant for his arrest. He'll be no good to Piper from a jail cell."

Trent made a call that he placed on speaker.

A moment later, Brent Maddox answered. "What do you need, St. Claire?" he asked.

"You're on speaker with Bravo and Piper. Sorry for the late call, boss. We have a situation."

"Talk to me."

Trent summarized the events since Piper, Simon, and Liam had arrived in Copper Ridge, ending with the necessity of traveling to Piper's hometown.

Maddox whistled. "You need more than Bravo to handle Barone and his crew. Let me make some calls. I'll get back to you as soon as I can. In the meantime, lay low and rest. Piper?"

She jerked. "Yes, sir?"

"I know you're anxious to have answers. Don't strike out on your own to get them. If I can't work it out for Liam and Simon to leave the area, I'll send another Fortress team with you."

Liam's jaw clenched. No. He didn't care who the boss had in mind, they weren't Liam and Bravo. He trusted his teammates to have his back and Piper's.

"Wouldn't going to Hartman with a team of operatives draw attention? My uncle hasn't threatened me, and Gavin only implicated Barone."

"Barone has a lot to lose. He's already rid himself of one problem. He'll be desperate to eliminate the remaining ones."

"Me and Liam."

"Trust me and Bravo or the alternate Fortress team. We'll protect you while you find this evidence. If we help the feds lock up Barone, you'll be safe. This will be a long, tough fight and cost more than you realize."

Piper looked at Liam. "As long as Liam and the rest of Bravo as well as their families are safe, I don't care about the cost to me."

Liam kissed the back of her hand. She might not care about the cost to herself but he did. If they didn't destroy

Barone's organization, the cost to Piper would be unbelievably high.

He glanced at his teammates and saw that they were aware of the consequences as well. Liam had preparations to make in case Fortress failed in Hartman.

A sleepy child's voice came through the speaker. "Daddy?"

"Did you have a bad dream?"

"I heard voices."

"I'm sorry, Alexis. I was working," he said to his daughter. "Tell Trent hello."

A soft gasp. "Hi, Mr. Trent."

A smile formed on Trent's lips. "Hi, sweetheart. Sorry to wake you."

"Is Grace there, too?"

"Not this time. When I see her, I'll tell her you asked about her."

"I wish I could talk to her. She's nice."

"She likes you, too. Would you like her to call you later?"

"Oh, yes. Thank you, Mr. Trent."

"You're welcome."

Maddox broke in. "I need to tuck Alexis into bed. Give me a few hours, Liam. I'll get back to you as soon as I know something."

"Yes, sir."

The call ended.

Trent stood. "We'll let the boss work his magic. In the meantime, we should set up watch shifts."

"I'll take the first shift." Liam was too worked up to sleep.

Cade scowled. "Not happening. You didn't sleep at the hospital last night and neither did Trent. I'll take the first watch. You can join the rotation tonight."

"I'll take over at four o'clock," Matt said.

Trent moved toward the suite door with Matt a step behind. "We have the two rooms across the hall if you need us." With that, he and the medic left the suite.

Simon turned to Cade. "Wake me if you need someone to spell you."

The EOD man rolled his eyes. "I can handle a three-hour shift." He waved him on. "Go sleep."

With a salute, Simon closed himself into the bedroom.

Liam drew Piper to her feet as Cade went to the kitchen for coffee. "Come on. I'll walk you home."

She grinned and slid her hand into his. "Your boss seems nice."

He chuckled at her description of the tough Navy SEAL who started Fortress Security. "He can be. Brent Maddox expects the best from his employees and tells us when we let him down."

Liam nudged Piper into her room, one lit only by moonlight filtering through the curtains, and closed the door. He wrapped his arms around her waist. "I made you a promise."

A slow smile curved her lips. "I remember."

"I don't break my promises."

Piper's arms circled his neck. "Good to know."

Instead of swooping in like the take-charge Marine he was, Liam reined himself in and nibbled his way across her delectable lips with a series of butterfly kisses before capturing her mouth for a deeper caress.

As soon as his tongue brushed against hers, Liam was lost in a storm of sensation and heat. He'd imagined how sweet her kisses would be many times. Reality was one thousand times better than his imagination. The kiss might have started out sweet but quickly morphed into sizzling heat.

Piper moaned and inched closer. As the minutes passed, Liam became aware that Piper Reece fit perfectly in his arms, as if made for him.

Liam eased back, his breathing as ragged as hers. "Good grief, woman. You have one killer kiss." Unable to resist the sight of her kiss-swollen lips, he dived back in for another series of kisses before forcing himself to ease up.

He changed the intensity of the kisses to affectionate rather than blow-the-roof-off hot. By the time Liam lifted his head, both of their bodies had calmed down, their breathing almost normal. He brushed her bottom lip with the pad of his thumb. "Dream of me tonight," he whispered and left, closing the door behind him.

Cade glanced over his shoulder where he kept watch at the French doors. His lips curved into a knowing grin. "Will you be able to sleep?"

Liam gave a rough laugh. "Doubt it."

"They're worth it."

Piper was a miracle. The women he'd dated to this point couldn't handle his job or erratic schedule. Piper appeared to take everything in stride even in the middle of her own problems.

Liam couldn't get over the fact that she'd been worried enough about him to forget the information she came to Copper Ridge to retrieve. She knew he was military trained and an experienced operative and still she was concerned about his safety. Maybe, just maybe, Piper Reece could go the distance with him. He prayed his assessment was right because he was more than half in love with her. Spending this much time with her had deepened his emotional attachment to the woman.

What if she didn't return his interest? He blew out a breath. He'd coax and persuade her into his arms. There was no other choice. Piper meant too much to him to let her go without a fight.

He turned toward the kitchen to pour himself a mug of coffee when his cell phone signaled an incoming message. Liam pulled out his phone to check the screen and frowned.

"Problem?" Cade asked.

"Maybe. Z wants me to call him."

"He's awake. Better find out what's going on so he'll go to bed."

His gut twisted into a knot as Liam called Zane.

"How is Piper?"

"Sleeping, I hope. She was shaken up by Gavin's death. What's going on, Z?"

"Trouble. I pulled the security cam footage from Wicks."

"And?"

"You were right to be concerned about Piper. The pushy tourist was Jared Spencer, your old nemesis from your military days."

The thought of the deadly Marine anywhere near Piper made Liam's stomach lurch. "Do you know what he wants?"

"He's been connecting with your old unit since he was released from prison two months ago."

Not good. "Did he contact Major Graham?"

"Unknown."

"One of the other unit members might tell me what Spencer wanted." Spencer approaching Piper and pressuring her to go on a date concerned Liam. If Spencer was around town for any length of time, he'd learn that Piper was important to Liam. The man was ruthless and wouldn't have a problem using Piper to target Liam.

"Don't count on it. I picked up online chatter from unit members saying you're a traitor and rat. The general consensus is you should have ignored what was happening instead of turning on a brother Marine."

Disappointment and hurt spiraled through Liam. He'd given blood and suffered bullet and knife wounds for the men and women in his unit. To be accused of betraying that brotherhood cut deep. "Do you know if Spencer is still in Otter Creek?"

"No electronic paper trail to follow. Your man is living off the grid."

Liam massaged the back of his neck. With his military training, Spencer could live in the woods where it would be impossible to find him unless he wanted to be found. "He could be anywhere, Z. If he's still in the Otter Creek area, the wives of Durango and Bravo need to be on alert in case he decides to use them to draw me out."

"I'll send a warning to the operatives."

"Cade's with me on night watch."

The EOD man turned, eyebrows arched. "All right. Anything else before I go to bed? My wife has looked in on me twice in the past ten minutes. She won't sleep unless I'm with her."

"Start gathering information on Barone's home in Hartman, Alabama."

Zane was silent a moment. "Planning to visit the crime boss?"

"Gavin had information to nail Barone for enough crimes to make the feds happy and told Piper he was leaving it for her. That's why we're in Copper Ridge. Unfortunately, someone killed him before we arrived. He hid an envelope with directions to another hiding place, this one in Hartman. If we want to put Barone away, we have to play Gavin's game and hope he hid the information well enough to elude Barone's people."

"Dangerous game, my friend."

"No choice." Liam glanced at Cade who continued to watch him. "One more thing. I may need alternate IDs for me and Piper as well as background data." If this situation couldn't be resolved and Barone and his cronies handed over to the feds, Liam would go into Fortress Security's private witness protection and relocation program with Piper.

CHAPTER SIXTEEN

As Liam ended the call to his mother, his gaze met Cade's. Her admonition to protect himself and Piper at all costs still echoed in his mind. His strong, protective mother agreed the private witness protection program was best if matters couldn't be resolved with Barone and his crew.

"How did she take it?" his friend asked.

"Better than I hoped. She insisted I find a way to communicate with her. If I was permanently relocated with a new name, I should expect her to ask Maddox to do the same for her and maybe my sister, too."

Cade gave a low whistle. "Your mother has a steel spine."

"I don't know if Marissa will uproot her life. If not, I'll find a way to keep in touch and make sure she's protected."

"You're lucky. Not every family would reinvent themselves for an adult child."

Liam's eyes stung. "I know. Mom wants to rock her grandchildren."

"What about your sister's children?"

"She's not married or dating, and she also can't have kids. Severe injuries from a car accident."

"Your sister could adopt. Many children need a great home."

"She won't consider adoption. Says it reminds her of the loss. Marissa plans to be the favorite aunt my children run to for comfort when they're angry at me. If this situation with Barone goes south, she won't have the opportunity to spoil my children."

Cade studied him a moment, speculation in his gaze. "Why consider going into witness protection for Piper? You've only dated a few months."

Liam poured coffee into a mug and sipped before answering. "I can't let Piper go alone. She's not trained in evasion tactics. One mistake and Barone's people will be on her in a heartbeat."

"You're talking about giving up your current life and losing everything you've worked for."

Liam glanced at Piper's closed door. "I'm falling in love with her. I can't let her walk out of my life. I need Piper."

A slow nod from his friend. "Then we obliterate Barone and his crew. Otherwise, we'll have to break in a newbie for Bravo. Does Piper know how you feel?"

"Would you tell a woman you've dated for a few weeks that you want to rush her down the aisle, place a wedding band on her finger, and change her identity? I need time without her being afraid of a Hartman thug will catch her alone and demand incriminating information. I won't have that time if we're constantly looking over our shoulder, on the run from Barone's henchmen."

"We'll help you." A pointed look from his friend. "We never leave a man behind."

Liam's eyes stung as he positioned himself on the other side of the French doors and kept watch while he sipped his coffee.

When Liam's mug was empty, Cade said, "You need sleep."

"I have research to do." So many problems and possibilities tumbled in his brain, he wasn't sure he could sleep.

"You didn't sleep on the flight home and once you reached Otter Creek, you were in bodyguard mode. You've been awake for more than 48 hours. Go to bed."

"Yeah, all right." Although he hated to admit it, fatigue dragged at him even with the coffee in his system. This tired, he could make a fatal mistake.

Liam placed his Sig within easy reach and stretched out on the couch. A moment later, the living room plunged into twilight as Cade turned off the overhead light.

"I have your back, Liam, and I'll protect Piper with my life. Let go and rest."

He closed his eyes and allowed himself to relax for the first time in two days. Three hours later, he roused when Matt and Cade traded places.

"I've got this, Liam," Matt murmured. "I'll wake you at the first sign of trouble."

Liam woke to the sound of Piper's door opening. He glanced at his watch and frowned. Five o'clock. He sat up. "What's wrong, Piper?"

"Nightmare. Go back to sleep."

Liam held out his hand. "Come here."

"You need to sleep."

"I will if I know you're safe and resting. Come here."

With a sigh, Piper settled beside him on the couch.

He spread the blanket over them, relaxed into the cushions, and propped his feet on the coffee table. After kissing her forehead, Liam leaned his head back and closed his eyes.

Two hours later, he woke to an incoming text signal. He glanced at Piper, pleased to note she was sound asleep.

Liam eased his cell phone from his pocket and scanned the screen.

Simon turned from the French doors, eyebrow cocked in silent inquiry.

"Zane has information," Liam murmured.

Piper stirred. "Is everything all right?"

"Not sure. Zane wants me to call."

"Need coffee, Piper?" Simon asked.

She wrinkled her nose. "I prefer hot tea or a soft drink."

"I'll ask for hot tea with our room service order. Soft drinks are in the refrigerator."

Piper hurried into the kitchen as Liam called Zane. When his friend answered, Liam said, "You're on speaker with Piper and Simon. What do you have for me?"

"The IDs will be ready by the end of the day. Still no lead on Spencer's location but online communication between members of your unit is heating up."

"More of the same?"

"Afraid so. Spencer seems determined to turn the unit against you."

To isolate him. Spencer didn't know he was closer to his Bravo teammates than he'd been to his Marine brothers. "Anything else?"

"I hacked the Copper Ridge police department's computer system. They're still processing evidence from the crime scenes. However, they cleared you despite the fact your service record makes them nervous."

"What about Simon?"

"Not willing to turn him loose. They want to pin Gavin's murder on him as well as the shooter's death."

"Nice," Simon said. "Do you have good news, Z?"

"Don't know if the news is good, but it's interesting. Piper's uncle is trying to find her."

Piper sat beside Liam with her soft drink in hand, brow furrowed. "I haven't talked to him since I left Hartman. Why is he anxious to talk to me now?"

"Definitely not a coincidence." Liam draped his arm around her shoulders. "What else, Z?"

"I crosschecked the prints of the shooters in Copper Ridge with the prints collected at your house and Piper's."

Liam's hand tightened around the phone. "And?"

"The shooters were busy. They trashed Piper's place."

"What about mine?"

"Spencer broke into your home."

"The PSI team finished searching the house?"

"They netted three cameras and five bugs."

Liam smiled. "Spencer must be furious that he spent so much money on surveillance equipment only to have PSI confiscate it."

Piper leaned closer to the phone. "Zane?"

"Yes, ma'am?"

"Do you know if my uncle is still in Hartman?"

"From what I can tell. Why?"

She sighed. "I hoped he was somewhere else. Has Liam mentioned Brandy Strickland to you?"

"He didn't but her name popped up when I dug into Gavin's background. What do you want to know?"

"Gavin had travel documents for her under a different name. Do you know where she is?"

"I don't, but I'll try to locate her."

"Thanks. Although we didn't part company on good terms, I don't want anything to happen to her. I'm worried."

"Considering what happened to you, and Gavin's death, you're right to be concerned."

"Z, it's Simon. You said the Copper Ridge cops want to pin Gavin's murder on me. Have they run a ballistics test on the bullet that killed Gavin?"

"Still waiting on the results of that. Their crime lab is backed up."

"What about the shooter in police custody? Have they checked his weapon against the bullet?"

"They submitted the test for that as well as testing for a match to your weapon. According to their interview notes, he insists he didn't kill Gavin and neither did the other shooter. He says you did it."

Simon growled. "The cops have to clear me, Z. I'm going with Liam and Piper to Hartman whether the Copper Ridge police approve or not. He needs someone to watch his back."

"You won't help him or yourself if they find out you're leaving and toss you in jail," Piper pointed out.

"She's right," Zane said.

Simon's jaw tightened. "Let's hope Maddox comes through."

One look at his face told Liam that Simon would go to Hartman with or without permission. Frustration gnawed at his gut. He didn't want his friends in danger from the law or the criminals. "Keep digging, Zane."

"Planned on it. I assigned the geeks to find schematics for Barone's house."

"Better add Gino's house to the list."

"Copy that. Anything else, Liam?"

"You might need to create two more sets of documents."

"For?"

"My mother and sister."

"Ah. I'll have them ready."

"Thanks." Liam ended the call and glanced at Piper. "What do you want to do about your uncle?"

"Find out what he wants. Should I use my new cell phone?"

He nodded. "He won't be able to trace the call and pinpoint your location. Put the call on speaker."

Piper retrieved her phone, called her uncle, and tapped the speaker button.

After five rings, a male voice answered.

"It's Piper."

After a few seconds of silence, he said, "I'm glad to finally hear from you. Three years is too long to sulk like a child."

Liam scowled. Three years was too long for Gino Romano to hold a grudge against his niece for not falling into line and marrying a man who would have treated her with disrespect.

"How are you, Uncle Gino?"

"Missing my only niece. When are you coming home?"

Piper glanced at Liam, an unspoken question in her eyes.

He gave her a short nod. He didn't know what game Romano was playing, but they'd be better off if Barone received word Piper was in town at the request of her uncle. Thin cover but Liam would take it anyway.

"I didn't think you wanted to see me."

"Come home. We'll talk. Sofia will make your favorite dinner to celebrate your return. It's time to put aside our differences. You have a destiny to fulfill."

Liam didn't like the sound of that and, from the expression on her face, neither did Piper.

"All right, Uncle Gino. I'll come for a short visit but I'm not staying in Hartman. I have a new life that I enjoy."

A snort. "In that little podunk town of Otter Creek? Ridiculous. You're wasting your life there, wasting your business degree in a small business."

Piper froze. "How do you know where I live and work?"

"Did you think I wouldn't trace your whereabouts with a private investigator? You're my only living relative. I was concerned about your welfare. When shall we expect you?"

"I'm not sure."

Liam held up one finger.

"Maybe tomorrow or the day after," she added.

"You can't be more specific?" Romano sounded irritated.

"I have a few things to wrap up before I can travel."

"I'll see if I can find Gavin. I'm sure he would love to renew your friendship."

Liam covered her knee with his hand and shook his head. Romano was throwing out a lure.

"I don't want anything to do with Gavin," Piper said. "He destroyed our dating relationship when he cheated on me. I will never trust him again. Besides, I'm bringing a friend with me to Hartman."

"A friend?"

"His name is Liam." She glanced at him, smiled. "He's amazing."

"Who is he?"

"The man I'm dating."

Long seconds of silence followed her last statement. "I look forward to meeting him. Plan to stay here. No need for a hotel room. This is still your home. Let me know when you will arrive. I want to give Sofia enough warning to prepare a meal for you and your guest." With that last command, Romano ended the call.

Piper drew in a deep breath and turned to Liam. "How did I do?"

"Perfect." Liam planted a quick kiss on her mouth.

"I hoped we could sneak in and out of Hartman without my uncle or Barone noticing."

"The chances of pulling that off were slim to none," Simon said, glancing over his shoulder at her. "This is better."

"How is announcing our intention better than sneaking in?"

Liam tucked her close to his side again. "Going to Hartman this way will create doubt in Barone's mind, and perhaps your uncle's, about our true purpose."

Maybe the tactic would keep them alive.

CHAPTER SEVENTEEN

Piper finished tying her shoe laces and stood, uncertainty swirling inside her. Going to her hometown, the epicenter of danger dogging her, seemed foolish. Barone's henchmen were everywhere in Hartman. She and Liam wouldn't be able to walk anywhere without tripping over at least one of them. Being spied upon while they were in town made her skin crawl.

The upcoming trip didn't intimidate Liam and Simon and made Piper wonder about their missions. Did they walk into similar danger all the time?

She thought about Liam's actions on Highway 18. He made himself a target to free her from the kidnappers. Were his actions out of character because she was involved?

Stupid question. Liam wouldn't shy away from danger. He was a protector at heart. His professional skill set highlighted his willingness to do the hard job of protecting his teammates by pulling the trigger and taking a life. How many people would fire that shot, knowing the results? Not many. Liam McCoy was one of the strongest men she knew, inside and out, and she was blessed that he wanted to be part of her life.

She grabbed her purse and walked into the living room where Liam and the others discussed options.

"How do you feel?" Matt asked.

Ever the medic. "Better. Have you spoken to Delilah?"

His eyes lit at the mention of his wife. "She and Molly have the shop covered."

"Molly is working there now?"

"She is Delilah's bodyguard."

Piper blinked. "Bodyguard?" She shifted her attention to Liam. "Did I miss something while I showered?"

He held out a hand. "Come sit with me while I explain."

Oh, boy. That didn't sound good. She took his hand.

"I'll keep watch from the balcony while you talk," Trent said. He gave a hand signal to the others and the rest of Bravo exited the suite, leaving Liam and Piper alone.

"Tell me what happened."

Liam pressed a tender kiss to the back of her hand. "Zane called."

"What did he say?"

"The man in Wicks who asked you on a date is Jared Spencer, the Marine I told you about. Z confirmed his identity with the security footage from Wicks."

Cold chills surged over her skin. The man with a grudge against Liam had tried to pick her up. Why? "Molly is working at Wicks in case Jared tries to hurt Delilah."

"That's right. The other wives of Bravo and Durango also have operatives with them for protection."

"Why did Jared want to take me out?"

"Using you to draw me out."

She nudged him with her shoulder. "Good thing I turned him down." Piper expected him to at least smile at her teasing.

Instead, he captured her mouth in a hot, deep kiss. Whew! The man could kiss. She was fast becoming addicted to his arms holding her tight against his chest and his mouth on hers.

When Liam lifted his head, he said, "I would have hunted Spencer down and killed him if he touched you."

One look and Piper knew he wasn't joking. She stroked his stubble-roughened cheek with the fingertips of one hand. "For your sake, I'm glad that wasn't necessary." He had too many deaths on his conscience. There would be more, she knew. A hazard of the job. If he wasn't excellent in his work, the members of Bravo wouldn't make it home from a mission.

He stared. "I believe you mean that."

"Good because I do mean it."

"You're more concerned with how this affects me than the impact on you."

"This surprises you?"

"You don't know the number of women who asked me how many people I killed in my military career and then with Fortress. You haven't."

"Why would I? You protect the public and your teammates. All I care about is how it affects you."

"Doing my job means I'll bring danger right to your doorstep."

"Teach me how to protect myself and you."

"Are you sure you want to be involved with me, Piper? You have to be sure because the more time I spend with you, the harder I'm falling for you."

Piper stared, heart hammering against her rib cage. Did that mean what she thought? "You're falling in love with me?"

"Hard and fast."

"Liam." How could she respond without giving away the secret she'd hidden in her heart for months?

"I won't walk away unless you tell me you don't feel the same." His lips curved. "Even if you do say it, I'll do everything in my power to change your mind. I'll use every skill in my arsenal to convince you to give me a chance to win your heart. Be sure, Sunshine."

Piper leaned in and kissed Liam, her arms circling his neck. After a long series of increasingly deep kisses, she looked into his eyes and took the gamble of a lifetime. "I've been sure for months."

Liam's eyes lit and he drew in a shuddering breath. "Thank you for trusting me. I'll guard that gift, and treasure your heart with every breath."

She might be falling in love with him but that didn't mean Piper had forgotten what she suffered at Gavin's hands. Where Gavin's rejection hurt, Liam's would devastate her. "Where do we go from here?"

"Forward, one step at a time. We enjoy our courtship. I want to warn off other men in Otter Creek so they won't attempt to steal you from me. Will I rush you to make a deeper commitment?" Liam shook his head. "The pace is yours to set. More than anything, I want you to trust me with your whole self, including your heart."

"That might take months."

He brushed his lips over hers. "Snipers are known for their patience," he murmured. "I'm excellent at my job."

She fanned her face. "I think the temperature rose by fifty degrees in here."

Liam chuckled.

"Can I ask you something?"

"Anything. I'll answer if I can."

"During your phone call to Zane, he mentioned IDs. What did he mean?"

His expression sobered. "Preparing for the worst-case scenario."

"Which is?"

Liam kissed the back of her hand and threaded their fingers together. "Are you sure you want to know the truth?"

"Always. Holding back information because of your job I'll accept. I can handle difficult news."

A slow nod. "I asked Zane to prepare alternate IDs in case Gavin didn't give us enough information to take down Barone and we aren't able to find what we need to finish the job."

A ball of ice formed in her stomach. "Why would we need alternate IDs?"

"Barone has a long reach. If we can't dismantle his organization, we'll have to go on the run."

"You can't be serious. This isn't a movie. We're talking about running from Barone for the remainder of our lives. Constantly looking over our shoulders, worried one of Barone's thugs is after us." Dismayed at the prospect, Piper shook her head in denial.

"It's a choice between living or dying."

"This is crazy. I don't know anything about Barone or his business operations. I left Hartman in my rearview mirror, Liam. I won't go back and take up my old life. I like where I live and what I've become. When I look at myself in the mirror each morning, I'm not embarrassed by the choices of the woman staring back at me."

"Barone thinks you know information dangerous to him and his empire. That's enough to send his goons after you. If he believes you have enough evidence to put him in prison, he won't stop until you're dead. Our safety may come down to two choices. Run or put a bullet in Barone's head or heart."

Feeling sick inside, Piper shook her head again. "This is my problem. You can't give up your life and go on the run with me. Think of your family. You'd never see them again. I can't do that to you or them."

His hands curved around her upper arms. "I refuse to let you go alone. You're not trained for it. If running is our only option, I'll keep you alive."

"But at what cost? No, Liam. The price is too high."

His hands squeezed. "I made my choice. I choose you."

"What about your family? You can't give them up. I don't have family who will miss me." Pain shot through her heart at the thought of her uncle's possible betrayal. If their suspicions proved true, she had no blood kin who would wonder at her absence except the uncle who raised her and might have set criminals on her trail.

Liam smiled. "My mother plans to ask Maddox to send her into hiding with us. She thinks my sister, Marissa, will also go into the Fortress version of witness protection, too."

"Liam." Tears trickled down her cheeks.

He brushed the tears away. "I'm falling in love with you, Piper Reece. I won't give you up. Whatever comes, we'll handle together. You're not alone anymore."

The hotel phone rang. Liam frowned and answered it. After a brief conversation with the front desk, he turned to Piper. "The package I've been expecting arrived a few minutes ago. I'll take a quick shower and go get it. Do everything Trent tells you to do."

"Go. I'll make more tea and help Trent keep watch on the balcony."

He looked through the glass in the French doors. "Sit on the right side. You'll be less visible." Liam dropped a quick kiss on her lips and went into the bedroom.

Piper filled her tea mug and joined Trent, sitting where Liam suggested. Since the solid brick wall blocked most of the view, she understood why he'd chosen that location.

Trent glanced at her over his shoulder before facing outward again. "You okay?"

"Did you know he's considering going into witness protection with me?"

"I'd do the same if Grace's life were on the line. There's nothing I wouldn't do for my wife."

"Liam and I aren't married."

"Yet," came the soft reply.

A host of butterflies took flight in her stomach. "Yet," she agreed with an equally soft voice. "I'm afraid, Trent."

Another look over his shoulder. "You have reason to be. Liam won't let anything happen to you."

"At the risk of his own safety."

"It's how we operate, Piper. The safety of those we care about is our first priority."

"I'm beginning to understand what that means. I don't want him to give up the life he's built."

"Not your choice."

"How do I stop him?"

"You don't. All of us will work together to find the evidence necessary to toss Barone in jail. That's the only way to prevent you from having to disappear."

They remained silent while Trent remained alert for trouble and Piper sipped her tea. By the time her mug was empty, Liam had returned with a package.

He crouched by Piper's chair and drew out a watch, a bracelet, a pair of earrings, and a necklace.

Piper smiled. Daisies.

"Fortress has five designs to choose from. I thought this set would suit you the best. Daisies are bright and full of life, like you." Liam strapped the watch on her wrist, then the bracelet, and necklace. He handed her the earrings.

When she was finished fastening them, Piper took a minute to admire the bracelet on her wrist. "This is perfect, Liam. Thank you."

"Now that I know Jared is nosing around, it's important that you wear these all the time. If you're ever taken from me again, I'll be able to find you."

"Do the other Bravo wives have the special jewelry?"

"They do," Trent answered. "Sasha, Delilah, and Grace chose different sets."

"How does Zane know which woman is in trouble if all the jewelry has GPS signal capability?"

"Each set assigned to the wives and girlfriends has a unique electronic signature."

"Where are the rest of your teammates?"

"Scouting the area, looking for anything out of the ordinary and keeping their eyes open for Brandy."

A heavy knock sounded on the suite door.

Between one heartbeat and the next, Piper was on her feet and hurrying to her bedroom, Liam's hand clasped around hers. Trent strode to the door, weapon in hand.

He peered through the peephole and turned with a scowl on his face. "Cops."

Piper's breath caught. Were the police about to arrest her and Liam?

CHAPTER EIGHTEEN

Liam clenched his jaw. He couldn't tell the cops more. The other information had been gathered through Z's computer hacking and netted results the cops couldn't use in court. "Let them in."

He glanced at Piper. "Stay here until I'm sure it's safe."

"The police are dirty?"

"I'd rather be safe than make a mistake that costs your life."

The rapping on the door came again, harder this time.

"Better open that before the cops become suspicious," Trent said. He took Liam's place by Piper's side.

Liam opened the door to Kerrigan and Barrett's scowling faces.

"What took so long to answer our knock?" Kerrigan snapped.

Liam's eyebrows rose. "Does it matter?"

Barrett held up a hand to restrain his partner's reply. "We need to speak to you and Ms. Reece."

Definitely something on the detectives' minds. At least they weren't making noises about taking him to the station. Not yet. Liam motioned for them to come inside.

The moment they spotted Trent, their hands edged closer to their weapons. At six foot four, Bravo's leader towered over the Copper Ridge officers.

"This is my friend, Trent. He's part of Piper's protection detail."

"Where is Simon?" Barrett asked. "We need to talk to him as well."

"Walking. Have a seat." Liam sat with Piper on the couch as the officers chose the loveseat. Trent returned to stand watch at the French doors, one shoulder propped against the wall. He angled himself to keep the detectives in view while he scanned the area at the back of the lodge. "What's on your mind, Detective Barrett?"

"We've been ordered to allow you, Simon, and Ms. Reece to leave."

Excellent. "You don't agree with the order."

"All three of you should be in jail," Kerrigan said. "You're not telling us everything. Obstruction of justice deserves jail time."

"You have some powerful friends, McCoy." Barrett watched him and Piper carefully. "Who did you buy off to score travel privileges?"

"Who called you?" he hedged. The last thing he wanted to do was drag Maddox or President Martin into the mix if their names weren't associated with the order. Liam had one of them to thank for the assist.

"The Copper Ridge chief of police. He's receiving outside pressure to turn you and your friends loose. Who do you know with that kind of pull?"

"Several high-powered people owe my team favors. We called in a marker."

"Team?" Kerrigan cocked her head. "Who's on your team?"

"Trent, Simon, and two others."

"Are they all here?"

"We have each other's backs. What do you think?"

A slight smile curved Barrett's mouth. "Are they well-armed like you and Simon?"

"Our jobs are dangerous. We have enemies who would love nothing better than to see us dead. We're heavily armed anywhere we go."

"What's your next stop?"

"Out of state."

A scowl from Kerrigan. "That's it? You won't tell us more?"

"I'm under no obligation to tell you. It's safer for you if you don't know too much."

"What if we have questions? And we will," she warned.

"Call Fortress Security's main number and leave a message. We'll call as soon as we're able."

"Are you leaving the country?"

"Do you think I would tell you if we were? Look, Kerrigan, we plan to stay inside US borders unless our unit is deployed overseas again." Unlikely, since they'd just returned from nearly a month out of the country. Still, he wouldn't discount that possibility.

The suite door opened and Simon walked inside with Matt close on his heels. "Detectives," Simon said in greeting. He shifted his attention to Liam. "Problem?"

He shook his head. "Our travel restrictions have been lifted to the dismay of Barrett and Kerrigan."

"Ah." Simon shrugged. "If you need us, call. We'll be in touch."

"I get the feeling that you know a lot more than you're telling us," Barrett said. When none of the men confirmed or denied his statement, he shifted his attention to Matt. "I'm Detective Barrett. This is my partner, Detective Kerrigan."

"Matt, team medic."

Barrett turned to Liam. "Anything you can tell us that might help our investigation?"

"Is the surviving shooter talking?"

"Not yet. Leverage would help."

"He's employed by a man not known for his tolerance of failure."

The detectives exchanged glances then refocused on Liam. "Anything else?" Kerrigan asked.

"Have ballistics tests come back yet on our weapons?"

"They'll be ready this afternoon. Why?"

"The bullet that killed Gavin won't match our weapons."

A scowl from the lady. "You had more than one weapon at your disposal."

"True. However, we didn't fire that shot."

"Which means you're searching for a third shooter," Simon added.

Barrett swore. "Copper Ridge had one murder last year. You boys are in town for less than a day and we have two bodies, one of which may have serious criminal connections."

Simon inclined his head.

"At least tell me if we should expect more trouble in Copper Ridge. We'd like to be prepared."

"Trouble will probably follow us out of town but you might experience an uptick in break-ins at the resort."

"What are they looking for?"

"The hottest commodity in town is information."

"What kind?"

Simon shrugged. "Don't know."

A snort from Kerrigan. "If you did, would you tell us?"

"Doubt it."

"Gavin's the key," Liam said. "Contact Detective Stella Armstrong with Otter Creek PD. She might have relevant information."

Barrett frowned. "She left a message on my cell phone to call her."

"You should," Piper said.

The detective and his partner rose. "Young lady, I don't know what you're mixed up in, but be careful. Whoever is behind this plays for keeps." With those words, Barrett and Kerrigan left.

"When do we leave, Trent?" Liam tucked Piper closer to his side when he noticed her hands trembling.

"Have to talk to Maddox before we leave for Hartman."

"Why?" Piper asked.

"We have to confirm our backup team is available. Taking on Barone and his crew requires more than five people."

"How many people does Barone have at his disposal?" Matt asked.

"That's the question of the day. Conservative estimate is thirty."

When a light tap sounded on the door, Matt peered through the peephole and admitted Cade.

"Which one of you ticked off the cops?" Cade's eyes glinted with amusement. "They snarled at each other and everyone one else who crossed their paths."

"Including you?" Trent asked.

"The lady cop took one look at me and said, 'You're one of them, aren't you? You have the same look as the rest of those mercenaries.'"

Simon rolled his eyes. "Kerrigan is ticked off that she can't throw me in jail."

"You're cleared?"

"Wouldn't say that. More like I received permission to travel until Copper Ridge's finest finds enough to evidence to arrest me for murdering Gavin James."

Cade's eyebrows soared. "Maddox's influence?"

"Let's find out." Trent called their boss.

"Yeah, Maddox. What do you need?"

135

"It's Trent. You're on speaker with Bravo and Piper. Liam and Simon have permission to travel. Who did you tap for the favor?"

"White House."

Liam whistled. The boss called President Martin. Guess that was the quickest way to garner the results Bravo needed. "It's Liam. Thanks for the assist."

"Martin was happy to call Copper Ridge's police chief. When are you leaving for Alabama, Trent?"

"How soon will our backup be available?"

"The Texas team's on standby."

"I prefer them close in case we need reinforcements."

"Probably best not to announce their presence by bringing them into Hartman."

"Barone has spies everywhere in town," Piper said. "Minutes after strangers register at a hotel, Barone or one of his lieutenants know. If the other team looks as dangerous and alert as Bravo, they'll draw plenty of attention, shooting down the element of surprise."

"Noted. Is there a town outside Hartman close enough for the team to be available if they're needed?"

"Amaretto. It's fifteen minutes away and in the next county. The town is large enough for the team not to blend in but small enough to be of little interest to Barone. Will that work?"

"Perfect. Trent?"

"Yes, sir?"

"Amaretto sounds like a good place for Bravo, too."

"Copy that."

"Zane will arrange for both teams to stay at a lodge. Looks like there's a large one near a forest. Should give you and the other team a good cover as old friends meeting for a week of hiking and catching up. What about Piper and Liam? Are they staying with the teams?"

"Gino Romano insists Piper will stay with him. Liam won't let her out of his sight."

"Check in every two hours, Liam," Maddox ordered.

"Roger that."

"Piper, do everything Liam tells you. You can't trust anyone in that house or town except Liam and the teams. Am I clear?"

"I understand."

"Is there anything I can do for you?"

Piper glanced at Liam, fear flickering in the depths of her eyes. "Would you prepare a safe house for us in case we have to run?"

"I'll have several ready. We'll take care of you, Piper.

"I don't want anything to happen to him."

"I understand, sugar." The tough Navy SEAL's voice was gentle. "We want both of you safe. We'll do whatever it takes to make that happen. We're well trained. Trust us to do our job. Trent?"

"Sir?"

"Expect Brody Weaver to contact you within the hour." With that, Maddox ended the call.

Piper twisted to face Liam. "Who is Brody Weaver?"

"Leader of the Texas unit."

"Does their unit have a name?"

"They chose Texas. Each team member is from the Lone Star state and that's how they wanted to be known." Liam turned his attention back to Trent. "Orders?"

"Pack your gear. Eat. I don't want you to stop very often on the way to Hartman. We'll be half a mile behind you in case you run into trouble."

Piper grimaced. "Room service again?"

Liam helped Piper stand. "Let's see if we have any interest from those in the lodge's restaurant or lobby." He glanced at his teammates. "We'll be back later."

Cade opened the door and followed them into the hall. "The Copper Kettle?" he asked, naming the main restaurant. When Liam nodded, he said, "I'll wait until you're seated before I enter the restaurant."

"Thanks."

"Enjoy your date." Cade veered toward the staircase as Liam led Piper to the elevator. He nudged Piper into the corner of the car and caged her in with his body, blocking her from the camera's view. "Even though we're on a date and I want you to relax, remember that we're on stage. Assume someone besides Cade is watching, waiting for us to make a mistake."

"This is what it's like on a mission?"

He trailed a finger down her cheek. "Yes." How could anyone's skin feel like crushed velvet? Delicate and beautiful. Piper was exquisite.

"How do you handle this long term?"

"Hide your true self behind the role. You become that person." He saw the exact moment when she realized why he insisted on going into witness protection with her. Slipping and letting the real Piper show through instead of the persona Fortress created for her would be easy. "We'll handle whatever comes together, Sunshine."

When the elevator stopped on the first floor, he gripped her hand as the silver doors opened and walked into the lobby with her by his side.

Cade lingered by the gift shop window, supposedly staring at the display. Based on the angle of his body and head, he watched the activity behind him using the reflection in the glass.

Liam requested a table for two with the hostess who seated them at the corner table at his request. When she returned to her station, Liam kissed the back of Piper's hand. "Order what you want. Act as normal as possible."

They finished the meal without mishaps or mistakes until the waitress brought the check. As she handed Liam the bill and turned to leave, her elbow knocked over Piper's glass. Tea spilled onto Piper's lap.

"Oh, no!" The waitress grabbed napkins to blot the liquid from Piper's legs. "I'm so sorry."

"Don't worry about it. Where's the restroom? I need to dry my jeans."

The woman gestured to the left side of the restaurant. "At the end of the hallway. Again, I apologize for my clumsiness. I'll clear your plates and glasses while you're gone."

When Piper rose, Liam stood to escort her.

"Stay. I'll just be a minute." She hurried toward the hallway.

He frowned, about to follow her when a man in black pants and a long-sleeved polo shirt with the resort logo stitched on the front approached their table.

"I'm Gene Derby, the Copper Kettle's manager. Is everything all right here?"

"It's my fault, Gene," the waitress said, cheeks flushing a bright red. "I knocked a glass of tea into a customer's lap. She's gone to the restroom to dry her jeans."

Derby turned to Liam. "I'm sorry, sir. We'll comp your meals and I'll speak to your companion."

From the direction of the hall, a woman screamed.

CHAPTER NINETEEN

Liam sprinted across the restaurant, dodging a waiter who turned into his path. Cade followed close on his heels. When he reached the hall, Liam drew his weapon and held it down by his side.

He and Cade ran down the hall to the women's restroom. He signaled Cade to take the right side while Liam took the left.

Shoving the door open, Liam quartered his side of the room while Cade scanned the right. Empty aside from Piper's pink purse on the floor. Windows in the bathroom were too small to climb through and located close to the ceiling. Piper hadn't come out of the hallway into the main restaurant. They would have seen her.

"Must be an exit close by." Scooping up her purse, Liam hurried to the hall and turned right. Fifteen feet away was a dimly-lit exit sign. His blood ran cold. Not again. He'd promised to protect her.

"Is something wrong?" Their waitress hurried toward them.

"My girlfriend is missing."

Blood drained from her face. "What? No. That wasn't supposed to..."

He thrust the purse in her hands, impatient to go after Piper. "Take this to Room 3217. One of my friends will take care of it."

He and his teammate ran to the glowing sign and hit the exit door at a dead run. A woman's muffled scream and a man's vicious swearing drew Liam's attention to a wooded area fifty feet away from the rear of The Copper Kettle.

He and Cade raced toward the trees. Liam's jaw clenched when he heard the sound of flesh hitting flesh. He put on another burst of speed. They had to reach Piper before the man who took her reached a vehicle. The man wouldn't be able to carry her a long distance, not with Piper fighting to free herself from her captor.

Cade signaled he was circling to the right and disappeared into the shadowy interior of the woods.

Liam shoved his fear for Piper behind a mental barricade and fell back on his training, divorcing his emotion from the task. He had to stay focused or risk losing Piper for good.

With careful steps, he tracked the noises for another quarter of a mile. Weapon up and ready, he peered around a large rock formation and saw Piper on the ground, hand pressed to her bleeding mouth. Five feet away from her stood a bald Caucasian male. He weighed three hundred pounds, easy, all of it muscle. Around six foot two, the thug had Liam by a good fifty pounds and five inches. Didn't matter. He refused to let this man take Piper.

"Where is it?" the man growled at Piper.

"Where is what?"

"The package your stupid boyfriend left for you."

"I have a lot of things from my boyfriend." She spread her hands. "Tell me what you're looking for."

"Don't mess with me, lady. I'm not in a good mood. You've been nothing but trouble in a job that was supposed to be easy, quick cash."

Liam frowned. Baldy was a hired gun? That didn't make sense. Why would Barone hire someone from outside his organization when he had plenty of blood-loyal talent at his disposal? Hiring an outsider posed a risk to Barone's security.

"Give me specifics so I can give you what you want."

Good girl, Liam thought. She stalled for time, trusting Liam to find her.

"Information." Baldy lumbered closer. "You're wasting time. I'm not a patient man and I have a mean, nasty temper."

"I keep important information in my purse, the purse you threw on the bathroom floor. You'll have to take me back to the lodge."

A snort. "I ain't falling for that." He aimed the weapon at Piper's chest. "I'm tired of your lies, lady. Where is the information? Tell me and I might let you live." A lazy shrug. "You'll tell me what I want to know. How much you suffer is up to you. Where is the information and how much do you know? Talk or the first bullet goes through your kneecap in five seconds."

He'd heard enough, and Cade was in place. Liam stepped out from cover. "Drop your weapon."

Baldy froze. "You won't shoot me. My finger's on the trigger and the gun's aimed at her head."

"You want information. Killing Piper before you're sure the information's in her purse risks mission failure. If you hurt her, I'll kill you. Drop your weapon and you live. Simple choice. Make it."

He looked at Piper and mouthed, "On three, move right." Out of Baldy's sight, Cade left tree cover, weapon up and ready.

Liam silently mouthed the countdown. At three, Piper threw herself to the right and rolled. Liam leaped, taking Baldy to the ground, trusting Cade to secure Piper.

An elbow shot to the ribs stole Liam's breath and shoved him off the thug who rolled to his back. Liam dove on top of Baldy and slammed his fist into the thug's face, breaking his nose. Howling in pain and rage, Baldy swung his weapon toward Liam.

He clamped a hand around the man's wrist with a punishing grip and pinned his arm to the ground. Liam stripped the weapon from his hand and tossed it aside. He dodged a blow to the throat and pressed his forearm against Baldy's carotid artery. His opponent's face reddened as he fought to free himself. The struggles weakened, then ceased as he slid into unconsciousness.

Breathing hard, Liam waited another few seconds to be sure he was down, then flipped Baldy onto his stomach. He secured his wrists behind his back with zip ties. That done, he stood and faced Piper.

When she threw herself into his arms, Liam hugged her tight. "Are you okay?"

She nodded but he knew adrenaline had poured into her system and blocked pain. Once she crashed, she'd notice any injuries.

Liam tilted her head up. His gaze zeroed in on her bleeding mouth. Jaw clenched, he turned his head and stared at Baldy, who was still unconscious.

"No." Cade moved between Liam and Baldy. "We need to know who sent him. Can't learn the identity if you kill him. Take your woman to the suite and send Simon or Trent. We need to interrogate this clown, hand him over to the cops, and leave Copper Ridge."

Liam shifted toward the fallen thug, fury riding him hard. Baldy had deliberately hurt Piper to scare her into cooperating. A soft hand on his forearm brought him to a halt.

"I need my purse. Hopefully, someone hasn't walked off with it." She scowled. "That's my favorite purse."

"I handed it to our waitress with instructions to take it to the suite."

She started to smile and winced. "Ouch. That hurts."

Liam took her arm. His need to take care of her trumped the desire to teach Baldy a lesson in manners. "We'll ask Matt to look at your lip."

"And you'll leave the bald man for the police to handle?"

"No promises." If her injuries were more serious than a split lip, he'd dole out a suitable punishment to the creep who enjoyed hurting women.

Liam slid his arm around Piper's waist, tightening his hold when he felt her body trembling. When they broke through the tree line, he guided her to the lodge's side entrance and into the stairwell. He lifted Piper into his arms and carried her upstairs despite her protests. "Indulge me, Sunshine. I need to hold you. You scared me."

Piper kissed his jaw. "Scared me, too. I knew you would find me, though. Did you activate the trackers?"

He shook his head. "The restaurant hallway had one exit that led outside. Cade and I heard you scream and tracked you."

"Having the jewelry gave me peace of mind."

He squeezed her gently, grateful she was alive. "I'd go to the ends of the earth to find you. With GPS help or not, I wouldn't stop until you were my arms."

Liam exited the stairwell on their floor and walked to the suite. He set Piper on her feet and unlocked the door.

Trent turned from the French doors and scowled when he saw the injury to Piper's face. "What happened?"

Matt entered the suite with his mike bag, Simon on his heels. "Cade texted me."

"Piper was kidnapped from the women's restroom at the restaurant. Cade requested you or Simon interrogate the kidnapper before we notify the police."

"I'll go," Simon said. "Coordinates?" Once he had the location, the spotter left the suite.

"While Matt checks Piper, tell me details."

Liam relayed the events of the last hour while he watched Bravo's medic assess Piper's injuries. As Liam finished his report, Matt grabbed a chemically-activated ice pack and pressed it to Piper's mouth.

"You need stitches. Would you prefer a hospital or me?"

"You."

"All right. While we wait for the lidocaine to numb your lip, I'll treat your scrapes."

Liam sat beside Piper and gathered her close when he heard her teeth chattering. "It's adrenaline dump, Piper. The shakes will pass soon."

"Afterward, you'll want to sleep." Matt wrapped a blanket around her. "All of us experience different reactions to adrenaline dump. The shakes and heavy, dragging fatigue are common."

She shivered and huddled deeper into the blanket and against Liam's side. "How do you and the rest of Bravo handle this when you're on missions?"

"We've experienced adrenaline dump so many times, the reaction isn't extreme." Liam kissed her temple. He held her while Matt cleaned the cut and slid the needle into her skin to administer the medicine.

The medic patted her knee. "Snuggle with Liam for a few minutes."

Liam unwrapped her blanket and positioned Piper against his chest. He draped the cover over her back and looped his arms on top.

She groaned. "Not only do you have superb kissing skills, you're as warm as a furnace. That's it, Liam McCoy. Your days of playing the field are over. I'm keeping you."

Matt and Trent grinned.

Liam chuckled. "Good to know I won't have to fight off other would-be pursuers."

"Not a chance."

Matt moved to stand behind the couch. "Extend your right arm, Piper." He treated the scrapes and cuts on her hands and arms. When he finished, he tossed the medical detritus in the trash and returned. "All right. Let's see if the lidocaine has kicked in."

He pinched various spots close to the cut. She didn't react. "Excellent. You'll have to turn around, Piper. The stitches will take five minutes, maybe less. Afterward, huddle with Liam until the shakes stop. We'll bring you a soft drink with sugar to help combat the shock. Are you ready?"

Piper nodded. She turned to face Matt who now stood in front of the couch.

Matt tugged on rubber gloves. "Lean your head back against Liam's shoulder. If you're not a fan of needles, close your eyes."

"Ha. I'd rather see that needle than be taken by surprise."

"You'll feel tugging and pressure. No pain."

"Go ahead."

Liam stroked Piper's hair as the medic worked. True to his word, five minutes later, Matt was finished.

"Shouldn't leave much of a scar. I used small stitches."

"Unlike what you do with us," Trent pointed out.

"I stitch wounds while we're on the move. Can't do delicate work when tangos are on our trail." Matt handed Piper the ice pack wrapped in a washcloth. "Keep this is place for twenty minutes. We'll repeat every two hours. The cold reduces swelling."

A knock sounded on the door.

Trent checked the peephole and admitted Cade.

"Cops will be here soon."

"What did you learn from the kidnapper?"

"He doesn't know who hired him."

Liam scowled at Cade as Piper huddled against his chest again. "How was he contacted and paid?"

"Anonymous email for the arrangements. Once he agreed to the terms, half the money was mailed to a P.O. box he uses for business. The other half would be collected on job completion."

"What was the job?"

Cade's gaze shifted to Piper. "Once he retrieved Gavin's information, he was instructed to kill her and hide her body."

CHAPTER TWENTY

Piper stared over her shoulder at Cade. "What did he plan to do? Shoot me and dump my body in the woods?"

"You don't want details," Cade said. "You'll have enough problems sleeping tonight as it is."

Smart man. Guess she'd be fighting kidnappers again in her sleep tonight. "Did he tell you his name?"

"John Baker. He offered to share the payout for his work if I let him go."

Liam stiffened. "He expected us to help him kill Piper?"

"Nope. He recognized that you were emotionally involved with her. The offer was for me. When I protested killing an innocent woman, he suggested a compromise. I get the information from Piper since she trusted me, pass it to Baker, and together we'd fake her death. A win for everybody."

Liam growled.

Piper smoothed a hand over his heart, comforting him as much as herself. Knowing who probably commissioned

Baker, she wasn't shocked at such cold bartering over her life.

Gavin should have approached the FBI or state police himself. Instead, he'd dragged her into this mess as well as Liam and his teammates, then planned to flee the country, leaving them to deal with the fallout. Liam would have taken care of the problem himself instead of thrusting Piper into danger.

She pressed her cheek against his chest again, holding the ice pack against her mouth. What had she ever seen in Gavin James? Compared to Liam, Gavin was a characterless worm.

"I should have killed Baker when I had the chance," Liam said. "The information he gave you wasn't enough."

Cade lifted a shoulder. "Baker was paid for his work so he's not one of Barone's people. That means a paper trail. Zane will follow the money."

"If we're lucky," Trent said. "The person behind this is careful. There might not be a trail."

Piper groaned. "That is not what I wanted to hear. We have to know who's behind the attacks to stop them."

"We'll find answers." Liam kissed her temple. "Even if we have to assume alternate identities, we won't quit."

The thought of Liam leaving behind his mother and sister made Piper's heart hurt. The only way to prevent it was to discover who wanted her dead, locate Gavin's information, and destroy a criminal organization. Piece of cake.

A hard rap rattled the door. Piper jerked.

"Easy, Sunshine." Liam rubbed her back.

Cade checked the peephole. "Cops."

Piper loosened her hold on Liam and wrapped the blanket around herself to keep the warmth he'd shared. The shakes were gone and all she wanted to do at the moment was curl into Liam's arms and sleep.

Liam threaded his fingers through Piper's. "Tell me when you want to stop answering questions." When she nodded, Liam glanced at his friend. "Let them in, Cade."

Barrett and Kerrigan entered. Kerrigan's gaze landed on Piper's lip. She frowned, attention shifting to Liam with suspicion in her narrowed eyes.

Piper's hand tightened around Liam's. "The kidnapper hit me, not Liam."

"You sure? Your boyfriend has bruised knuckles."

"He punched the kidnapper."

Barrett sat on the loveseat, studying Piper's face. "Did one of you take a picture of Piper's injuries before treatment?"

"I did," Matt said.

The detective rattled off his email address. "Send me the picture for our files." He turned to Piper and Liam. "Start at the beginning. We left your suite after seven. What happened, Piper?"

"Liam and I ate breakfast in the Copper Kettle. The waitress knocked a glass of tea onto my jeans."

Beside her, Liam went stock still. She glanced his direction and caught the slight shake of his head. Guess she would ask questions later.

Piper resumed her recitation of events. "I went to the bathroom to dry my jeans. Someone followed me in, moving fast. A bald, muscular man grabbed me and carried me out the back door of the restaurant with his hand clamped over my mouth."

"How tall was he?"

"Over six feet."

He glanced at Liam, eyebrow raised in silent question.

"Six two, at least 300 pounds."

"What did he do when he took you outside?" Kerrigan asked, pen poised over her notepad.

"He carried me into the forest at the back of the lodge." Goosebumps surged over her skin at the remembered panic and certainty she was going to die without having told Liam she was in love with him. She needed him to know the truth. She planned to fix that soon.

Liam rubbed her arm. "He can't hurt you now."

True. Baker, however, was only the next round of thugs waiting for a shot at her. What if next time Liam couldn't get to her? She wanted to protect herself and knew the perfect person to teach her. Liam.

"Keep going," Barrett prompted.

"I'm not sure how far he took me. I know I would have a hard time finding my way back without help. Every tree looked alike to me out there."

The detective turned toward Liam again.

"A quarter of a mile," he said. "Baldy was in good shape."

"Baldy?" Kerrigan frowned.

"You haven't seen the kidnapper?"

She shook her head. "One of the patrol cops drove him to the hospital. We'll interview him after he's received medical attention since he took a beating." She glanced at Liam's hands.

He snorted. "If I'd beaten up the guy, he'd have more injuries than a broken nose. Baldy kidnapped my woman and pulled a gun on me. He's lucky to be alive. Anyway, he didn't introduce himself. We had to call him something, Baldy was the default name."

"So Baldy took you into the forest, Piper. What happened when he stopped?"

"I broke free and ran. He caught me and punched me. Baldy threatened to kill me if I didn't give him what he wanted."

"Which was?"

"Information. He said he wanted the information my boyfriend gave me and didn't mind hurting me to get it."

Kerrigan turned her accusing gaze toward Liam.

"Baldy meant Gavin, not Liam," Piper insisted.

"What information?" Barrett asked.

"I don't know. He wouldn't tell me and neither did Gavin. Like I told you before, I haven't spoken to Gavin in three years."

"What happened next?"

"I asked questions, stalling to give Liam time to find me. Liam told Baldy to drop his gun but he refused. He tackled Baldy, took away the gun, and restrained him. Then Liam brought me to Matt."

His gaze dropped to her mouth. "Did Matt stitch your cut?"

She nodded.

Another frown from Kerrigan. "Doesn't he need a license?"

"I'm a certified EMT as well as a medic for Fortress Security," Matt said.

"You carry medical supplies with you?"

"Sometimes we're deployed at a moment's notice. I carry my mike bag wherever I go."

"Handy." Her word dripped with sarcasm.

"Do you have anything to add, Piper?" Barrett asked.

"No." She leaned her head against Liam's shoulder. Man, she needed a long nap. "I've told you all of it."

Barrett turned to Liam. "How did you know Piper was in trouble?"

"I heard her muffled scream. Cade and I ran to check on her and found Piper's purse on the bathroom floor. She was nowhere in sight."

"What did you do?"

"Checked out the back door of the restaurant and heard Piper scream again. We tracked her and Baldy to where your patrol cops found him with Simon." Liam continued to recount events until they returned to the suite.

Barrett watched Liam for a moment. "Why do I think you're not telling me everything?"

"You have to go through proper channels. We don't."

"Hints or suggestions?"

"Run a ballistics test on his weapon."

"Planned to, but why?"

"I didn't shoot Gavin. Neither did Simon. We know there's a third shooter involved. Perhaps he's our mystery shooter."

"Why are you asking for help?" Kerrigan demanded of her partner. "We're the professionals, not this band of mercenaries."

A shrug. "Saves time. Liam's right. He doesn't have to follow our rules. If he says something that sends us in the right direction, we'll catch the killer sooner."

"He could be misleading us to protect his own hide."

Anger heated Piper's blood. Some of her fury must have communicated itself to Liam because he glanced down at her and winked.

"He hasn't so far. Why start now?" Barrett looked at Liam again. "Anyone else I need to talk to about this latest incident?"

Liam inclined his head toward Cade. "Cade was my backup."

After the detectives questioned them a second time, the detectives left to view the crime scenes in the bathroom and the woods.

As soon as they were gone, Liam turned to Cade. "We need to talk to the waitress."

"Caught that, did you? I wondered when you'd remember what she said." Cade smiled. "I'll track her down." He waited until the detectives left the floor, then searched for the waitress.

"What's that about?" Trent asked.

"The waitress was upset when she learned Piper was missing. She said that wasn't supposed to happen."

"What does that mean?" Piper asked.

"I don't think she knocked over the tea by accident. I believe someone asked her help in getting you to the women's restroom."

"I might have gone to the suite instead of the restaurant's restroom."

"Baldy still would have targeted you," Trent said. "Attack Liam in a deserted hallway and he's free to grab you before anyone interferes. Or, better yet, incapacitate Liam at the door to the suite, force you both inside, and interrogate you without interruption."

Piper frowned. "I would have screamed until I attracted someone's attention."

"Not if drawing attention meant a bullet in Liam's head." Trent phone signaled an incoming call. His face lit. "It's Grace. I'll take this on the balcony."

Matt took the ice pack from Piper. "We'll apply another in two hours. In the meantime, rest. I'll be back in a minute with a soft drink. Drink part of it before you sleep."

When he left, Liam turned Piper's face gently toward him. "How do you feel?"

"You were right about the adrenaline dump. I'm tired and my muscles ache."

"You fought hard to escape."

Matt returned and handed Piper the drink plus a straw. When she finished half, he placed the bottle in the refrigerator. "I didn't have a chance to ask about your injuries, Liam. You have injuries I should check?"

"Bruised ribs, nothing that needs attention."

"I want to check." Matt had Liam strip off his shirt.

Piper's breath caught at the sight of his discolored rib cage. Her fingertips brushed over the mark. "You should have mentioned you were hurt."

"The bruise will disappear in a few days. If I'd sustained a serious injury, I would have told Matt."

The medic examined Liam's ribs, his fingers checking each rib for breaks, then listened to his breathing. He straightened. "Bruised but you'll live. An ice pack every two hours will help but I won't browbeat you into it this time. I'll check on you two later." He left.

Liam shrugged into his shirt, then cupped Piper's face between his palms. "I'm sorry." His gaze dipped to her injury. "I messed up, Sunshine. It's my fault you were hurt. I promised to protect you and I failed. Again."

"You saved me a second time, Liam."

"I should have accompanied you to the restroom. If I had, Baker wouldn't have taken you."

"No matter what you did, Baker was determined to force me to give him the information. I wish Gavin had been man enough to handle this himself instead of dumping the problem on me. If he had, he would be sunning himself on a beach somewhere with Brandy."

"You sure he'd go to the beach?"

"Gavin avoided the mountains unless he was in the mood to ski. He preferred sun, sand, and surf. This isn't your fault, Liam. Don't blame yourself."

"I wasn't responsible for the incident in Otter Creek. This one, however, was on me. I wasn't careful enough with your safety. Why would you trust me after that colossal failure?"

"Easy. I was in the kidnapper's hands for ten minutes before you found me. You're the reason I'm alive." Piper kissed him gingerly. "Half my mouth is numb."

He chuckled, the shadows disappearing from his eyes.

Now or never, she thought. Liam needed to hear the words and Piper needed to say them. The operative had more courage than ten men. He could handle the truth. "When Baker took me into the forest, I thought I would die before you found me."

He flinched and started to respond.

Piper laid her fingers against his mouth, her touch light. "Hear me out. I didn't say that to hurt you. In those minutes when I was on the ground and Baker had his gun pointed at me, I realized if he killed me, my biggest regret would be not telling you how I feel about you."

Liam pressed his forehead to hers. "I know your feelings run deep, Sunshine. So do mine."

"I love you, Liam. You're so deep in my heart I'll never let you go. I dream of a future with you, a home, a family, a dog or two." She kissed him again. "I dream of growing old with you, greeting each morning with my arms wrapped around you, and falling asleep with my head pillowed on your chest. My life was empty without you. I never want to go back to that emptiness."

Piper fell silent, running out of steam and courage. What if he rejected her? He'd said he was half in love with her and that gave her hope.

"Thank God," he whispered and brushed a long series of butterfly kisses over her lips, careful to avoid her stitches. "I love you, Piper. I dream of that same future with you. I'd love a house full of children and a pack of dogs." Liam smiled against her lips. "No cats, though."

That gave her pause. "You don't like cats?"

"I'm allergic to them. Ten minutes around one and my eyes are bloodshot, itchy, and swollen."

"Wow. No felines in the McCoy clan."

"Piper McCoy," he murmured. "I love the sound of that." Another kiss, then, "You will marry me, right? I didn't just imagine you calling yourself a McCoy?"

"Piper McCoy sounds like the perfect name. I'd love to marry you."

"Soon after we're home, I'm buying you a ring. I want the men in Otter Creek to know you belong to me. I also want you to meet my mom and sister. They'll love you."

"I'd like that." She couldn't wait to meet the woman who raised Liam to be a man of honor and strong character. "What if we can't go home again, Liam?"

He shrugged. "There are jewelry stores in every city across America. If Mom and Marissa don't come into witness protection with us, I'll ask Maddox to work out a meeting with them. As long as I know you love me, I'll make it work."

Trent opened the French door and stopped, eyes twinkling. "Should I leave and come back later?"

Liam smiled. "Not necessary. How's Grace?"

"She told me to hurry and save the world and come home. She misses me."

"Sounds good." He shared an intimate smile with Piper. "We have plans to make."

Another knock sounded on the door. After a speculative look at Piper and Liam, Trent opened the door for Cade.

"What did you find out?" Liam asked as soon as the door closed behind his teammate.

The operative sat nearby, his expression grim. "We need to get Piper out of here as soon as possible."

REBECCA DEEL

CHAPTER TWENTY-ONE

Liam straightened, his gaze locked on Cade. "What did the waitress tell you?" Based on the EOD man's expression, his news wasn't good.

"Baker approached Darla, your waitress, and asked her to dump either a plate of food or Piper's drink in her lap. He claimed to be Piper's brother, back from a fourteen-month deployment in the Army and wanted to surprise her. He said he and Piper pulled practical jokes on each other and she wouldn't be angry. Darla didn't know he intended to kidnap Piper."

He frowned. "That's what we guessed. What's the problem?"

"Baker wasn't alone. Another man was with him."

Liam dragged a hand down his face. Great. Barone was hiring outside talent in pairs. Even if Zane unearthed pictures of Barone's crew, he wouldn't have photos of the hired talent.

Cade was right. He needed to take Piper away from Copper Ridge. Unfortunately, he was taking her to Hartman and her uncle. At least there, though, he'd know everyone except his team was a potential enemy.

He glanced at Piper. "I'd feel better about your safety if we're on the road rather than here in Copper Ridge."

"I'll do whatever is best for me and your teammates."

He kissed her forehead. "Thanks. As soon as Simon returns, we'll leave."

"I'll pack." Piper set aside the blanket and walked to her room, closing the door behind her.

"Is she all right?" Cade asked.

Liam jammed a hand through his hair. "She's shaken up by the kidnapping and half afraid her uncle is behind it. We have to end this, Cade. She'll won't be safe until we uncover every secret."

"And if it turns out her fear is correct, that her uncle is responsible for this chaos?" Trent asked.

"At least she'll know the truth. She's strong. She can handle whatever comes."

"She'll have to be if she wants a relationship with you, Liam." Trent folded his arms across his chest. "Don't think I didn't notice the hot looks going back and forth between you two. What gives, buddy?"

He could blow off the inquiry but why? His teammates were his friends and they knew him better than anyone, including his family. "She loves me, and we're unofficially engaged."

Both men congratulated him and clapped him on the shoulder. "Good job, man." Cade grinned. "Sasha will be thrilled to hear the news."

"Grace, too," Trent said. "When can we tell them?"

"I want to give Piper the chance to tell Delilah first. After that, you're free to tell the news."

"Excellent." A pointed look from his team leader. "Tell Piper to call Delilah before we leave. Grace and the others need something good to talk about to distract them from what we might face in Hartman."

"Copy that." He'd be searching for good things to tell Piper when he was in harm's way. If he could keep his job.

A sharp pain speared Liam's heart at the thought of giving up the job he loved. He'd do it in a heartbeat to keep Piper safe. He hated to lose touch with Trent, Matt, Cade, and especially Simon.

The suite door opened. Simon walked in, followed by Matt. "How is Piper?" Simon asked.

"Five stitches in her lip, cuts and scrapes on her hands and arms," Matt answered as he handed a makeshift ice pack to Liam. "Ice the ribs. You can't afford to be immobile."

Trent frowned. "How bad are the ribs?"

Liam waved his concern aside. "Bruised. What did the cops say, Simon?"

"Not much since I wasn't involved in Baker's takedown." His eyes gleamed with amusement. "Copper Ridge's finest isn't impressed with you leaving the scene of the crime with their star witness."

"I was more interested in Matt checking Piper's injuries than waiting for the cops. Besides, we answered Barrett and Kerrigan's questions here in the suite. Now that I know we have another man involved, I'm glad I made that call."

Simon's eyebrows rose. "Another man?"

"I talked to Piper and Liam's waitress, Darla," Cade said. "Baker asked her to dump a drink or food on Piper to get her into the bathroom alone. He had another man with him when he talked to Darla."

"I didn't see signs of another tango out there. I looked around while we waited for the cops to arrive." He turned to Liam. "What do you want to do?"

"Spirit Piper out of Copper Ridge as fast as possible. The detectives know how to reach us if they have more questions."

A slow nod from his friend. "I'll grab my gear." He strode to the other bedroom.

Cade, Matt, and Trent looked at each other. Trent motioned to the door. "Let's go. We'll meet back here."

As soon as they left, Liam called Zane.

"What do you need?"

"Tell me you have new information." He had more questions than answers.

"So far, I have zip. We're still digging. You have anything for me?"

He summarized the previous two hours, ending with, "We'll leave Copper Ridge as soon as we're packed."

"You're heading straight into the lion's den."

"I know. Look into John Baker. He said he doesn't know who hired him. Maybe you can discover who made inquiries about hiring him."

"I'll see what I can do. Tell Trent the Texas team is on the way to Amaretto. I reserved five rooms at the lodge on the outskirts of town. If you and Piper need to hide, Amaretto should be safe enough for one night. I sent a list of safe houses to your email."

"I hope we don't need them." If they did, he and Piper were in deep trouble and their mission to find the evidence to use against Barone was a failure.

"I'm almost finished with the papers for your mom and sister, and Maddox is scouting a new location for you, Piper, and your family to start a new life if necessary."

"I appreciate it, Z. If my family agrees to the relocation, my only regret would be leaving my team behind. I love my job. I don't know how to do anything else."

"The boss and I have been brainstorming about that. How do you feel about heading up a new team training facility?"

He sat up straighter, winced at the pain the movement caused. "Are you serious?"

"We can't keep up with demand for our services. Maddox wants to establish another training facility on the west coast. If you have to relocate and you're willing to take on the task, the boss will work it out. He doesn't want to lose you, Liam. I don't know if Bravo would be willing to move. If they aren't, you'll create a new team. Consider it if you have to go into hiding. Anything else I can do?"

"Not right now. Thanks, Z."

"Yep. I expect a check-in in two hours."

Liam smiled. "Yes, sir."

With a chuckle, Zane ended the call.

As he stood at the French doors to scan the area, he thought about the potential job opportunity if he had to reinvent himself. The idea of starting another training facility wasn't one he'd considered. He enjoyed his role in Bravo. If he had to relocate, though, the job would be an interesting challenge.

"Liam?"

He turned and smiled at Piper. "Everything packed?"

She nodded. "I heard you talking to someone."

"I called Zane. He's still digging. I asked him to check John Baker's background and his accounts. If we're lucky, he'll learn who made inquiries about hiring him and his partner."

Piper studied him a moment. "What else?"

"He and Maddox have been brainstorming about ways to keep me with Fortress if we go into hiding." He told her about the training school and his role in the endeavor.

"Is that what you want?"

"I'd rather work with Bravo. If I don't have that option, a new school would be interesting."

"Would you go on missions?"

He turned toward her, his gaze assessing. "Would you rather I didn't?"

Piper cupped his cheek with her palm. "I want you to be happy, Liam. If that means going on missions, you should go."

"You'll worry."

"Of course. I'll survive. The other wives and girlfriends of Fortress operatives handle the separation and worry. So will I."

He wrapped his arms around the woman he adored. "You're an amazing woman, Sunshine."

Simon opened his door and stopped. "Should I come back in a few minutes?" Humor filled his voice.

"Not necessary." Liam released Piper and retrieved her luggage and his gear. Within twenty minutes, the cargo areas of the SUVs were packed and the key cards for the resort turned in.

"We have your six," Trent told Liam. "Stop when you need to. When we reach Amaretto, the rest of us will stop at the lodge to check in, then do reconnaissance on Barone's place as well as Romano's. I talked to Brody Weaver. Either one of Bravo or one of his team will be near you and Piper at all times. I'll send you the contact information for the Texas team in case you need to speak to them. Input the same information into Piper's phone."

"I'll take care of it." His hand tightened around Piper's. If she had to reach out to Texas for help, every member of Bravo would be down, and Piper's chances of survival were nil.

CHAPTER TWENTY-TWO

Piper glanced around the gas station on the outskirts of Amaretto. From here, the rest of Bravo would travel to the lodge and unload their luggage while she and Liam continued to Hartman.

Seeing Liam's teammates in the rearview mirror the past few hours had been a comfort. The team would still be near, but not close enough to dispel her fear for Liam's safety.

Liam walked from the convenience store with bottles of water in one hand and snack food in the other. He climbed into the driver's seat, deposited drinks in the cup holders and handed Piper the snacks. "I bought several things. Hopefully, one of them will appeal to you." He slid her a pointed look. "You aren't eating enough."

She seized a pack of salted peanuts. "This is perfect. Thank you, Liam."

He squeezed her knee and started the engine. "You ready?"

"Would it matter if I said I wasn't?"

He glanced at her, concern in the depths of his eyes. "Your uncle isn't expecting us today. We could go with

Bravo to the lodge for tonight. I'll introduce you to Brody and his team."

Delaying the inevitable was tempting. But she wanted an end to this nightmare. The only way to accomplish that goal was to locate Gavin's information and go straight to the feds. Liam and his friends must know government agents who would take the information and use it against Barone. The part of her wanting to end this and move on to the next phase in her life was stronger than the part hoping to hide for a few more hours.

"I wish. I have to know who's behind the attempts to kidnap and kill me. The attacks won't stop until we bring the person to justice." What if Barone's henchmen wanted revenge? This nightmare might never end.

Piper shoved that thought behind a thick wall in her mind. She and Liam would find a way to end the threat. No other outcome was acceptable. Piper wanted a life with Liam in Otter Creek. She didn't want to look over her shoulder the rest of her life, expecting a hit man with orders to snuff out her life or those of her children.

Grim determination filled her. No one had the right to threaten her or her family. Going to Hartman was the next step in shutting down the danger to her, Liam, and their future children.

He lifted her hand to his lips and kissed her knuckles. "All right. Let's do this." After a short conversation with Trent and a promise to report in two hours, Liam drove from the gas station and traveled the final few miles to Hartman.

The closer they drove to her hometown, the more Piper's stomach knotted.

"We'll be okay, Sunshine." Liam threaded his fingers through hers. "I won't let anyone hurt you again."

"I'm not worried about that."

He glanced at her, skepticism in his eyes.

"Okay, that's not my only concern. I'm more concerned for your safety than mine. You will step into the line of fire to protect me."

"We have backup, but we can't mention that my teammates are near to anyone. We have to act as though we're alone. Otherwise, Bravo and Texas lose the advantage. Act as though you have all the confidence in the world. After all, you're here because at your uncle's request. At the moment, no one knows Gavin's clue led you here."

"They'll figure it out."

"The trick is to stay several steps ahead of them and be out of their reach by the time they figure out what we're doing."

"Sounds simple. Why do I think achieving that goal will be harder than it sounds?"

Laughter rumbled from his chest. "Probably Because you're as smart as you are beautiful. Remember what I told you about mission planning?"

"Have backup plans. A lot of them."

"Right. The reason is things always go wrong."

She hoped the mission went according to plan this time.

Fifteen minutes later, Liam stopped at the black wrought-iron gates. A security guard swaggered up and motioned for Liam to roll down his window.

"Got an appointment?" The guard's eyes narrowed when he saw Piper. "Do I know you?"

"We've never met." Of that, she was sure. This man's eyes were as cold as a snake's.

"Mr. Romano is expecting us," Liam said. "I'm Liam and this is his niece, Piper."

A grunt. "Wait here." He lumbered off a few feet and pressed his cell phone to his ear, gaze locked on Liam and Piper.

"Uncle Gino won't be happy we didn't give him some warning."

"Why? He ordered you to come home."

"He doesn't like surprises, including surprise visits."

"To have you here, Gino will deal."

What did her uncle want? He'd maintained silence for three years, displeased with her for refusing to marry Gavin. Did the attempts on her life have anything to do with why he wanted her in Hartman now?

Her heart skipped a beat. Maybe she and Liam had looked for the culprit behind her problems in the wrong place. Was Gino to blame? He had the money. Motivation? When he realized Gavin was dead, his motivation would disappear.

If her uncle set up the attacks, she was taking Liam into the heart of danger by staying in Gino's home.

The guard returned. "You'll be met at the front door and escorted inside."

"If I park in front of the house, my SUV will stay there. No one drives my vehicle except me."

Another narrow-eyed look. "Drive to the front door." He retraced his steps to the guard shack and pressed a button. The black gates opened inward.

"I'm not impressed with the security."

She frowned. "Why not?" When she was growing up, the guards were everywhere, watching each move she made. Her uncle had bragged to his friends about his top-notch security team.

"The guard didn't ask for identification or demand to search us and the vehicle for weapons."

"Would you have let him search us?"

"Not a chance. The point is he didn't insist. If your uncle is innocent of wrong doing, he needs better security to keep him safe."

Piper smiled. "Should be an interesting conversation. He thinks he knows best about everything."

"That's what I wanted to see."

She blinked. "What?"

"Your beautiful smile." Liam parked at the front steps, turned off the engine, and came around to open Piper's door. Leaning in, Liam kissed her.

When he eased back, Liam tucked her hair behind one ear. "Remember that we're on stage."

"Even in our rooms?"

"Until I determine if cameras or bugs are in the rooms, yes. No matter what happens, know that I love you, Piper."

Tears stung her eyes. "I love you, too."

Liam hugged her, muscular body shielding her from the view of others interested in their arrival. "Don't cry. Your uncle will think the tears are my fault."

His gentle teasing brought a smile to her lips. She wrapped her arms around him and leaned in to nuzzle his neck. "How do we approach this?" Her uncle's security cameras were positioned to track visitors approaching the house. Although Piper didn't remember the security people having the ability to read lips, Gino's had new guards now. One of them might have the lip-reading skill.

"You're here because Romano asked you to come home. When we search for Gavin's information, we'll tell people you want to show me your hometown and introduce me to your friends." He kissed her temple. "We have an audience."

Piper looked toward the front door. Two guards watched them, their jackets open to reveal guns in holsters at their hips. Her uncle waited at the top of the stairs, a frown marring his handsome face. Uncle Gino was not happy with her. Nothing had changed.

"We should go before Uncle Gino grows more irritated." She released her hold on his neck. "Thank you for coming with me."

"I wouldn't let you do this without me." He helped her from the SUV. After locking his vehicle, Liam laid his hand at the small of her back.

They walked up the stairs under the watchful eyes of her uncle's security detail. As she and Liam drew closer, Piper realized Gino Romano had aged and lost a lot of weight. He didn't look healthy, his skin sallow. Gino's wrist bones protruded and his fingers resembled thin sticks.

An invisible band squeezed Piper's heart. Was her uncle sick? "Uncle Gino."

"I'm glad you're here, Piper." He held out a hand to Liam. "Gino Romano."

"Liam McCoy. Thanks for opening your home to me."

A small smile curved Gino's lips. "Piper didn't leave me a choice."

"Still, I appreciate the hospitality, sir."

After a short nod, he turned his attention to Piper. "Come. We have much to discuss. Your friend can bring luggage to your rooms while we talk."

Liam stiffened.

Piper shook her head. "I don't have secrets from Liam. No offense, Uncle Gino, but after the past two days, I don't trust anyone except Liam."

Gino's brows beetled. "You're perfectly safe in your own home, Piper. I have more security than ever."

"He comes with me."

"I suppose the luggage can be dealt with later. Follow me." He turned on his heel and led the way into the house.

As they passed through the lobby and headed toward Gino's office, Piper caught glimpses of various rooms and realized nothing had changed since she left.

When Gino entered his office, one of the security guards barred the way before Liam and Piper crossed the threshold. "You armed?" he asked Liam.

"I'm in private security. What do you think?"

The guard snorted and held out his hand, palm up. "No one goes armed into a closed-door meeting with Mr. Romano. Hand them over."

"No." Liam cupped Piper's arm and turned her away from the office.

"Wait." Gino laid a hand on the guard's arm although his gaze remained fixed on Liam. "You don't plan to harm me, do you, young man?"

"As long as you aren't a threat to Piper."

"There. You see?" The older man motioned for the security guard to step aside. "I'll be fine. If it makes you feel better, wait in the hall."

With an unspoken warning, the guard moved enough for Piper and Liam to pass.

Once he closed the door, Gino waved them to chairs in front of his desk. "Have a seat. Who do you work for, McCoy?"

"Fortress Security."

Gino's eyes widened in surprise. "That's an elite group. How long have you worked for them?"

"A few years."

"I understand why you're hypervigilant. It's not necessary here."

"Piper was kidnapped twice and had shots fired at her. I don't trust anyone with her safety."

"Kidnapped? Why would anyone kidnap my niece?"

"That's what I plan to find out."

"Uncle Gino, we haven't spoken in years. Why insist that I come home now?"

After a lingering speculative look at Liam, Gino shifted his focus to Piper. "There's no easy way to tell you this, child."

Piper's nails dug into her palm. "Just say it."

"I'm dying."

CHAPTER TWENTY-THREE

Of all the things Liam expected Romano to say, this wasn't in the list. The old man was dying. A ploy or the truth? No matter what Romano claimed, Liam would ask Zane to confirm. "The doctors are sure?"

"No question. They've given me three months. After losing your parents when you were young, Piper, I thought it best to tell you in person."

Piper's pallor made her bruised and puffy lip more noticeable. "Is experimental treatment an option?"

He shook his head. "The cancer is too advanced. My body is riddled with it. I've come to accept the inevitable. You should, too." Romano inclined his head toward Liam. "I'm glad you have a friend who will be here for you when I'm gone. You'll need him."

Liam didn't like the sound of that. "Why do you say that?"

"It's why I asked Piper to come home."

Uneasiness roiled in Liam's gut. Romano's words and tone hinted at Piper's permanent presence in Hartman. Her living in the middle of Barone's turf wasn't happening.

"Tell me, Uncle Gino." Piper's voice sounded thick.

Liam threaded his fingers through hers. Small comfort, but better than nothing. He'd give anything to take the pain from her. Since he couldn't, he'd comfort her however possible.

"You're my only living relative. When I'm gone, the estate will be yours. I've named you as executor of my will. You will also be given the presidency of my company."

Piper was shaking her head before he finished speaking. "I'll settle your estate but I'm not moving back to Hartman. I have a life I love in Otter Creek. Besides, I know nothing about the video game industry and don't have any interest in learning."

He waved her protests aside. "We'll talk tomorrow. I'll take you to the company and let you see what we've been doing while you were away. Dinner will be ready in two hours."

Gino opened the door to the hall and signaled one of the security guards. "Todd, show Piper's friend where he'll sleep, then help with their luggage." He glanced over his shoulder at Piper and Liam. "I'll see you at dinner."

"This way," Todd said, his voice holding a hint of a growl. He strode down the hall and up the curving staircase to the second floor. He turned right, pausing in front of a room at the end of the hallway. He threw open the door and glanced at Liam. "This is your room. The lady is across the hall. Mr. Romano thought you'd prefer to stay close together. Give me your remote and I'll bring your luggage."

"You have more important things to do. I'll bring our gear inside. Thanks for the offer."

A shrug of the massive shoulders. "Suit yourself." He turned and left.

"Liam, I..."

He turned and kissed her with gentle thoroughness, cutting off the flow of words. "Wait," he whispered against her lips.

Liam nudged her inside the room, closed the door to the hall, and searched. Fifteen minutes later, he'd disabled two bugs and one camera. "Now your room," he murmured. "Knowing someone is listening and watching us is creepy."

And puzzling. If Romano was honest about his health, why would he spy on his niece and her guest? Was he involved in the abduction attempts and Gavin's murder?

Liam was sure he'd find devices in Piper's room to keep tabs on her and her conversations. The search yielded two bugs and two cameras, one of them in her bathroom. Burning with fury, he disabled the devices. Liam held her close. "You okay, Sunshine?"

She shuddered. "I might never be okay again. My uncle is spying on me. I can understand spying on you even though it's insulting. You're a stranger to him. But his own flesh and blood? What's he involved in that he's making sure I haven't turned on him?"

His arms tightened. "We don't know Romano is responsible for the electronics. Could be anyone with access to his estate."

"That would include the security guards, the maids, the housekeeper, my uncle's personal assistant, and the chef that comes in for special events. Even the lawn care people come inside the house on occasion."

Liam blew out a breath, frustrated at the revolving door of Romano's home. How was he supposed to narrow down the list of suspects when so many people trekked in and out? "That can't happen at our home. The security risk is too great."

"No problem. I want to take care of our home and children myself. I don't want our home to be like this one. Don't misunderstand me. I love my uncle and I'm grateful he took me in instead of letting me grow up in the foster care system. But as close as I thought we were, Uncle Gino left most of my care to Sophia. He lavished praise on me when I did what he wanted. The minute I deviated from his plan, he pressured me to give in. I couldn't marry Gavin, Liam, even to make my uncle happy."

"I'm glad you stood up for yourself. Otherwise, I wouldn't have met you."

"What do we do now?"

"Bring our gear inside." Well, most of his gear. Liam wouldn't unload his Go bag or the case containing his sniper rifle. Whoever installed the bugs and cameras in their rooms would nose around in their belongings. "Each time we leave the rooms, we'll have to search them again. If we're not vigilant, someone will slip in more devices to keep track of us."

"When should we go after the information Gavin left?"

"Is the information inside a building or outside?"

"It's in a botanical garden on the outskirts of Hartman. Archer Botanical Garden is one of my favorite places to visit. Gavin and I spent a lot of time there."

He eyed her. "Have you ever been to the Opryland Hotel in Nashville?"

Piper's eyes lit. "No, but I've heard it's incredible."

"The hotel has an atrium you'd enjoy."

"Maybe we can visit one day." She smiled. "If we find time to travel between your missions and my job."

"We'll make time." Opryland was the perfect place to spend part of their honeymoon. From there, they'd fly to their ultimate destination. Maybe the Bahamas. He'd think about that.

Liam dropped a quick kiss on her lips. "I'll be back in a minute."

"I'll go with you."

Recognizing her uneasiness, he wrapped his hand around hers and led her from the room. Together, they retrieved part of their gear. "Would you give me a tour of the house and estate?" Liam had studied the schematics Zane unearthed. Didn't mean the house still matched the schematics. Many homeowners remodeled their living spaces.

"Where do you want to start?"

He glanced out her bedroom window. "Outside while we still have light."

The minute they walked outside the house, a security guard trailed them. Although Liam kept an eye on the guard, the man stayed twenty feet behind them during their tour.

He listened to Piper talk about changes in the estate since she left home and noted the security measures around the grounds including the placement of guards and security cameras and the hum of an electric fence. To Liam, the estate resembled a prison more than a home and wondered if that was a factor in Piper's vehemence at living somewhere other than Hartman.

When they returned to the front of the house, the guard waited at the foot of the stairs until they walked inside. "The grounds are beautiful and well-maintained. Your uncle must have a landscape team to keep everything looking so lush and beautiful."

"He has a team of five who care for the plants and trees and trim the lawn." She tugged on his hand. "Come on. Let me show you the home I grew up in."

Piper resumed her running commentary on the changes in the house as they wandered from room to room. Part of her conversation included funny stories about things that happened in different rooms.

Those stories gave him insight into the woman he loved. Love for her uncle was obvious from the affection in her voice when she mentioned him in the stories.

More significant was the role Sophia played in her life. Piper looked on the housekeeper as a beloved aunt, a woman she held in high esteem.

They finished the house tour in the kitchen. When they crossed the threshold, an older woman with salt-and-pepper hair turned from the stove. Her dark eyes lit the moment they saw Piper.

"Welcome home, Piper." She hurried across the kitchen and embraced Piper, joy in her smile.

"Thank you, Sophia. It's good to see you again."

Her gaze dropped to Piper's mouth and her smile faded. "What happened?" She turned accusing eyes toward Liam.

Piper patted Sophia's arm. "Not his doing. A little accident. It's a long story. I'll be fine in a few days."

The woman released Piper and turned to Liam. "Introduce me to your friend."

"This is Liam."

"It's nice to meet you, Sophia. Piper's been telling me how much she misses you."

The housekeeper teared up. "Oh, Piper. You shouldn't have stayed away so long."

"You know why I couldn't return."

She waved aside Piper's comment. "Stubborn pride on both your parts. At least you returned before Mr. Romano passed. It's so sad. He's a good man and too young to die."

Seeing Piper's jaw tighten, Liam decided a subject change would be wise. More of Piper's tears would gut him. "Something smells good. What's for dinner?"

"Lasagna, garlic bread, salad, and an apple cobbler with ice cream for dessert."

He gave a low whistle. "Wow. I'll have to run an extra mile tomorrow morning to work off the extra calories."

The housekeeper's gaze swept over him. "You don't have an extra ounce of fat anywhere. Why are you worried about gaining weight?"

"I'm an instructor at a bodyguard training facility. Can't let my students outrun me. It's hard enough to keep up with trainees several years younger than I am. Extra weight makes it more difficult to do my job."

Wide eyes stared at him. "A bodyguard trainer. Are you a bodyguard?"

"Sometimes. I'm in private security. We do various jobs."

"Do you need help, Sophia?" Piper asked.

"The food is ready and the table is set. If you'll tell me your drink preference, I'll carry them to the table in a minute."

"Iced tea is perfect for both of us. We can take our own glasses, though." Piper hugged the housekeeper again. "I'm not used to someone waiting on me unless I'm in a restaurant."

Sophia tilted her head. "Do you eat out a lot?"

She glanced at Liam, lips curving "More since I started dating Liam."

"We'll have to send your young man on an errand so you can tell me all about him."

Liam grinned. "What about having coffee with us after dinner here in the kitchen? You can tell me stories about Piper when she was younger after she spills my secrets." Maybe Sophia would become an ally. Domestic staff knew what was going on inside a household because the family treated them as if they weren't there. If something odd was happening in this house, Sophia would know.

Pleasure brightened the housekeeper's face. "I'd love to catch up with Piper and hear about your romance."

"It's a date, then." He picked up two glasses, filled them with ice, and poured tea for himself and Piper. While the housekeeper rang the dinner bell, Liam escorted Piper into the dining room.

He stopped short at the entrance. "That is quite a display," he murmured. A large flower arrangement graced the center of the table. Candles were already lit and music played softly in the background. A snowy white tablecloth draped over the table. Glass and silver glittered in the light of the ornate crystal chandelier hanging over the table, and a fire crackled in the fireplace.

"Isn't it?" Piper looked uncomfortable. "I'm sorry. I didn't think to warn you this would probably happen."

Liam chuckled. "I can handle a formal dinner. I would have included dress clothes if I'd known."

Piper brushed his lips with hers. "I think you look exceptionally good in jeans or cargo pants and a long-sleeved t-shirt."

"I'm glad since that's my standard uniform." He leaned in to press his lips to her temple. "Remember, eyes and ears are everywhere," he whispered.

She nodded slightly. "Uncle Gino sits near the fireplace." She frowned as she studied the table. "Four places are set. I wonder who else is expected for dinner?"

At that moment, the doorbell rang.

"We'll find out in a minute." Liam seated Piper. He remained standing, preferring to be on his feet to meet the newcomer.

Voices murmured and footsteps heralded the approach of the visitor. Romano walked into the dining room with a dark-haired woman about Piper's age on his arm.

Piper drew in a sharp breath, her gaze locked on the woman.

Liam frowned. Her face had lost all trace of color. He laid his hand on her shoulder and waited for someone to confirm the woman's identity.

Romano escorted her to the seat across from Piper. "Sit here, my dear," he murmured. Once she was seated, he sat at the head of the table. "This is Piper's friend, Liam."

He extended his hand across the table. "Ma'am."

She gave a flirtatious laugh. "Call me Brandy."

CHAPTER TWENTY-FOUR

Piper stared in disbelief. Why did Gino ask Brandy to dinner? He had to know Piper would be uncomfortable with Brandy's presence at the table. Maybe her uncle thought enough time had passed that she wouldn't mind.

Thinking of Brandy and Gavin's betrayal no longer brought sharp pain. From the time Liam walked into Wicks, he'd captured her interest.

Being in the same room with Brandy made Piper conscious of her rough appearance. She cast a glance at Liam. Would he think Brandy was attractive? Of course he would. The woman was beautiful. She hadn't met a man yet who wasn't captivated by her.

She sighed, aggravated with herself. Liam loved her. He never said anything he didn't mean, and he was loyal. Piper wouldn't have to worry about him straying. Liam believed he was the luckiest man on the planet because she loved him.

Liam's handshake was just long enough to be socially acceptable as he introduced himself. He sat and wrapped his hand around Piper's.

Brandy looked disconcerted a moment before turning to Piper. "It's been a long time."

"You look beautiful." The other woman always took time to look her best before venturing into the world.

"Wish I could say the same. What happened to your face?"

Wow. She still had claws and didn't mind sharpening them on Piper. "An accident. I'll be fine in a few days."

"Have you been in town long?"

"A few hours."

"I suppose you haven't seen Gavin."

Liam's hand tightened around hers in silent warning.

Everyone in town would know the truth about Gavin's absence soon. The Copper Ridge police would notify Barone before much longer.

Grateful Liam didn't allow her to see Gavin in the cave, Piper shook her head without having to hide a lie. "I don't want to see him."

An eyebrow rose. "You're still hung up on him." She smiled, satisfaction gleaming in her eyes.

"No, Brandy. I have no interest in him. I haven't talked to him since I left Hartman." Another truth.

Sophia brought a pitcher of iced tea and filled Brandy's and Gino's glasses.

Brandy frowned. "Don't you have anything besides tea? Something stronger, perhaps?"

"After dinner, my dear." Gino patted her hand. "Sophia is catering to Piper's preferences tonight."

With a shrug, the other woman sipped the drink, grimaced, and set it aside. "I'll stick to water," she muttered.

And so began a long string of complaints from Brandy about everything from the food to the decorations and candles. Dinner progressed with conversation between Gino and Brandy. Piper and Liam contributed little although the other pair didn't seem to notice their lack of participation.

Throughout the meal, Liam found opportunities to touch her. A brush of fingertips over her cheek, a gentle squeeze of her hand, a wink when she glanced his way, an intimate smile. Although he remained alert and aware of Gino and Brandy, Liam's focus centered around Piper. With every passing minute, she fell deeper in love with the handsome operative.

When the meal ended, Gino said, "Liam, escort Brandy into the library for a stronger drink. Get to know her better."

Piper's hand tightened around her fork. Uncle Gino was determined to separate her and Liam. Did he think Liam would succumb to Brandy's charms, leaving the path clear for Gavin to move into her life? If so, he'd be disappointed.

Liam smiled. "I have a coffee date with two beautiful women as soon as the table's cleared and the kitchen cleaned. I'll have to pass."

Brandy's forehead furrowed. "A coffee date?"

"Sophia promised to share stories about Piper's childhood with me."

She scowled. "You prefer spending time with a servant than me?"

"He didn't mean it that way." Gino stood and held out his hand. "I'll go with you. Perhaps when they finish their coffee, Liam and Piper will join us. We'll get reacquainted."

As she walked from the dining room on Gino's arm, Brandy said, "You haven't told her yet. You promised to talk to her as soon as she arrived."

Piper and Liam exchanged puzzled glances. Why did Uncle Gino want to talk to her about Brandy? From the way things looked, she'd spent a lot of time with him.

Sophia walked into the dining room to see them at the table. "You didn't go to the library for drinks?"

Liam smiled. "I'm not letting you wiggle out of our date, Sophia. I want stories about Piper more than I want to spend time with Brandy and Mr. Romano. An added bonus is spending more time with the love of my life."

The housekeeper's eyes softened. "You have to share the story of your romance with me."

"If I can have more apple cobbler while we talk."

"Deal." Her eyes twinkled. "You might have to run two extra miles tomorrow."

Liam chuckled. "You're an amazing chef, Sophia. Mr. Romano is lucky to have you in his employ."

Piper pushed back from the table. "We'll help clear the table, then we'll catch up."

"That's not necessary." Sophia glanced toward the hallway, as though worried she'd be overheard. "It's not your job."

"We're family. Family works together to accomplish tasks faster."

They cleared dining table and wiped it down before shifting their attention to the kitchen. While she and Liam loaded the dishwasher, Sophia prepared the coffee maker.

By the time the carafe was full, Liam and Piper had loaded the last of the dishes and taken a seat at the kitchen table. Sophia placed a steaming mug of coffee in front of Liam and returned for the mugs of tea she'd prepared for Piper and herself. One more trip netted the apple cobbler for Liam.

"Don't keep me in suspense any longer. Tell me how you met and when you realized you were meant for each other."

Piper paused with her mug halfway to her lips. "How do you know we're meant for each other?"

Sophia laughed. "The joy in your eyes, sweet girl. You adore that man and he feels the same about you. It's exactly how my Julio and I looked at each other for forty years. Tell me the story, Liam."

"I met Piper soon after I arrived in Otter Creek a few months ago. Hate to burst your bubble about a slow-growing romance with an epiphany of love but I took one look at Piper and every other woman faded into the background. No one interested me except her. Took me a while to work up the courage to ask her out. I'm not good enough for her."

"That's not true," Piper protested. "Don't listen to him, Sophia. He's exactly what I need. The same thing happened to me. No one caught my eye except Liam."

"How did you meet?"

"His teammate is married to my boss. The training staff at Personal Security International spends time together outside of work, building a strong team rapport. Delilah dragged me to every dinner or cookout the team held because she knew we were fascinated with each other. While Liam worried about not being good enough, I struggled with trust issues after what happened with Gavin."

Sophia shook her head. "He's a foolish man who takes after his father. How serious are things between you?"

Liam kissed the underside of Piper's wrist. "I haven't purchased a ring yet, but Piper has consented to be my wife. I'd love to marry her in the spring."

Piper's heart skipped a beat before surging ahead at greater speed. "I like that idea. We'll figure out a date that works with your schedule when we return home. My schedule is more flexible."

Liam turned to Sophia. "How do you feel about coming to Otter Creek next spring?"

"You want me to come to your wedding?" Sophia's voice sounded faint.

"You're my second mother." Piper clasped the older woman's hand. "Please say you'll come."

"If I'm able to get away, I'd love to attend."

She squeezed Sophia's hand. "Great. We'll give you three or four dates. Hopefully, one of them will work with your schedule as well as ours."

"Do you plan to work after you're married? You told me often how much you want to start a family."

Piper's cheeks heated at the thought of having family with Liam. "I'll work for now. When we're ready for a baby, we'll talk about the feasibility of me staying at home."

Yet another thing she and Liam hadn't discussed. They had time. First, Piper wanted to build a solid marriage with the man she adored.

Brandy's laughter rang out, drifting into the kitchen.

Piper frowned. "Why did Uncle Gino ask Brandy to dinner tonight? He must know I haven't talked to her since I found her in bed with Gavin."

Sophia looked uneasy. "You should discuss this with Mr. Romano."

"I will but I'd appreciate your take on the situation so I don't blunder and cause Uncle Gino undue distress."

Although Sophia still didn't seem comfortable with the conversation, she said, "Brandy is spending more and more time with Mr. Romano at work and at home."

Stunned, Piper stared at the housekeeper. Why was her uncle spending so much time with Brandy?

"When did this start?" Liam asked.

"Not long after Piper left Hartman."

She frowned. "Wait. What do you mean about Brandy spending time with my uncle at work?"

"Oh, that's right. You don't know. Brandy got a job at your uncle's company soon after you left." She leaned closer and dropped her voice. "I don't know what's going on except Brandy has been promoted several times over the past three years. She's one of the vice presidents of the company now." A pointed stare at Piper. "Your job if you'd stayed instead of running from your problems."

"Leaving was the best thing I could have done for myself, Sophia. If I'd stayed, I wouldn't have met Liam. I don't have one ounce of regret for leaving Hartman and Gavin in my rearview mirror. I wish I'd parted on better terms with my uncle, though."

Sophia patted her hand. "You're here now. That's what matters. Mend your fences while you can."

"Do you know why Brandy insists on Mr. Romano talking to Piper tonight?" Liam asked.

Another guilty glance toward the hall, then, "I shouldn't say. Mr. Romano won't be pleased if he finds out I'm gossiping."

Piper squeezed her hand again. "You're giving me advance warning. We know Uncle Gino plans to talk to me. Help me out."

"I think it has to do with the company. I overheard Brandy on her cell phone, bragging to Mr. Gavin."

"What about?"

"She said Mr. Romano is going to make her CEO of his company."

CHAPTER TWENTY-FIVE

Liam walked Piper to her room and closed the door behind them. With a finger to his lips indicating the need for silence, Liam pulled an electronic signal detector from his pocket and searched the room for bugs and cameras.

His gut clenched when he discovered three bugs and one camera had been planted in Piper's room. Once the equipment was dismantled, he wrapped his arms around Piper.

"I can't believe this," she whispered.

"Even if we lock the rooms, the security team will have keys. It's easy to plant more bugs while we're out."

"Is my uncle responsible?"

"I don't know, Sunshine but I'll learn the truth before I'm finished. How is your lip?"

"The medicine Matt used to numb my mouth has long worn off."

That explained the small amount of food she consumed at dinner. He reached into his pocket and drew out a packet of capsules. "Mild pain meds, courtesy of Matt. Should help you sleep."

"I'm not sure I'll be able to sleep tonight. I don't feel safe in this house."

Liam cupped her nape. "I'm right across the hall. If anything scares you, come to me or call out. I'll hear you."

He bent and captured her mouth. Although Liam's kiss was thorough and filled with sizzling passion, his touch remained gentle in deference to her injury.

When he lifted his head, Piper said, "I can't wait until my lip is healed. I want a real kiss."

"Is that right?" Pleasure zinged through his bloodstream at her words.

"I'm addicted to them."

"Same here." After a soft brush of his thumb over her bottom lip, Liam released her. "You need ice. I'll bring you more along with a bottle of water."

He returned to the kitchen and found it lit by a light over the stove. A quick search netted him a plastic bag which he filled with ice and kitchen towel. Liam grabbed a bottle of water, then went to Piper's room and knocked one the door.

A moment later, Piper let him inside. "Thank you, Liam."

Because he couldn't resist her tempting mouth, Liam stole another series of soft kisses before going to his own room. Inside, he searched the room and dismantled a camera and two bugs.

He called Zane.

"You're late," was his greeting.

"Needed to take care of Piper and get rid of bugs and cameras from our rooms."

A soft whistle sounded over the speaker. "Bold."

"This is the second time I've cleared electronics from both bedrooms."

"Suspects?"

"Too many to count. You wouldn't believe how many people work at Romano's estate. What do you have for me?"

"The ballistics test came back from the incident in Copper Ridge. The bullet that killed Gavin James didn't come from the weapons carried by you, Simon, or the three tangos you and Simon captured or killed."

"Either Gavin's killer is Baker's partner or someone else from Hartman drove to Copper Ridge to ensure Gavin didn't pass on the information he discovered."

"Given his history, is it possible an angry Copper Ridge husband or boyfriend took exception to Gavin hitting on his woman?"

"Maybe. The shot was precise, though, and Gavin didn't have defensive wounds. If an angry spouse or boyfriend went after Gavin, I think he would use his hands and fists in a fit of rage. This feels like cold-blooded, premeditated murder. Anything from Otter Creek?"

"The only fingerprints that shouldn't be in your home came from Jared Spencer. The rest belong to members of Bravo, Durango, and their wives or girlfriends."

He rubbed the back of his neck. "Not what I wanted to hear, Z."

"You'll like this bit of news even less. Spencer made a play for Delilah."

Liam stiffened. "Is she all right?"

"She's fine. Molly was in the back room, putting stock away. She arrived in time to stop him from doing more than scaring Delilah. As soon as Molly appeared, Spencer left Wicks."

"I need to convince my teammates to go home. They and their families are in danger because of me."

"Funny. Matt thought you'd say that. He said should concentrate on ending the threat to Piper. PSI personnel and trainees have the families covered."

He'd be wasting his breath trying to send his teammates home. They had each other's backs in firefights and out. Bravo wouldn't leave Hartman until he and Piper left. "Copper Ridge police have anything else?"

"They still want to charge Simon with murder but can't. Someone anonymously sent them traffic cam footage showing his journey to the resort, complete with time stamps in the corner. Once the ME confirms time of death, Simon will be off the hook for James's murder. No question Simon killed the thug after you arrived at the resort and wounded the second one. To this point, the wounded man won't talk."

Liam frowned. "He's not claiming Simon shot him for no reason?"

"That's right. He also hasn't lawyered up."

"Is their crime scene team any good?"

"I don't know. Why?"

"If they are, the techs should find multiple bullets and shell casings from the two thugs shooting at us. I didn't fire and Simon fired twice." Both shots hit their mark.

"Makes your story more viable. Anything else I can do?"

"Did you get the contact information for the members of my military unit?"

"I did. You'll be disappointed if you get in touch with them, Liam. Spencer did a great job convincing your buddies that you're responsible for his unjust imprisonment."

"Thanks for the warning. I'll call you in six hours."

Liam took a quick shower. A short time later, he sprawled on top of the covers fully dressed and fell into a light sleep.

He woke three hours later to the sound of a floorboard shifting with a soft squeak. Before the sound disappeared, his hand wrapped around the grip of his Sig. Fabric brushed against a wall.

He waited for the intruder to open his door. He relished the coming confrontation. Perhaps by the end of it, Liam would have answers to lingering questions and Piper would finally be safe.

Instead of entering Liam's room, the intruder passed by his door. Sliding from bed, Liam moved with soundless steps across the room.

Liam turned the knob, opened the door a crack and checked the hall. Nothing. He frowned. Someone had passed his door. He'd heard the intruder trying and failing to be stealthy. Where was he?

His gaze shifted to Piper's door. Liam's eyes narrowed. Her door was ajar. Had Piper left the room? His hand tightened around the grip of his weapon. Holding the gun at his side, Liam crossed the hall to Piper's room and pushed open the door as a muffled cry came from inside.

A black-clad figure with a mask stood over Piper, hands clamped around her throat. Shoving his weapon into his MOB holster, Liam sped across the room and tackled the man fighting to control Piper's panicked struggles, forcing him away from her.

He took the intruder to the floor and thumped his head against the hardwood twice. When the man groaned and went motionless, Liam pulled a zip tie from his pocket and cinched his wrists together behind his back.

He stood. "It's Liam. Are you okay?"

Piper scrambled from the bed and threw herself into his arms.

Liam moved her further away from the downed intruder. "Piper, are you hurt?"

"No."

He frowned at her raspy voice. "I'll turn on the light."

Keeping her against his side, Liam circled to the opposite side of the bed and turned on the lamp. The dim light gave him just enough vision to see the red marks on her throat.

Liam growled. Was his aim to kill her or knock her out? Either way, this clown would be sorry he'd laid a hand on Liam's woman.

He nudged Piper to a nearby chair. "Stay here."

"Why?"

"I don't want you close when I take the mask off his face in case he's faking unconsciousness."

"Can't we just call the police?"

"How did he get into the house? This place has security crawling all over it."

"I wish I knew."

"We have two possibilities. Either the security measures are subpar, or he was already on the estate. I want answers before we call the cops."

Liam flipped the intruder onto his back and yanked off the mask. His lip curled. No wonder he knew where Piper was sleeping tonight.

"Who is it?"

"The guard at the front gate."

"Why would he want to hurt me?"

"Let's find out. Still have water in the bottle I brought you?"

Piper retrieved the bottle and tossed it to Liam's outstretched hand.

He unscrewed the cap and dumped the contents on the guard's face.

The man choked and sputtered, his eyelids fluttering up. He saw Liam and scowled. "You're a dead man," he snapped.

He ignored the threat. "What are you doing in this room?"

A sullen glare was his response.

Liam considered his options. On the house tour, he'd discovered Romano's room was in the other wing on the first floor. Should be far enough away to keep Piper's uncle from investigating a muffled scream. However, the guards roamed the house at thirty-minute intervals. In fact, the guard's sweep should be occurring in the next ten minutes, not enough time to get as much information as Liam wanted from this clown.

Fine. He'd get what he could from this guy, then leave him for the cops when the guard appeared. When the gatekeeper tried to get up, Liam shoved him down. "Stay."

The guy cursed at him.

Liam crouched and gripped the area between the man's neck and shoulder, pinching one of the nerves. The other man gasped, his face losing all trace of color. "Watch your mouth," Liam said, voice soft. "There's a lady present." After receiving a nod of compliance, Liam asked, "Name?"

"Rusty."

"Here's how this is going to play out, Rusty. You tell me what I want to know or you'll wish you had never been born. What are you doing in Piper's room?"

The man clammed up.

Liam sighed. "We're doing this the hard way, huh?" He glanced at Piper. "Lock yourself inside my room, baby."

"I'd rather stay with you." Fear glimmered in her eyes.

He hoped she wouldn't regret her choice during the interrogation or in agreeing to marry Liam. "No matter what, don't interfere." He turned back to Rusty, clamped a hand over his mouth and bore down hard on the same nerve he'd pinched a minute before.

The response was immediate. Rusty's body bowed as pain wracked through his body. His scream was muffled by Liam's hand. When he eased his grip on the nerve, the guard moaned, breathing rapid.

"Why were you in Piper's room?" he asked again and lifted his hand for the man to answer.

Another round of cursing.

Liam repeated the same procedure, this time holding the grip long enough that tears left trails down Rusty's face before he eased up. "You should know I love Piper," he said, voice soft. "I'll do whatever I have to do to protect her. I won't blink at killing you right here, right now. I have the perfect cover story, after all. I walked inside this room to see your hands around her throat. The bruises you left behind will attest to my version of events. It's too bad you were hurt in my struggle to protect the woman I love. How do you think I feel right now?" Liam let the fury and determination to protect what was his show in his gaze.

Rusty swallowed hard, fear growing in the depths of his eyes.

"That's right. Wouldn't take much to convince me to rid the world of one more lowlife. Piper will tell the cops you attempted to kill her. Total justification for my actions when the cops show up. You think the officers will have much sympathy for a man who breaks into an unarmed woman's bedroom and attacks her? I'll ask you one more time. Why were you in this room with your hands around my woman's throat?"

"I wasn't trying to kill her, I swear."

"Doesn't take much pressure to crush a windpipe. Want a demonstration?"

A fast head shake.

"Too bad. Talk to me before I decide you aren't worth keeping alive." He was almost out of time. The guard making the rounds would be coming in another three or four minutes.

"I was supposed to scare her into talking."

"About what?"

"Her boyfriend."

Liam's smile was more a baring of his teeth. "I'm her boyfriend. Are you talking about her ex, Gavin?"

"Yeah."

"What were you to find out?"

"Where he hid the information he stole. I was supposed to get it back. That's all."

"Who sent you?"

"Don't know. Just an email contact with money dumped into my account." His gaze shifted to the left as he said those words.

Liam stared at him. The idiot was lying through his teeth. "You expect me to believe you took on a job without knowing who your employer is?"

That brought his glare back to Liam. "Hey, the money was good. What do I care where it came from as long as I don't have to do nothing illegal?"

"Breaking into a woman's room and threatening her with bodily harm isn't legal anywhere, dude."

Footsteps approached the room. Liam was out of time. He turned to see the guard in the doorway.

"What's going on in here? What did you do to Rusty?" The guard's hand edged toward his weapon.

"Don't do it," Liam ordered. "I'll kill you before your weapon clears your holster."

The guard froze.

"Your friend broke into Piper's room. I found him with his hands around her throat."

The other man's mouth dropped open.

"Don't believe him, Ed," Rusty spat out. "The lady invited me in."

"Liar," Piper said, disgust lacing her voice.

Liam turned his head to look at Rusty. "This is your only warning," he murmured. "Close your mouth."

Rusty paled again and fell silent.

"Call the cops, Ed." Liam stood. "Your buddy, Rusty, is going to have a long talk with the police."

"But he said the broad invited him."

"If you won't help, go back on your rounds and I'll notify the police."

Ed raised his chin, defiance in his gaze. "I ain't calling the cops on a friend."

Liam pulled out his cell phone and made the call himself. He also sent a text to Simon who was on watch outside the estate grounds so he'd know what was happening.

Simon called. "Need help?"

"I've got it."

"Is Piper all right?"

"More bruises to add to her collection."

"What do you need me to do?"

"Update our team leader and the boss."

"You can't talk freely?"

"That's right."

"I'll take care of it. Let me know if you need me."

Within a couple minutes, sirens sounded in the distance. Now the fun would begin.

CHAPTER TWENTY-SIX

Piper huddled against the couch in the sitting room attached to her bedroom, wrapped in the blanket Liam had grabbed from the foot of her bed. Liam's arm tugged her closer to his side as the EMT approached Piper.

"Let me look at your throat," the woman said.

"I'm fine," Piper insisted.

"All the same, I'd rather check." Her gaze flicked to Liam. "I'm sure your boyfriend wants to know if you need a trip to the hospital. It's better to be safe, ma'am."

Liam squeezed Piper's shoulder. "Do it for my peace of mind."

She preferred to have Matt check her, but that wasn't possible unless the members of Bravo made their presence known. They couldn't do that without giving away their advantage. "All right."

The EMT smiled. "Great. This won't take long." After answering a series of questions and allowing the woman to prod her throat, the medical technician pronounced her good to go. "Your throat will be sore for a few days and you'll have bruises. Other than that, you'll be good as new in a week or so. If you have problems with your throat, go to the hospital to be checked out by a doctor, ma'am."

"I will. Thank you."

The EMT gathered her equipment and followed her partner from the room, leaving the police behind with Liam and Piper.

One of the men dressed in a suit sat across from them in a straight-backed chair. His partner leaned against the wall by the door, notebook and pen in hand.

"I'm Detective Tate Haynes." He inclined his head to the man at the door. "That's my partner, Detective Wallace. What happened here tonight?" he asked Liam.

Piper relaxed at the knowledge Liam would be questioned first. His version of events would guide her in relaying her own version.

"I heard someone walk past my door at 2:15. When I checked, the hall was empty but Piper's door was open. When I looked inside her room, I saw the gate guard leaning over Piper with his hands wrapped around her throat. I tackled him, restrained him, and called you guys."

Nice. Nothing about the persuasive techniques Liam used to question Rusty. Something told Piper the gate guard wouldn't have a mark on him to prove his version of events.

"You carry zip ties around?"

Liam smiled. "I'm in private security. We're prepared for anything."

"What outfit are you with?"

"Fortress Security."

The detective's eyebrows soared. "Tough group to get into. How long have you worked for them?"

"Five years."

"What did you do before that?"

"Marines."

"Thank you for your service." Haynes took Liam through his side of events a few more times, asking more detailed questions. When he was satisfied, he turned to Piper. "Tell me what happened, ma'am."

"I was asleep. Something woke me and I realized someone was in the room. I thought Liam might be checking on me at first."

"Is there a reason he'd come into your room in the middle of the night?"

She frowned. The detective sounded as though he was accusing Liam of something. Did he think Liam attacked her and she covered it up?

"My uncle told me some upsetting news before dinner. Liam is protective. I wouldn't be surprised if he peeked into the room to be sure I was okay."

"I see. Go on."

His words were neutral. His voice, however, said he didn't believe her explanation for Liam's possible presence in her room in the middle of the night. "I knew before Rusty put his hands around my throat it wasn't Liam."

"How?"

"Liam doesn't wear cologne. Rusty does." She wrinkled her nose. "A nauseating musky scent. I started to call out for Liam. Hard hands wrapped around my throat and choked me." Her voice broke off at the remembered pain and panic.

"You're safe, Sunshine," Liam murmured. "Rusty won't touch you again."

"Did Rusty say anything while he held you down?" Haynes asked Piper.

"He wanted to know where the information was."

A frown. "What information?"

Liam squeezed her shoulder.

"I don't know. I fought to get his hands off my throat but his grip was too strong. Liam tackled Rusty and restrained him. We called you."

Haynes watched her a moment, then took Piper through the attack several times, asking more detailed questions. Finally, he asked. "What aren't you and your friend telling me?"

She stilled. "You think we're lying?"

"Not lying. Holding back. There's more to this story. I want all of it. If my investigation is hampered, I might be bad tempered enough to haul you in for obstruction of justice."

Again? She heard the same threats from Barrett and Kerrigan in Copper Ridge. Unsure what to say, she said nothing. Trusting the wrong people would be hazardous to her health and Liam's.

Liam stroked Piper's arm. "We ran into a little trouble before we came to Hartman."

"What kind and where?"

The operative gave the detectives the bare bones of events in Copper Ridge. "Gavin James left information for Piper but we don't know where it is or what it's about. If Gavin was still alive, I'd have a heart-to-heart talk with him about endangering my girlfriend because of his own cowardice."

Haynes glanced at his partner who shrugged. "You're sure James is dead, McCoy?"

"A bullet pierced his heart. I'm sure. The Copper Ridge police will confirm his death."

The detective dragged a hand down his face. "The news will be all over town soon. You think Rusty's attack on you has something to do with James's death, Ms. Reece?"

"Nothing else makes sense. I work in a candle shop in Otter Creek, Tennessee. The most dangerous thing I do all day is pour hot wax into molds and decide which scents to add to the mix. I have no idea what Gavin discovered. Whatever it was got him killed. I don't want to be the next victim or drag Liam into this mess."

After reviewing their statements one more time, the detective stood. "Come to the station tomorrow. We'll have more questions and you can sign your statements. In the meantime, be careful and watch your backs. If you think of anything else that might help, call me."

After he took pictures of her neck, Haynes and his partner left.

Gino walked into the room. "Piper, what's going on? One of the guards said you were attacked in your bed."

"I'm sorry the commotion woke you, Uncle Gino."

"You should have sent someone for me. I have a right to know someone attacked you in my home." His words came out clipped, tone harsh.

"I planned to tell you when you woke. I didn't want to disturb you."

He waved her explanations aside and glanced at Liam. "Tell me what happened. Don't leave anything out."

Liam gave him a sanitized version.

Gino shook his head. "I don't understand. He's worked for me for two years and I've never had trouble with him. This doesn't make sense." He sighed, his attention shifting to Piper. "I understand if you prefer to stay somewhere else. I doubt you'll feel safe after this."

"Piper and I will talk." Liam kissed her temple. "We'll let you know what we decide to do."

All the anger seemed to drain from her uncle. "I'm sorry, Piper. Perhaps I shouldn't have asked you to return home. I hoped you and Gavin would mend your relationship and continue where you left off."

Piper gripped his hand and urged Gino to sit beside her. "He cheated on me while we dated, Uncle Gino. Not once, but over and over. I couldn't trust him after that. Besides, I love Liam."

Gino's eyes widened. "I see."

"I plan to marry Piper, sir. I'd like your permission and blessing."

A small smile curved the old man's mouth. "And if I won't give it?"

Piper's breath caught at the mischief dancing in her uncle's eyes. This was the uncle she adored. But was it the real Gino? The possibility that he was behind her troubles remained. He had means, motive, and opportunity.

Liam's own lips tipped up at the corners. "I'll be sorry to cause you distress but that won't change my plans. I love your niece."

A soft sigh. "I'm disappointed in Gavin. He turned out to be like his father."

Piper frowned. "You knew Gavin was like that but you still encouraged me to be with him?"

"The match would have been a good one."

For who? Not for her.

"Some women wouldn't mind a wandering husband if they had access to a life of luxury."

"I'm not one of them," she said flatly.

"I see that. Liam, you and Piper have my blessing. I hope your marriage is blessed with children and many years of love and laughter." With a pat of Piper's hand, Gino rose. "I'll return to bed for a few more hours of sleep." He pierced Liam with a pointed look. "I expect to hear if anything else happens in my home."

"Including if we find more listening devices and cameras planted in our rooms?" he asked.

Gino's jaw hardened. "Including that. Looks like I'll be talking to my security people later today. Do you have recommendations for security improvements?"

"Several, if you're interested."

"We'll talk later." With a wave of his hand, he walked to the hallway and spoke with one of the security guards who hurried off to carry out his orders.

Piper leaned her head against Liam's shoulder. "What are we going to do?"

"For now, nothing. We're staying on this couch where I can watch over you for the rest of the night. No one will get through me to hurt you."

"You need to sleep."

"So do you. I'm used to staying awake for days at a time on missions. Staying awake for one night won't hurt me."

"You have to sleep sometime."

"We'll figure something out." He squeezed her shoulder, his gaze intent.

They hadn't checked this room for bugs or cameras. Piper swallowed hard, flinching at the soreness in her throat. The thought of sleeping with possible bugs or cameras keeping track of every breath or movement made her skin crawl.

She shook her head. "I can't," she whispered.

"Then sit with me and let me hold you." Liam palmed the remote and channel-surfed until he found a station running episodes of a cozy mystery series she enjoyed. "Just relax," he murmured. "I think we should count this as another date and another step in my attempt to romance you."

Piper tilted her head back. "Watching old episodes of a television series?"

"I prefer shows with more action in them. This is a real sacrifice, Sunshine."

She burst into laughter, a surprise considering a moment ago she felt no humor at their situation. Piper snuggled close to Liam's side. "That's quite a sacrifice. I'll give you credit for a date."

"Awesome. I promise to come up with something better for the next date."

"My turn to choose the date and I have a perfect place."

"Hmm. Sounds intriguing. What's my reward for going along with your plan?"

"Your choice."

He chuckled. "That's easy. Another kiss."

"Deal." Her plan would work if Liam was as good as she thought he was. If not, they'd be leading the enemy to Gavin's next clue.

CHAPTER TWENTY-SEVEN

Liam's eyebrows rose when he saw the sign. "Hartman Museum?" He eyed Piper who sat in the passenger seat of his SUV. "Why are we here?"

"If someone listened and watched us in my sitting room, we might have a tail."

His lips curved. Smart lady. "We do."

She shuddered. "Can't say I wanted to hear confirmation of my theory. Anyway, I didn't want to lead the bad guys to Gavin's hiding place. The museum grounds are adjacent to the botanical gardens. Gavin and I found a natural passageway through brush and trees leading to the gardens. It's hard to spot. You have to know where to look. There are many places to disappear on both properties. We can lose the tail while we visit the museum, then go to the gardens."

He parked in the lot at the back of the museum. Based on the number of cars around the building, he and Piper might be the only visitors to the museum. After sending Trent a text to report the plan, Liam circled the hood and opened Piper's door. "Good plan, Sunshine."

"It's only good if it works." She led the way toward the museum entrance.

Liam paid the admission price and escorted her inside the quiet building. He glanced around, slowing his steps as he took in the stairs and vaulted ceiling in the entryway. "This looks like someone's home."

Piper smiled. "That's because it was. The founding family built this house. George Hartman's granddaughter, Emeline, hates the house. Since she's the last remaining Hartman and has sole possession of the Hartman estate, she sold the building and grounds to the town for a tidy profit and then moved to Key West, Florida."

Liam whistled. "Beautiful place to live. Pricey, too. Why did she choose Key West?"

"She loves Ernest Hemingway's work."

As good a reason as any to move there, he supposed. "Is the museum one of the places you visited often when you lived here?"

She nodded. "I've always enjoyed history." Piper led him on a tour of the large house, pointing out items she thought might be of interest to him. The gleaming weapons displayed in glassed-in cases was fascinating.

"Arthur Hartman was quite a collector," Liam said as they left the weapons room and wandered down the back stairs to the grounds of the museum.

"Is it a good collection?"

"Oh, yeah. Some of those weapons are antiques and worth several thousand dollars on the open market."

"I had no idea."

He caught movement out of the corner of his eye. Liam wrapped an arm around Piper's waist and angled himself to place his body between her and the potential threat. "You're not into weapons. You impressed me with your knowledge of the candles around the museum."

"I thought it best to learn all about candles since I work in a candle shop. Did you know the first wicked candles were created by the ancient Egyptians by dipping rolled papyrus into tallow or beeswax?"

Liam grinned despite his growing uneasiness, amused by her enthusiasm. "Can't say I've ever heard that."

When they strolled into a grove of trees, Liam pressed a forefinger to Piper's lips to ask for silence and guided her deeper into the shadowy coverage. He urged her toward a large tree and nudged her back against its shelter. "Where is the passageway?" he whispered.

She inclined her head to the left. "A quarter of a mile from here. The grounds are pretty extensive."

"Good. Gives us time to lose our pursuer. Walk where I walk." Clasping her hand in his, Liam led the way toward the natural tunnel, choosing his steps with care to minimize the sound and tracks.

He lengthened his stride to put enough distance between them and their pursuer to lose him. Liam urged Piper to move faster.

She tugged on his hand and pointed to the dense greenery and stand of trees to the left. Piper moved ahead of him and dropped to her hands and knees. She crawled between a large bush and a jutting boulder.

Huh. If he hadn't seen her disappear between the two objects, Liam would have missed the gap. He wasn't sure he could slither through there as easily as Piper.

He glanced over his shoulder. Their pursuer was too close to hunt for another way into the tunnel. If Piper's plan was to work, he needed to move now.

Liam eased into the opening. Limbs and sticks grasped at his clothes. He frowned. The last thing he wanted to do was leave a trail a two-year-old could follow. Angling his shoulders more and pressing close to the rock, he made his way through the opening and out the other side into the natural tunnel where Piper waited for him.

He caught her arm and guided her deeper into the shadowy interior. When he heard twigs snapping and muffled swearing, Liam nudged Piper to stand with her back to a large tree. He slid the Sig from his holster and held it by his thigh.

The rustling of bushes grew louder. Liam aimed his weapon at the tunnel opening. With his left hand, he reached behind him and drew Piper up against his back, then went motionless.

Movement drew attention. If their tail found the tunnel and walked inside, Liam didn't want to give away his position. Both he and Piper were dressed in dark clothes. The follower's vision would take a few seconds to adjust to the sudden dimness, seconds Liam could use to take action to protect Piper.

Liam followed the stranger's progress through the small gaps in the bushes. Instead of entering the tunnel, the stranger stood, turning this way, then that, searching for signs of their passage.

More swearing. A moment later, a voice drifted their direction. "Yeah, it's me. I lost them." A pause. "How should I know? They're walking around the museum at the old Hartman place. Looks like she's showing her man around town." Another pause. "I think it's a waste of time, but you're the boss. I'll let you know when they come out again."

Piper's breath caught.

Liam glanced at her as the stranger's footsteps indicated he was leaving. "What is it?" he whispered.

"I know him."

His eyebrows rose. "Who is he?"

"Well, I don't know his name, but I know who he works for. Matteo Barone. He works with the estate's security team."

A good indication of who wanted the information Gavin left for Piper. Liam wasn't surprised. He held her close and waited five more minutes in silence before he believed it was safe for them to resume their journey to the botanical gardens.

"Let's go before he comes back." He'd prefer to retrieve the package or whatever Gavin had left and walk out of the museum estate the way they came in. Otherwise, they'd raise the other man's suspicions. Speculating that they'd retrieved a package from Gavin was one thing. Confirming that fact by acting out of the norm was stupid.

Clasping Piper's hand, Liam walked toward the far end of the tunnel where the trees and brush thinned and winter sunlight filtered through the leaves. When they neared the open space of the botanical gardens, he held up his fist in a silent order for Piper to wait until he was sure it was safe for her to move into the open. She stopped at the edge of the clearing.

Relieved he didn't have to explain his actions when the need for silence was imperative, Liam walked a few feet from the foliage and scanned the area for signs someone had anticipated their plans and waited for them. He let his gaze scour the shadows and landscape. Nothing out of place and he didn't feel the weight of someone's gaze on him.

Satisfied Piper was reasonably safe, he turned and held out his hand to her. She threaded her fingers through his. "Where to now?"

"This way." She led him toward a path to the right. The walkway wound through lush gardens dressed for winter.

He'd always thought gardens were dormant during the winter months. This part of Alabama, though, seemed to have mild winters because the gardens were vibrant and alive with color. Liam frowned, eying the blooming flowers on both sides of the path. Mums, maybe. What he knew about flowers would fill a bullet casing.

A few minutes later, the path curved and Liam saw a gazebo fifteen feet ahead. "The gazebo?"

"The bench along the rock wall behind the gazebo."

When Piper began to hurry, Liam held her back. "We don't want to draw attention to ourselves. We're supposed to be enjoying our time together while you show me your favorite places in Hartman. Moving fast draws the eye. We can't be in a hurry."

"I want this over with so we can go home, Liam." As she slowed at a more sedate walking pace, Piper smiled at him. "I have a wedding to plan."

"I like the sound of that. How long will I have to wait before I slide a wedding band on your finger?"

"You mentioned the spring. I was thinking April. I'd love to marry you in an outdoor ceremony with glorious flowers blooming everywhere."

He pressed a kiss to the back of her hand. Five months. He would deal. "Sounds perfect."

Liam urged her to sit on the bench beside him. "Let's wait to see if we have company before retrieving the package."

"How long do we wait?"

"Until I'm sure you're safe. Tell me about the botanical gardens. How long have they been here?"

While Piper told him about the history of the gardens, Liam scanned the area, looking for anything out of place, for movement that caught his eye. He waited for his own senses to tell him they were being watched. At the ten-minute mark, he said. "Let me take your picture. Sit where you can reach the package. I'll use my body to block you from view in case we have an observer that I've missed."

Piper moved to the opposite end of the bench and turned at an angle to smile at Liam.

His heart skipped a beat. Man, she was gorgeous. All he wanted to do was drag her close and kiss her until she forgot her own name. Liam pulled out his phone and tapped his camera app. "You're beautiful, Piper."

Her smile widened and her face lit. "There's that charm again."

He chuckled and snapped her picture. "Where's the hiding place?"

"There's a loose rock in the stone wall behind me."

"Can you reach the rock without turning around?"

She shook her head.

"Which rock?"

"The one that has natural markings in the shape of a tepee. Pull the rock out straight and reach into the small opening."

Liam studied the wall behind her and spotted the rock. "I see it." He slid his phone away and knelt in front of her. "How sore is your lip, Piper?"

"Not sore enough to deter me from sharing a kiss with you. It's good cover, after all."

He laughed and pulled her close to his chest. "Kiss me, sweetheart."

Piper wrapped her arms around his neck and pressed her lips to his. Her kiss was gentle and sweet, filled with the tenderness of her heart, and made him fall further in love with her. He was the most blessed man on the planet to have this woman in his life.

Dragging his attention back to the matter at hand, he let Piper take control of the kiss while he reached for the rock. Liam worked it loose and removed it. With his arms wrapped around Piper's waist, he used her body for cover and shifted the rock to his left hand.

He tilted her head to a different angle to see the interior of the opening. A white envelope or package protruded from the back of the crevice.

Liam pulled the package free. He lifted his mouth enough to whisper, "I have the package. It's small enough that I'll slide it into your front pocket."

Piper inched closer to him. "Go ahead." She initiated another kiss, this one hotter and deeper.

When she flinched, Liam eased back to alleviate the pressure on her injury. He maneuvered his hand between their bodies and slipped the package into Piper's pocket. "Keep kissing me while I replace the rock."

Her lips curved. "Such a hardship," she teased and dived back in for another kiss.

Liam called on years of discipline drilled into him by the Marines and Fortress to concentrate enough to position the rock in the same place. Once he'd finished, he took a minute to fully concentrate on Piper.

Liam broke the kiss and shifted his weight to his haunches. Piper's swollen lips, heavy-lidded eyes, and flushed cheeks made him smile. "Let's get out of here." The sooner he had Piper in a safe place, the better. Liam's gut told him that trouble was coming for both of them before long. He hoped they were ready.

CHAPTER TWENTY-EIGHT

Piper strolled hand-in-hand with Liam from the museum, feeling the weight of someone's stare on them. She fought the urge to glare at the man sent to retrieve Gavin's information. Barone must be desperate if he resorted to having them tailed and intercepted in broad daylight.

What information was worth this much effort to retrieve? She scowled. The information wasn't worth Gavin's life or Liam's. Maybe she should leave Hartman and encourage Liam and his teammates to do the same. Zane was resourceful. The Fortress tech genius would uncover Barone's secrets without Gavin's information.

Piper sighed, knowing that option wasn't possible. Barone had to pay for murdering Gavin and Piper wanted to be part of his downfall. Gavin was a good friend before their relationship fell apart. She'd fulfill his request as a tribute to the good memories they shared.

If the security guard thought they had the information, he'd confront her and Liam, then take them to Barone. The crime boss wouldn't let them go if they handed over the envelope in her pocket. They knew too much.

"I want to run," she muttered to Liam. "And that's saying something since I hate jogging."

Liam chuckled. "You're doing great. You're a perfect partner in crime."

Her lips curved. "We did steal the package without Barone's security guard seeing us."

"He's not a sterling example of private security. He wouldn't make the cut at Fortress or PSI. We'd have booted him from the school by the end of the first week."

Liam unlocked his SUV and tucked Piper inside. He handed her the seatbelt and leaned in for a brief kiss. "You up for a field trip?"

"If the trip takes me out of this town and away from our creepy watcher, you bet I am."

He flashed her a grin and shut the door. The operative took his time circling the back of the SUV and climbing behind the steering wheel. Liam slid the electronic signal detector into his pocket and cranked the engine.

"That's a neat gadget. After this is over, I might ask your boss for one." The thought of Liam's enemies tracking her movements and threatening their children made everything inside her protest. No, she didn't believe danger would dog her steps every minute. At the same time, she couldn't afford to slack off on the vigilance. Liam depended on her to protect their family while he was on missions.

"It's an important tool in my line of work." He glanced at her before cranking the engine. "Are you worried about this man in particular or in general? I promise I'll protect you until my last breath."

She hadn't meant to give Liam the impression that she didn't trust in him or his protection measures. "I believe you. I was thinking about protecting our future family while you're on missions. Having a signal detector would help me be sure no one followed us around Otter Creek or kept track of our movements with a tracking device."

"You are one in a million, Sunshine," he said, voice huskier than normal.

"Did you find a tracking device?"

He nodded. "I'll go to a gas station and fill the tank. While I'm doing that, I'll remove the tracker that clown slapped on the undercarriage of my ride."

She smiled at his disgruntled attitude and words. "Won't the guard become suspicious if the tracker shows we're parked at the gas station for more than a few minutes?"

"Not if the tracker is moving."

She stared a moment. "You're attaching the tracker to another vehicle."

"Yes, ma'am. Hopefully, it will be a vehicle that's passing through town on the way to somewhere else. Won't keep the goons off our tail for long but we'll have enough breathing room to discover what information we have and how to pass it to the feds before Barone's crew catches up."

"Where are we going?" she asked as Liam drove from the lot.

"Amaretto. It's the safest place I can think of to see what Gavin left for you and figure out our next move."

She reached for her pocket, intent on pulling the envelope free and checking the contents.

Liam wrapped his hand around hers. "Wait until we're in the lodge with my teammates. If we have access to traffic cams, so does Barone. My windows have a special protective coating on them to blur pictures taken with a camera. Still, someone will see you have something in your hands which would incite a feeding frenzy."

Piper grimaced. Nice visual. Reminded her of sharks circling their prey, waiting to move in for the kill. Instead of giving in to her curiosity about the envelope's contents, she contented herself with holding Liam's hand.

Minutes later, he parked beside a gas pump on the opposite side of town from Amaretto. "Are you hungry?"

"Not yet."

"You should be. You didn't eat breakfast." He gave her a knowing look. "You're not a stress eater, are you?"

"Afraid not. When I'm stressed, I don't want food."

"You need the calories even though your stomach isn't giving you hunger signals. We'll find something your stomach will tolerate when we reach the lodge." He exited the vehicle.

While the nozzle deposited fuel in the tank, he grabbed a handful of disposable towels and rubbed away dirt on his SUV. At one point, he disappeared from view. When he stood, he glanced at Piper and winked.

Some of the tension eased from her body. He found the tracker and removed it.

He opened her door. "I'm going inside for soft drinks. Lock the doors. I'll only be a minute. If something spooks you, honk the horn." Another quick kiss and he closed the door again. When she activated the lock, he walked to the convenience store, stopping a moment to admire a sports car. He touched the bumper as though checking out the finish and went inside the store.

Piper grinned at the smooth transfer of the tracker from his SUV to the sports car. True to his word, he was back in less than two minutes with two drinks in his hand.

He handed her a soft drink that contained ginger and cranked the engine. After entering the lodge's address into his GPS, Liam drove from the gas station. "We're taking a circular route to the lodge. I don't want to lead Barone's henchmen to Bravo or Texas."

For the next hour, Liam made random turns, asking Piper questions about various sites they passed. When he deemed it safe to proceed to the lodge, Liam followed the GPS directions.

"What do you know about the Texas unit?" Piper had heard them mentioned by Bravo and Durango but no one gave details about the group. Maybe they didn't talk about other units for security reasons.

"Bravo worked a few missions with them. They're an interesting bunch."

"I know they're from Texas."

"They're also from various branches of law enforcement and have some very unique skill sets. It's unusual for one of our units not to have former military members in their ranks."

"What are their skills?"

He shook his head. "Oh, no. I'm not telling their secrets. Find out for yourself what they can do."

Piper frowned. "It's not fair to whet my curiosity and refuse to tell me. I won't be spending much time with them."

"Don't worry. You'll figure it out."

She huffed out a breath. "Hurry up, then."

His laughter filled the cabin as the SUV leaped forward. Within thirty minutes, he parked at the back of the lodge next to the trio of Fortress SUVs. Liam circled the hood to open Piper's door. "Come on, beautiful. Let's get you inside in case I missed an unfriendly tail."

Holding hands, they walked to the back entrance. Halfway down the corridor toward the bank of elevators, the back door opened again and Cade entered.

"Anything?" Liam asked his teammate.

"Nope. You're clear."

"What does that mean?" Piper asked.

"No one followed us from Hartman except Cade. You're safe here."

"We're safe here," she corrected. "I'm as concerned about you as you are about me."

"We have your back, Piper." Cade caught up with them and pressed the call button for the elevator. "Let us worry about your safety and Liam's."

She didn't think Liam would cede control of the situation to his teammates. He was a hands-on kind of man. Her cheeks burned. Very hands on. She loved the frequent touches, the hand holding, and the kisses.

They rode to the fourth floor in silence and Cade led the way down the hall toward the back of the lodge. He stopped in front of one door and knocked.

A moment later, the door opened to reveal a man whose height topped six feet four inches with a chest that seemed as broad as the span of Piper's outstretched arms. If she'd seen this guy on the sidewalk at night, she would have crossed to the other side of the street to avoid him.

The stranger's lips quirked. "About time you got here." His voice was deep and rich. "We were about to send out a reconnaissance party to escort you to safety."

Liam snorted. "I'm touched by your confidence in my skills, Jesse. You planning to let us in?"

The mountain of a man stepped back. "The party's in the living room."

"Did you order room service like I asked?" Cade motioned for Piper and Liam to go ahead.

"Took four carts to bring in all the food. The bellhop made a bundle in tips for this delivery."

Piper pressed a hand to her stomach. The idea of eating made her feel nauseous.

Jesse's gaze dropped to her hand for a second before returning to her face. His eyes narrowed. "You haven't eaten, have you?"

Did she have a sign plastered to her forehead? "I'm not hungry." Still.

He turned accusing eyes to Liam.

The sniper stiffened, muscles bunching in his jaw. "I'll find her something she can handle or I'll go buy food for her. I take care of those I care about, Phelps."

Liam pressed his hand to Piper's back and urged her inside a suite. Bravo and four other men ranged around the living area and the small kitchen. They stood when she walked inside.

Wow. Talk about testosterone overload. They all looked tough with muscular builds and eyes that missed nothing.

Liam wrapped his arm around Piper's waist, the hold proprietary as though warning off competitors. "Piper, this is Brody Weaver, Logan Fletcher, Sawyer Chapman, Max Norton, and Jesse Phelps, better known as the Texas unit. Guys, my girlfriend, Piper Reece."

Matt moved closer, frowning. "Does your throat hurt?"

Her cheeks burned at being the center of attention. "Some."

"What happened?" Jesse asked.

Liam ushered Piper to the couch and brought both teams up to date on the incident earlier in the morning.

A man who looked as though he belonged on a movie set or a magazine cover scowled. "Is that clown still alive?"

"Hard to get answers from a dead man," Liam replied.

"Did you learn anything we can use?" Logan asked.

"Not much except Rusty was paid to find Gavin's information. He doesn't know who hired him."

"Is he lying?" This from the man called Max.

"Oh, yeah. He knows exactly who hired him and he's not saying."

"He's too afraid of Barone to name his employer," Piper said. "I don't work for him and I'm scared of the man."

"You're smart enough not to work for a crime boss," Sawyer pointed out.

Matt went to his medical bag and grabbed a packet. He dropped two capsules onto Piper's palm. "Mild pain meds. You need to eat and take them." He pointed his finger at her when she opened her mouth. "Don't argue. You won't help Liam if he has to carry you around because you're weak from fasting."

She glared at her friend. "How did you know I was going to protest?"

"Your face shows every thought in your head. You'd be a terrible poker player."

"Yeah, yeah." He was right. She was a terrible liar. Piper happened to think that was a good trait. She looked up when Jesse handed her a soft drink.

He tapped the cap. "Drink and take your pain meds. I'll fill a plate with food I think your stomach will tolerate while Liam tells us the rest."

"Sit rep," Trent said to Liam.

Piper drank part of the soft drink and swallowed the pills while Liam told the teams about their encounter with Barone's security guard and finding the tracker on the SUV.

By the time he finished, Jesse had brought a plate covered with small portions of several bland foods as well as what looked to be a large slice of pound cake. Lemon from the looks of it. The cake looked and smelled fabulous.

"What did Gavin leave for you?" Simon asked Piper.

She paused with her fork halfway to her mouth, pulled the envelope from her pocket, and handed it to Liam.

Liam ripped open the envelope and unfolded the short note inside. He was silent a moment, scowl deepening the longer he read. "I don't believe this."

The food Piper had already eaten threatened to make a reappearance. "What did he say?"

"He gave you another location to visit."

"I told you. He was a gamer. He was all about the quest."

Liam turned his head toward her, fury burning in his eyes. "If he wasn't already dead, I'd hunt him down and kill him myself."

She blinked, surprised. "Why?"

"His next hiding place is in his suite."

Piper felt the blood drain from her face. Her appetite disappeared in a flash. "Oh, no."

"What's wrong with that?" Brody asked.

"Two things. One, I bet his suite was the first place his father's cronies looked for the information. Obviously, they didn't find it or we wouldn't be having to look over our shoulders all the time. Second, the suite is in the heart of Matteo Barone's house. Gavin lived with his father."

In order to get the information they needed to have a life, Piper and Liam would have to face their worst nightmare in the flesh.

CHAPTER TWENTY-NINE

Liam leaned against the railing of the balcony, his hands gripping the wrought iron. Gavin was crazy for leaving the next clue in his father's mansion. How did he expect Piper to retrieve it? He shuddered to think what might have happened if she'd faced this treasure hunt on her own. At least with the two of them working together, he could protect her.

He thought through various scenarios and tossed them out almost as soon as they appeared in his head. He couldn't come up with anything safe enough to take Piper into Barone's stronghold. The problem wasn't going in. It was surviving long enough to leave the estate grounds.

If he couldn't come up with anything, Liam and his teammates would plan a nighttime foray onto the estate. He wasn't risking Piper's life for another clue.

Simon came out on the balcony. "How are you holding up?"

"I'm not." He turned toward his best friend. "I can't let her do this, Simon. I could lose her. If that happened, I wouldn't survive." He wouldn't want to. Piper was necessary for his survival. If he lost her, he'd break apart.

Some big, bad Marine and black ops soldier he was. For a man whose strength had been honed in the hottest firefights, Piper's strength left him breathless. She knew she was outmatched in training and experience for this job, yet she forged ahead because she had no choice. Most women of his acquaintance would have cut and run long before now. Piper never would. She wanted justice for Gavin even though his betrayal cut deep.

"We'll take precautions."

Liam snorted. "Might look suspicious if I take her to Barone's place dressed in full body armor and a combat helmet."

A quick smile. "Probably." Simon gave him a sidelong glance. "What about getting an invitation to the estate?"

"What do you mean?"

"If you received an invitation to visit Barone, you could spread the word around town that you were going to the estate grounds."

He stared at his friend. "I don't love this idea. It still leaves too much opportunity for danger to Piper. Besides, how do you expect us to wrangle an invitation to the crime boss's home? Piper can't call him and ask to come for a visit."

Simon was silent a moment. "Word should be spreading about Gavin's death. Piper doesn't need an invitation to pay a condolence call to Gavin's father since she's in town. She'll draw more attention if she doesn't go. This is a small town. Her visit will be expected. Better still, she can take you with her as well as her uncle. No one will question your presence since you're engaged and want to support the woman you love."

Liam stared out at the landscape again, a ball of ice in the pit of his stomach. The last thing he wanted to do was take Piper to Barone, but he couldn't see a way around it. He and the other Fortress operatives could slip onto the estate in the middle of the night. However, the likelihood of a confrontation while outnumbered by the enemy was near one hundred percent. Barone would claim his security force had protected him against armed intruders. A law enforcement community in the crime boss's pocket wouldn't question Barone's version of events.

If by some miracle they made it inside the house without encountering at least one of the numerous guards, Piper was the only one who knew how Gavin's mind worked. Liam and the others might find the next clue but wouldn't be able to decipher it. He wouldn't have known where to look for the other two clues if not for Piper.

Besides, he'd read the clue directing them to the Barone estate. Gavin hadn't left enough obvious information for Liam and his teammates to know where to start looking. The longer they stayed in the mansion searching for the clue, the greater risk they took of being discovered in a confined space.

"I know you don't want to take her to Barone's estate. A condolence call is the most natural way to take her where she needs to be for the next clue."

"How did Gavin expect her to get onto the estate grounds?"

A shrug from Simon. "Her uncle."

Made sense. If Piper mended fences with her uncle, Gino Romano could wrangle that invitation with no trouble. One man visiting an old friend and bringing his niece along for the visit wouldn't raise suspicion.

"Liam?"

He turned and held out his hand to Piper. Liam wrapped his arms around her. "Feeling better?" He hadn't liked how pale she'd been earlier, grateful the two medics had taken care of her while Liam came to the balcony to call Maddox.

Simon used a hand signal to indicate he and Liam would talk more later.

Piper nodded. "You were right. I needed to eat." She tilted her head back and smiled. "Don't tell Jesse, but I'm pretty sure it was the pound cake that did it, not the rest of the food he piled on my plate."

Amused, he dropped a quick kiss on her mouth. "I thought your secret vice was chocolate."

"Preferred vice, although it's not a secret. I think sugar in all forms is my downfall." She cupped his jaw with a soft palm. "Talk to me, Liam."

"Reading my mind again?"

"I know you're upset. You weren't able to find a way to get me inside Barone's estate?"

"Simon and I thought of a way."

"But you don't like it."

"I don't want you within a hundred miles of that mansion or Barone."

"I'll be safe because I have you with me."

"Too many things could go wrong, Piper. One bullet would kill us both."

Her brows knitted. "I don't understand."

"If Barone or one of his men took your life, I would do my utmost to kill every one of the thugs on that estate. I wouldn't survive against odds in the enemy's favor."

She leaned up and pressed a soft kiss to his lips. "Then we make sure that doesn't happen. Brainstorm with your teammates and find a way to accomplish the goal. I know you, Liam McCoy. You don't quit without a fight."

Liam tugged her closer to his chest. She didn't understand. "It's not worth the risk to your life, Sunshine."

"The alternative is a life on the run. I don't want that for either of us. We deserve to live without fear. If the only way to accomplish that goal is to beard the lion in his den, then we conquer that great cat and let the feds cage him."

His lips curved. Courage in spades. No wonder he adored this woman. Unfortunately, she was right. He wanted to be free to love and live with her in Otter Creek, surrounded by their friends and colleagues. "All right. We'll talk to the others, come up with a plan, and a billion contingencies."

Inside the suite, the operatives gathered with Piper and Liam when he explained what he needed.

"Can you draw a rough sketch of the Barone mansion, Piper?" Brody asked.

"I'll try. It's been a while since I've been there. Matteo might have remodeled the place."

"It's a place to start."

"What happens if there are changes?"

He smiled. "We'll adjust. It's what we do."

For the next hour, the operatives bounced ideas off each other, pointing out the strengths and weaknesses of each option until they settled on the strongest plan of attack.

"What do you think, Piper?" Trent sat against the wall and stretched his legs out in front of him. "See any flaws in our plans?"

"I can't think of anything better. I say we go for it. I'm ready to hand the feds everything they need to send Matteo to prison. What's the first step?"

"Talk to Romano," Liam said. "We need him on board. He'll play a crucial role in helping us gain access to parts of the house off limits to town visitors."

"Should I call him now?"

"I'd prefer to broach the subject away from the house. Your uncle has security cameras everywhere. Some of the cameras may not be connected to his security system."

"Let's take him out to dinner. There's an Italian restaurant he loves on the opposite side of town. We'll talk to him as we drive to the restaurant."

Simon nodded. "I like it."

"Who's on night watch?" Liam asked.

"I'm pulling first shift, Matt has the second."

The knot in his stomach smoothed out. He trusted the members of the Texas unit to have his back. Liam trusted his own teammates more. "I need to drive Piper back to her uncle's place. Romano goes to bed around 9:00."

Simon slid off the barstool. "I'll grab my gear and be ready to go in two minutes." He left the suite.

Liam turned to Trent. "Orders?"

"Get as much information as you can about Barone's place from Romano while you're out of the house. Have Piper call me and leave the connection open so I can hear the information firsthand. Check in every two hours unless you're asleep. We'll let you know when the shift changes."

Simon returned with his Go bag in hand.

Liam escorted Piper to his SUV, scanning the area for threats. To this point, their location hadn't been compromised. After helping her inside, he climbed behind the steering wheel. "Call your uncle and invite him to dinner."

He listened to one side of the conversation as he headed for the highway. When she ended the call, he glanced her way. "He agreed?"

She nodded. "He was surprised by the invitation but pleased we wanted to spend time with him."

Liam heard guilt in her voice. "I planned to invite him to dinner before we left town, Sunshine. We moved it up a day or two."

"You were?"

He wrapped his hand around hers. "Even though you and Romano were at odds, he's your family. I want to know him and I want you to know mine. They're going to love you."

"I hope so. I'd feel terrible if your mother didn't think I was good enough for you."

"You're the best thing that's ever happened to me."

Liam circled around Hartman to come into town the same direction they'd gone out. He didn't want to point observers toward Amaretto.

Minutes later, he parked in front of the Romano residence and traipsed to the front door to assist Piper's uncle to the SUV. As soon as he stepped on the landing, the front door opened and Romano walked outside.

"Where are we going to dinner?" the older man asked.

"Ricci's."

Romano's eyes lit. "Excellent. It's my favorite restaurant."

"Piper told me."

The other man glanced at Liam as they descended the stairs. "Want to tell me what's really going on?"

Liam flashed him a grin. "Dinner and a favor. We didn't want to talk inside your home."

"Because of the bugs."

"Yes, sir." He opened the SUV's back door and waited for the older man to climb inside before getting into the driver's seat.

Liam started the vehicle and drove from the estate grounds. As he turned onto the street toward the center of town, he glanced in the rearview mirror. "Let's talk, Mr. Romano."

CHAPTER THIRTY

Piper stood in the circle of Liam's arms as her uncle conversed with the owner of Ricci's following their meal. They stood in an alcove and watched the interaction between two long-time friends. Eating the wonderful Italian food in the warm, familiar atmosphere brought back good memories of many meals she and her uncle shared in this restaurant. Those memories were tempered by the knowledge of the pending separation from her only living blood relative.

From his body language, Antonio Ricci knew Gino didn't have long to live. "They've been friends for forty years," she said. "Both men are hurting." So was she. Despite her uncle's disappointment with her, she loved him.

"Ricci has family here?"

She nodded. "He grew up in Hartman. His parents moved here from Italy."

"He'll have the support of friends and family when your uncle's gone." His arms tightened around her. "So will you."

Tears stung her eyes. She didn't want to imagine a world where she couldn't pick up a phone and call her uncle when she wanted. Three years she'd wasted, waiting for him to understand her decision to leave Gavin and Hartman behind.

"I can't fight this battle for you, Piper, but I'll be by your side. You aren't alone anymore."

She turned, wrapped her arms around him, and laid her head against his heart. "You don't know how much that means to me." Piper wanted to say more but couldn't, her throat tight with repressed emotion. She didn't want to call attention to herself or Liam by giving in to the tears threatening to spill down her cheeks.

When Gino finished his conversation, the three of them walked from the restaurant together. They remained silent until they settled in the SUV and drove toward the Romano estate.

"How is Mr. Ricci?" Piper asked.

"He is like many of my friends. Sad because my body is failing."

He wasn't the only one. At least she'd had time to see and talk to him.

"Antonio also was of some help in the other matter we discussed on the drive to the restaurant."

Liam glanced at her uncle in the rearview mirror. "What did he say?"

"Matteo made changes to his estate. He added additional security to the house. He also allowed a large building to be built half a mile behind the house on an adjacent piece of property with an access road between the two places. The new building resembles an oversized garage."

Piper frowned. "Wait a minute. I thought he already had a garage. Why would he need another one?"

"That's the question many are asking."

"He bought more property?" Liam asked.

"Not officially. According to scuttlebutt around town, Bluefield Industries bought the property."

"How do you know Barone is behind the purchase?"

"Matteo has been seen at the job site and is the one approving the work. Doesn't take a genius to realize there's a close relationship between Matteo and Bluefield even though his name isn't on the paperwork. You're in security. I'm sure you will confirm the connection."

"I'll look into it."

Piper glanced at her uncle. "Did Barone bulldoze the miniature forest behind the house? From what I remember, the tree line started about ten feet from the edge of the driveway and went on for a mile or more."

Gino smiled. "That's what I asked Antonio. Matteo's property has a clearing two hundred yards from the house. You can't see it because of the dense tree cover. I've walked the property with Matteo several times. The trees thinned at the northeast end which is where the Bluefield Industries property begins. That's where Matteo put the access road that leads to the garage."

"Barone's driveway leads to the Bluefield property?"

"He says it's not a driveway since it doesn't connect to his concrete drive. It's more of an access point in case there's a fire on either property. The interesting thing about this is according to Antonio's son who was on the construction crew, no cars were moved to the new garage although that's what the plans labeled the building. In fact, as far as he knows, that building will never be used to house vehicles."

"How does he know that?" Liam asked.

"There aren't any garage doors installed, just one large metal door like the ones used for warehouses. Giorgio said part of the space seemed to be wired for occupancy."

He frowned. "Heating and air conditioning?"

"That's right along with plumbing and small rooms."

"Offices."

"It's possible. Giorgio was afraid to ask too many questions. It wouldn't have been good for his health."

Piper eyed her uncle. "If you know how dangerous Barone is, why are you still friends with the man?" She'd known and avoided being in the same room with the crime boss.

"We've been friends for sixty years, Piper. I didn't know for a long time how ruthless he is. By the time I learned the truth, Matteo and I had a long history and we were in business together."

Her heart skipped a beat. Was Gino hinting at the criminal activity that the feds were accusing him of?

"We are from the same neighborhood. We fought back-to-back against those who hated us simply because of our ethnic heritage. We beat the odds to become successful businessmen. My business enterprise is legal. Matteo's view of ethical business practices is more liberal than mine. In any case, I can't turn my back on a lifetime friend."

Time to move the discussion forward. Liam would be turning into the estate grounds soon and their opportunities to talk without fear of being overheard limited. "Back to the oversized garage. The building inspectors didn't question the odd arrangement for a garage?"

Gino looked troubled. "No one questions Matteo. I'm afraid my old friend wields much power in this town."

"Do you mind helping us get into Gavin's suite, Uncle Gino?"

"No, child." His laughter was wry. "If Matteo discovers the ruse, what can he do to me that won't happen in the next few weeks anyway?"

Pain speared Piper's heart at the thought of the impending loss. "I want you to have those weeks to visit with friends and me. I'd love to take you to Otter Creek for a few days. I want you to see the life I've built, Uncle Gino."

He was shaking his head before she finished speaking. "You know I can't, Piper. I'm under a doctor's care even if they cannot do more than hold my hand. I also have a business to run, one I must prepare you to take over when I'm gone."

Another glance from Liam in the mirror. "I'm marrying your niece in a few months, Mr. Romano," he said. "My job requires me to stay in Otter Creek. I can't move here. Call me old fashioned, but I don't want to be separated from my wife."

Her uncle waved their protests aside. "There are ways around the problem. Piper will own the company, a company many hundred workers in Hartman depend upon for their livelihood. That doesn't mean she can't have someone manage the company for her."

Her uncle had effectively laid the livelihood of hundreds of workers on her shoulders. Yeah, no pressure. "What do you mean I can have someone manage the company for me?" Piper asked.

"A team of managers you trust or a team of advisors. You'll need to come to Hartman several times a year to keep an eye on things. I'm sure Liam will be happy to come with you."

"He's gone frequently."

Gino shrugged. "Come home when he's available. You can choose the times except when stockholder meetings are scheduled. I have a few names to suggest for the management team. Ultimately, however, the choice will be yours."

She and Liam exchanged glances before she turned back to her uncle. "Give me the list along with their work histories and their track record with the company. I'm not promising to hire any of them, but I'll give them a fair evaluation."

Another glance from Liam. Piper reached for his hand, aware she had just committed to running a multimillion-dollar company for the duration without consulting the man she planned to marry. She knew him well enough, though, to understand that Liam would support her decision and work with her to keep her uncle's legacy alive and healthy.

Gino gave her a thoughtful look. "I hope you mean that, dear, because one of my recommendations is to place Brandy on your management team."

Sophia had been right. Gino had been grooming Brandy to take over leadership in the company. The question was why. Brandy hadn't been close to Gino when Piper lived in Hartman. What changed? "I'm not sure how wise it would be to appoint someone I don't trust with keeping your legacy alive."

"You said you would be fair. I expect you to uphold that promise for the good of the company. If you find others with more experience and credentials, we'll talk."

Wow. So much for handing over leadership to her. Gino Romano wasn't planning to let go of the company until he had no choice. Suited Piper fine. She didn't want to take away the business giving him the will to fight cancer a little longer.

"When will people begin paying condolence calls to Barone and his wife?" Liam asked.

"Tomorrow." Gino sighed. "I already spoke briefly with Matteo this afternoon. Since he's unsure when Gavin's body will be returned to Hartman, he can't give a date or time for his son's funeral. He's considering a memorial service in a few days. If he follows that plan, then the burial would be a family-only event when Gavin's body arrives. Already the town dignitaries are asking when they can offer their condolences. Matteo felt that it would be less disruptive to his work and comforting to his wife to receive people tomorrow evening."

"We'll go to Barone's estate about 7:00 p.m. It will be full dark and better for our safety if we have to leave quickly."

Better for Liam's teammates to enter the estate under cover of darkness if they were needed as well, Piper realized. She prayed that wouldn't be necessary.

"I don't know what information Gavin left for you, Piper, but Matteo will be relentless until he gets what he wants."

Liam reached over and squeezed Piper's hand.

"I know, Uncle Gino. I haven't forgotten how ruthless he can be."

"He isn't a good man to have as an enemy."

"We'll be fine. Liam will make sure of it."

"Are you as good as you claim to be, Liam?"

"Better. I know what I'm doing, Mr. Romano. I'm well trained with years of experience. Nothing and no one will harm Piper as long as I'm breathing."

He gave a slow nod. "I'm glad to hear that, young man. Many people have gone up against Matteo and come out losers in the skirmish." He patted Liam's shoulder. "You must call me Gino. You'll be marrying into the family soon."

"Yes, sir."

The rest of the drive to Gino's house was completed in silence. To Piper, her uncle looked exhausted. Hopefully, she wouldn't have surprise visitors tonight. Gino needed to rest. Tomorrow might prove interesting and dangerous.

Soon after they walked into Gino's house, Piper's uncle excused himself to retire to his suite. She turned to Liam. "What would you like to do now?"

"Spend some time with my computer and you. I need to work for a while and I'd love your company while I do it."

Relieved she wouldn't be alone in a house she no longer felt safe in, Piper led the way upstairs toward their rooms.

Liam nudged her toward his room where he retrieved his laptop. He set it on the coffee table in her sitting room and held his finger to his lips as he pulled out his electronic signal detector.

Right. He had to check their rooms for more bugs and cameras. Hopefully, the person planting them would grow tired of dumping money into the bugs and cameras only to have Liam find and dismantle them.

Ten minutes later, he declared her suite clean. No one had planted devices to keep tabs on her. Some of the tension twisting her stomach into a knot disappeared. At least for now, they didn't have to worry about someone listening to their conversation.

Liam sat on the couch with her and reached for the television remote. "Find something to watch. When I finish working, I'll watch a movie with you."

A slow smile curved her lips. "You're giving me control of the remote?"

He tapped the tip of her nose with a light touch. "Don't get used to it. My hand gets twitchy without the remote."

Piper laughed. "You can hold my hand when the emptiness overwhelms you."

"Hmm. I like that plan." His smile faded. "Do you mind if I work for a bit?"

"Of course not. I don't need to be entertained, Liam. I'm happy just to be with you."

He pressed his forehead to hers. "I love you, Sunshine."

"I love you, too." While Liam booted up his laptop, Piper turned on the television and surfed for a program that wouldn't distract him while he worked. To be honest, she would have been content to sit with her head against his shoulder while he worked even if the television was turned off.

Finding a cozy mystery movie she loved, Piper settled against his side. To her delight, Liam frequently stopped to share a brief kiss with her before returning to his research.

Ninety minutes later, Liam's cell phone chirped with an incoming text. He checked his screen and frowned.

Piper sat up. "What's wrong?"

"Not sure. Zane wants me to call him as soon as possible." He called his friend, tapping the speaker button. "It's Liam. What's up?"

"Where's Piper?"

"Beside me. You're on speaker."

"You in a secure place?"

"I checked her suite. It's clear. What's going on, Z?"

"Two things. One, someone blew up Piper's car."

Piper gasped. "When?"

"About thirty minutes ago. I have bots scouring the Net for any mention of your name and Liam's. The explosion hit the town's newspaper website a few minutes ago."

"What's the second thing?" Liam asked, his arm around Piper's shoulder.

"There's a contract on Piper. Someone wants your woman dead."

CHAPTER THIRTY-ONE

Liam's grip tightened around his cell phone. "What can you tell me about the explosion?" he asked Zane.

"Professional job. The bomb was simple but effective. A blasting cap and C-4. The interesting thing is the explosion was just powerful enough to take out her car."

Beside him, Piper shuddered. "I'm glad my car was parked in the lot a block away from Wicks. Was anyone else's vehicle damaged?"

"No vehicles were parked next to yours. The damage to two other vehicles was limited to cracked windows."

Liam kissed her temple. "Spencer was EOD, one of the best bomb technicians I know. It had to be him. No way the clowns who tossed Piper's place could blow up her car with such precision. They would have used a Molotov cocktail."

"Why did Spencer destroy my car?" Piper asked.

"He hopes you go back to Otter Creek to deal with the aftermath."

"You wouldn't let me go back alone."

"That's what he wants. At the moment, he doesn't know where I am. If he's impatient to finish this, he'll use any means necessary to draw me out. Z, are we sure the other women are covered?"

"Don't worry. With this latest volley, the women will be double covered. You just worry about Piper."

"What about Stella?" Piper edged closer to Liam. "She travels all over town. If she's sent on a call, Stella will be vulnerable. We have to warn her."

"Don't worry," Zane said. "Stella Armstrong is one tough cookie. She was a US Marshal and dealt with the worst criminals. Anyone who comes after her will wish he hadn't. Aside from that, Stella has company anytime she leaves the station until Spencer is behind bars."

Liam frowned. "A partner?"

"Her husband. Since this case involves an explosives expert, Ethan thinks having Nate, an EOD expert, ride with the investigating detective is a wise precaution."

Otter Creek's police chief knew the value of good assets in the community and didn't mind utilizing them. The news of Spencer's escalation made Liam want to take Piper to a remote location until the former Marine had been run to ground. Unfortunately, Spencer would simply wait him out. If Liam wanted to smoke out Spencer, he couldn't stay off the grid.

"What about the contract on my life?" Piper asked. "Is Spencer behind that, too?"

"I'm afraid not. I've been looking for connections to the Marine since I caught wind of it. I can't find any indication he's connected to the hit."

Not surprising. He wouldn't use a third party to do his dirty work. Spencer would want to make Liam suffer by taking the life of the woman he loved. "Barone?"

"I'm still checking that possibility. So far, I can't find a connection there, either. However, Barone's financial empire is extensive and buried behind multiple firewalls."

"Have you updated Maddox?"

"As soon as I end this call. Watch your back, Liam. This situation has many layers."

"Copy that." When he ended the call, Liam set aside his computer and wrapped his arms around Piper. "Are you all right?"

She turned toward him.

Liam expected fear and maybe reprisal in the depths of her beautiful eyes. Instead, he saw anger. At him? Man, he hoped not although her ire would be understandable. "I'm sorry," he murmured, cupping the nape of her neck. "I never meant to bring danger to your doorstep."

"This isn't your fault, Liam. The blame falls to your demented former co-worker." She dropped her head against his chest and growled. "He has stellar timing. I just paid off my car. I doubt my insurance will cover bomb damage."

"I'll arrange for another vehicle through Fortress."

She leaned back to look at him. "Why?"

"Our vehicles are reinforced and have bullet-resistant glass. For my peace of mind, I need you in a safer vehicle."

"I don't know, Liam. That sounds expensive."

"You driving one of our SUVs is the only way I'll be able to concentrate on my job when I'm on missions. If I'm worried about your safety while deployed, I'll be distracted. That's not safe for me or my unit. Besides, in a few months, you'll be the owner of a multimillion-dollar company. That will make you more attractive to those who are looking for a soft target."

Piper frowned. "Dirty pool, McCoy."

"Get used to it, Reece, soon-to-be McCoy. I want you and our family to be safe. Let me do this for both of us, Sunshine."

She kissed him. "All right. Thank you for taking care of me."

"You are and always will be my top priority. I'll do whatever it takes to keep you safe, legal or not."

After sharing another kiss, Piper inclined her head toward the laptop. "What did you find out? Anything you can tell me?"

"Barone is the power behind Bluefield Industries. The mysterious warehouse belongs to him. The question is what he's doing with it."

"Maybe the feds know."

He considered that possibility. "I have a few contacts I can ask to see if they know anything. In the meantime, we need to sleep. Tomorrow will be interesting and you didn't sleep much last night."

"Neither did you."

"I don't need much sleep."

She frowned. "How much do you sleep each night?"

"Four or five hours. It's a leftover from my years in the military. I'll be fine. Focus on yourself. I want you a hundred percent when you meet my family."

"When will that be?"

"As soon as we return to Otter Creek, I'll call Mom and tell her we're coming to visit her and Marissa for a few days. I'll arrange to take a few days off. Shouldn't be a problem since Bravo just returned from a mission." He tugged Piper to her feet. "Get ready for bed."

"What will you do?"

"Grab my gear and move into the sitting room. I want to be close overnight." After a thorough kiss that pushed the boundaries of his control, Liam nudged her toward the bedroom. "I'll be here if you need me. Lock the door to the hallway but leave your door to the sitting room open."

"I feel guilty about you sleeping on the couch."

"This is luxurious compared to the nights I've spent in a tree, on a stone slab, or on the dirt."

With one last lingering look over her shoulder, Piper walked into her bedroom and closed the door.

Minutes later, Liam had transferred his Go bag and his duffel into the sitting room and was on the phone with Maddox. "Thanks for taking care of the SUV, boss."

"I need your head in the game when you're deployed. Arranging for Bear to prepare an SUV for Piper is a small price to pay to have you in top form. How is she holding up?"

"Better than I'd hoped. She was shocked at first by the news about her car. Now, she's furious. I don't know what I did to deserve a woman like her, but I won't take the gift for granted."

"I understand, my friend. I feel the same way about Rowan and Alexa."

Liam grinned, hearing the love in his boss's voice for his wife and daughter.

"Keep me posted, Liam. We've prepared the papers you need for Piper, your mother, and sister. The safe houses are also ready. You can access the locations with the link I sent to your email. You'll have to input your security code to see the file."

Liam doubted anyone could break Zane's encryption program. He appreciated the extra precaution anyway. "Thanks."

After ending the call to his boss, he texted Simon who was still on watch, giving him an update. He touched based with Trent, then decided to call it a night. Although he didn't want to admit as much to Piper, the short nights of sleep since he'd returned from deployment were catching up with him.

Once Piper opened her bedroom door and crawled into bed, Liam stretched out on the couch with his Sig close at hand. If anyone tried to break into her room tonight, he would take them down.

The night passed peacefully, and Liam was awake two hours before Piper. While he waited for her to wake, he pulled up everything he could find on her uncle's company.

Galactic Games was a powerhouse in the video game industry and rumors were flying around the market about the company launching a new game soon. His eyebrows rose at the estimated value of the game. Piper would have her hands full when her uncle passed away.

Movement in the bedroom doorway drew Liam's attention. He smiled. "Good morning, Sunshine. Sleep well?"

She nodded, the damp strands of her hair clinging to her shirt. "Turns out all I need to fall asleep is knowing you're close."

Satisfaction filled him. "You ready for breakfast?"

"Actually, I am. How about a breakfast date?"

"Have a place in mind?"

"A diner on Main Street. They serve the best eggs I've ever eaten."

"Sold." Liam grabbed his gear and slung it over one shoulder.

"Are we relocating to a hotel?"

He shook his head. "I don't trust anyone in this house. It's safer to store my gear inside the SUV."

After breakfast, he drove Piper to Galactic Games for a meeting with her uncle. He'd called during their meal to schedule the appointment.

As soon as they walked through the front doors, Liam knew the employees were aware of who their new boss would be. The deference Piper was shown made her uncomfortable.

"Ms. Reece." The receptionist beamed at her. "Welcome back to Hartman and Galactic Games. How may I help you?"

"I have an appointment with my uncle. Tell him I'm here, please."

"Yes, ma'am." She activated her headset and made the call. After speaking quietly to the person on the other end of the line for a moment, the woman ended the call. "Mr.

Romano is on a long-distance phone call. He'll be available in about fifteen minutes. Would you like coffee or tea while you wait?"

Footsteps drew near as the receptionist asked her last question. "I'll take them to the executive floor," a woman said.

Liam turned to face Brandy. The woman's earlier hostility seemed to have disappeared. In its place was a stoic resolve. Interesting. Did she plan to make nice in order to keep her job?

Brandy motioned for them to follow her and walked toward the elevator.

"Your choice," Liam murmured to Piper.

She squared her shoulders and trailed the other woman.

All right, then. Looked like Piper was going to take on the other woman. They rode to the third floor in silence.

Brandy led them to her office. "Have a seat. Would you like coffee or tea?"

"Water for me," Piper said.

"Coffee for you, Liam?" Brandy asked.

"Thanks."

"Cream, sugar?"

"Black."

She nodded. "I'll be right back. Make yourselves comfortable."

He stared at the door she'd closed behind herself.

"Brandy is up to something."

Liam turned to Piper. "Oh, yeah. But what?" Was she protecting her job or was something more at stake?

CHAPTER THIRTY-TWO

Piper watched Liam for cues as he accepted coffee from Brandy. Instead of sipping the drink, the operative cradled the mug in his hands. Clear enough. Don't drink anything handled by Brandy. Following his unspoken lead, she held the bottle of water without drinking.

Brandy sat behind her desk. "Gino will be free soon. I thought this would be a good time to talk before your meeting," she said to Piper. Her gaze slid to Liam. "I'm sure you won't mind waiting in the other room. This is company business, after all."

His eyebrow rose although he didn't say a word.

"Say what you have to say, Brandy," Piper said.

Irritation in her eyes at Liam's refusal to leave, Brandy turned to Piper. "I know we've had our differences in the past. I'd like to put that behind us in the interest of Galactic Games and the people who depend on us to feed their families."

She stared. "You're characterizing the gulf between us as differences? You slept with the man I was dating."

"I'd go back and change things if I could. I'm sorry, Piper. I didn't mean for that to happen but you know how persuasive Gavin could be."

Nice. Shifting the blame to Gavin who couldn't defend himself or explain his actions. "It's a little late for apologies. However, in the end, you did me a favor. Because you helped me see the true Gavin, I left Hartman and met Liam. For that, I am grateful."

Yes, Gavin had hurt Piper. In the end, though, she'd met the love of her life. Liam was worth every moment of pain and tear she shed three years ago.

Brandy relaxed in her chair. "Frankly, I'm surprised you're dating someone else. Gino wasn't aware that you moved on. I thought you would hold a grudge forever. I'm glad to see that's not the case."

"No grudge. But don't make the mistake of believing I'll trust you again. That won't happen. You showed your character and I won't forget that."

The other woman's face blanched. "Gavin is dead. What does the past matter now?"

"Uncle Gino is leaving his legacy to me. I need a management team who is loyal to the company and me."

Brandy's eyes glittered. "I see. Should I expect a pink slip when Gino dies?"

"I'm not ruling out anything." Piper stood, leaving her untouched bottle of water on Brandy's desk beside Liam's mug. "We'll see ourselves out."

"This isn't over, Piper. Not by a long shot."

She paused on the threshold and glanced over her shoulder at Brandy. "No, it isn't. By the time I'm finished, every secret will be revealed."

Brandy gaped at her. "What does that mean?"

Instead of answering, she walked away from the office with Liam at her back, ignoring the shrill demands for an explanation by Brandy. By the time she and Liam reached her uncle's outer office, Piper's hands shook. That woman had some nerve, insinuating Piper was an immature brat who refused to act like an adult. Piper wanted to fire her greatest nemesis on the spot, despite her uncle's wishes.

"Breathe," Liam murmured, wrapping his arms around her and tucking her against his chest.

"She's a piece of work."

"You handled her with class, Sunshine."

"Would you be able to forget the past and take her at face value if you were in my place?"

"In my line of work, I can't afford to have an operative at my back who isn't trustworthy. It's a great way to end up dead. So, no, I wouldn't trust that woman with anything or anyone I valued."

"Are you just saying that because she hurt me?"

As soon as the words came out of her mouth, she realized Liam would never sugar-coat things to spare her feelings. She held up a hand. "Don't answer that. I know you. You're reacting on instinct, aren't you?"

"She's a snake in the grass, waiting to strike at unwitting prey."

Piper relaxed in Liam's hold. Brandy was waiting to strike. How long before Piper felt the sting of the other woman's bite? Fine. She silently urged Brandy to do her worst. If the other woman showed her true colors, Piper would easily convince Gino to fire her.

Gino's administrative assistant approached them. "Mr. Romano will see you now. Come with me, please." The pleasant woman led them down a short hall to the familiar office with double doors, one of which had an engraved brass nameplate with Gino's name. "May I bring you a drink? Coffee, water, a soft drink, something stronger?"

"No, thanks, Caro. We're fine," Piper said as the assistant opened the office door.

"Piper and her friend are here, sir." Caro stepped back and allowed them to pass, then closed the door behind her as she left.

"Come in." Gino motioned to the sitting area with leather furniture. "Have a seat. Let's talk."

By the time the meeting and tour of the business concluded three hours later, Piper's head hurt and she felt overwhelmed with the responsibility of keeping afloat a corporation the size of Galactic Games. One thing she'd realized during the tour. Piper needed people who understood the gaming business inside and out.

She waited until they were seated inside Liam's SUV before she asked the question that had popped into her head near the end of the company tour. "Would Zane know people I could trust to advise me in running Galactic Games?" One thing had become clear as the tour progressed. Gino's employees would do and say anything to protect their own best interests. Those interests didn't necessarily coincide with the best interests of Galactic Games.

A slow smile curved his mouth as he started the engine. "I'm sure he does. Let's ask him." He activated his Bluetooth and called his friend.

"What do you need?" Zane asked when he answered the call.

"Tell Piper what you do in your spare time for fun."

"I create video games. What's going on, Liam?"

"Gino Romano is leaving Piper his company. She'll need management help, someone she can trust."

A soft whistle from the other man. "Sweet. Galactic Games is a fantastic company. How can I help?"

Relief swept through Piper. Maybe Zane could help her figure out how to run this titanic corporation and stop criminal activities she felt sure most of the workers knew nothing about. Piper was also beginning to wonder if Gino knew about the suspicious activities. "I need a list of names of people who'd be willing to serve on an advisory council at Galactic Games. Know anyone?"

"Several people. How many do you want?"

"Seven. Eight if you're willing to serve."

"Are you kidding? I'd love the chance to help. Your uncle's company bought my black ops games."

Even better. Piper drew a deep breath for the first time in hours. "Fantastic. Give me a list of names of people you trust and can work with, Zane. Most of the advisory work will be done online. The council should plan on meeting at least once a quarter. We'll work out the best time which will coincide with Liam's leave times." She wouldn't return to this viper's nest without Liam by her side.

"I'll get back to you with my recommendations along with their resumes. Thanks for asking me to participate."

"You sure you have time, Z?" Liam asked. "You don't sleep as it is."

"I'll make it work."

"Thank you, Zane," Piper said. "Any words of advice to get me started?"

"I know you asked for a full list of advisers to fill out the council. The wisest course of action might be to create a council of eight members, half of them in-house, half of them outsiders. That way you have the best of both worlds."

"That's a good idea. I'll keep that in mind."

"When will the council begin work?"

"Not sure. The doctors have given Uncle Gino three months or less to live. The council needs to be in place by that point, but they won't be active until my uncle passes away."

"Understood. When I talk to the people on my list, I'll tell them the probable timeline. What else can I do, Liam?"

"Nothing right now. Later, Z." Liam ended the call and glanced at Piper. "What do you think?"

"He's a life saver. I'll send him the list of candidates my uncle recommended along with their resumes and let him weigh in on the Galactic Games team members." She was silent a moment, then said, "I'll also ask HR for a list of first-line supervisors and their employees and pass those names to Zane as well. I'm not sure how much I trust the list of executives my uncle compiled. The supervisors and employees are less likely to be involved in questionable activities."

A slow smile curved his mouth. "Excellent idea. Are you hungry?"

She nodded.

"Let's eat dinner before we pick up your uncle."

Two hours later, Liam dropped Gino off at the front steps to Barone's house before returning to the street to find a parking place. The town's citizens had turned out in force to support the crime boss and his wife. No one wanted to be seen as ignoring the suffering of the most powerful man in town.

He found a place two blocks away and turned to Piper. "Are you ready?"

"I'm ready to find the information, hand it to the feds, and go home."

"I hope it's that easy." Liam circled to the passenger door.

Minutes later, they walked into the mansion. The home was so familiar to her that Piper felt as though Gavin would appear any moment. She scanned the crowded space for Barone and his wife.

She found the couple at the far end of a long receiving line. Gavin's mother was red-eyed, her skin blotchy from frequent tears. Barone, however, appeared the same as always until she and Liam moved near to the grieving couple. The closer they drew, the more apparent the crime boss's grief and fury became.

When Piper approached, icy contempt filled his gaze. "What are you doing here?" he said, his voice curt.

Gino moved up to stand beside her. "Offering condolences just as I am, my old friend." Piper's uncle gave

Barone a one-armed embrace, murmuring something softly into the other man's ear.

A slight nod from Barone. "Go anywhere you wish, Gino. Treat my home as yours. How do you feel?" Concern shadowed his eyes.

"Tired and weak. I may need a place to stretch out for a few minutes."

"If you need anything, you have only to ask one of my staff. They'll take care of you."

Gino squeezed Barone's shoulder. "Thanks, Matteo. I appreciate your hospitality." He moved on to speak to Gavin's mother in a soft voice, wrapping her in his arms when she dissolved into tears.

Piper held out her hand to Barone. "I'm sorry to hear about Gavin."

His lip curled as he dropped her hand. "Let's not kid each other, Piper. You hurt my son. I won't forget that offense." His gaze shifted to Liam. "And you are?"

"Liam. I'm sorry for your loss, sir."

A snort. "If you weren't with Piper, I might believe you." Barone's gaze shifted to the person behind Liam, dismissing him.

Piper turned to Gavin's mother and embraced the woman. She mentioned two things Gavin had admired about his mother. "I know we drifted apart these last few years, but I will miss him."

Tears sparkled on the other woman's lashes. "Thank you for your kind words," she whispered. "He didn't mean to hurt you, Piper. Gavin just couldn't help himself."

Not wanting to lie to Gavin's mother, Piper merely patted her back and stepped aside for Liam.

After Liam murmured his condolences, he and Piper joined her uncle.

"Come with me," Gino said. "Mrs. Baxter will be happy to make you a cup of hot tea."

Piper smiled. "Thanks," she said, noting many people close to them listening to their exchange. Excellent. Word should spread soon enough that she and Liam were in the Barone kitchen. From there, she and Liam would take the back stairs to Gavin's room.

They followed her uncle to the back of the house. As soon as the cook, Maggie Baxter, turned and saw Piper, her face lit up.

"Piper! Oh, it's so good to see you." The sixty-something woman hugged her, then turned her speculative gaze on Liam. "Now, who is this handsome man?"

"This is Liam. We're getting married in the spring." Piper still found it hard to believe she was planning a wedding to the man of her dreams.

Maggie threw her arms around Liam. "Congratulations, Liam. You're marrying a wonderful woman."

Liam patted her back. "Believe me, I know. I'm blessed."

When she released Liam, the cook turned back to Piper. "Is there something you need?"

"A cup of tea for my niece," Gino said.

"Coming right up. What about you, sir, and Liam?"

Liam shook his head. "I'm fine. Thanks for offering. Mr. Romano?"

"A bed, I'm afraid. I need to lie down for a few minutes, Maggie. Matteo said it would be all right for me to go upstairs for a bit."

"Of course, sir. Do you need assistance?"

"Piper and her young man will accompany me."

Maggie prepared Piper's tea and pressed the mug into her hands. "Can I get you anything else, dear?"

She shook her head. "This is perfect. Thanks, Maggie." Piper and Liam escorted Gino upstairs. On the second-floor landing, Liam held up his fist and slipped into the hall.

A moment later, he returned. "Two cameras in the hallway. You'll have to make it look as though you need help to walk, Mr. Romano."

The older man grimaced. "Unfortunately, I could use the assist. I didn't lie to Matteo or Maggie. I could use a few minutes to rest."

Piper and Liam exchanged glances. Maybe they shouldn't have asked Gino to help with their ruse. "Gavin has a sitting room attached to his bedroom. You'll be able to rest for a few minutes."

Liam opened the door to the hallway. Once Gino and Piper had cleared the threshold, he gripped one of Gino's arms while Piper supported her uncle on the opposite site.

When they'd nearly reached Gavin's suite, Gino stumbled and would have fallen if not for Liam's grip on her uncle's arm. "The door to your left," Piper whispered to Liam.

Liam shifted his hold on Gino so it appeared he was practically carrying her uncle toward the sitting room.

Piper hurried ahead and opened the door, holding it open for Liam and her uncle to pass. Once they were inside, she shut the door. Liam assisted her uncle to the couch and slid a pillow under his head when the older man stretched out.

"This is perfect." Gino patted Piper's hand when she knelt beside the couch. "I'll be fine in a few minutes, my dear. You'll see."

As they'd planned on the drive to the restaurant the night before, Piper got to her feet and walked into Liam's outstretched arms as though needing comfort in the face of Gino's failing health.

He nudged her to a chair and crouched in front of her, gathering her close again. "The signal detector is in my right inner jacket pocket," he whispered.

Concealed from view by his body, Piper retrieved the gadget and turned it on as he'd showed her. After watching the lights flicker for a moment, the light turned green.

"We're clear," he murmured. Liam turned to Gino who watched them. "Stay there in case someone checks on us. We won't be long."

He waved them on. "If we have company, I'll delay them as long as possible."

"Don't put yourself in danger, Mr. Romano."

"Go. I'll be fine."

Piper and Liam headed for Gavin's bedroom.

CHAPTER THIRTY-THREE

Liam held Piper back from barging into Gavin's bedroom. From this angle, the room looked clear, but his instincts screamed that something was off. This whole thing was too easy. He'd expected some resistance to their plan. Maybe they were just lucky.

He frowned. Maybe they were being lulled into thinking no one watched.

Liam turned on his electronic signal detector again and watched until the green light appeared. He still didn't like it. "Let's go. We need to hurry. Someone from security will be checking on us soon." If they didn't, the security team needed to be fired.

Piper went to the wall of video games and movies. She scanned the titles for a few minutes until she came to one near the end of a shelf crammed with movies.

She pulled the movie off the shelf and opened the cover. The silver disk gleamed in the dim light of the lamp Piper had turned on.

"How did you know which one to choose?"

"This is my favorite movie but Gavin wasn't fond of it." She frowned. "I don't understand. The information should be here."

Liam walked up behind her. "Check behind the disc," he murmured. He glanced around the room, uneasy. He needed to get Piper out of this house.

Piper popped the disc free. She turned it over and there, taped to the back, was a folded slip of paper with her name on it.

Liam snapped a picture of the writing on the paper and sent it to Zane and Maddox. "Come on." He turned off the lamp and propelled her from the room.

Gino sat up. "Well?"

Piper gave him a short nod. "Ready to go?"

"I'm better now."

She and Liam helped Romano to his feet. When she'd retrieved her tea mug, the older man slid his hand into his pocket and walked from the sitting room ahead of them.

As Liam suspected would happen, they were met in the hall by a security guard, suspicion in his gaze.

"Everything all right here?" he asked.

Romano clapped the man on his shoulder. "Matteo kindly allowed me to lie down for a few minutes. Cancer is taking its toll, I'm afraid."

A scowl. "This is Gavin's suite. You shouldn't be here."

"I was walking to a guest room when my legs gave way. Gavin's sitting room was the closest place for Liam to take me. We disturbed nothing. Check for yourself." With that, Romano moved toward the staircase. "I think I should return home now, my dear," he said to Piper. "Feel free to stay and visit with your Hartman friends if you wish."

"I've already expressed my condolences to Gavin's parents. There's nothing more for me here. Besides, I don't want to leave you alone."

Liam gripped Romano's arm and assisted the older man down the stairs. As much as he tried to hide his weakness from Piper, Romano was trembling with fatigue and weakness.

He needed to talk to Matt about Romano soon. Liam had a feeling Piper's uncle wouldn't last as long as the doctors projected.

As they entered the stairwell, Liam glanced back to see the guard slip into Gavin's sitting room. After returning the tea mug, Piper, Liam, and Romano left the mansion.

Outside on the stairs, Liam turned to the older man. "I'm parked two blocks away. Can you make it or should I bring the SUV to you?"

Romano walked down the stairs. "We shouldn't remain on the grounds. More chance to be stopped and searched if security becomes more suspicious."

Ten minutes later, Liam drove toward the Romano estate. He activated his Bluetooth and called Zane. "You're on speaker with Piper and Gino Romano, Z."

"Copy that. I checked the information you sent. It's enough to take care of your problem."

Thank God. The ball of ice in his stomach melted. "Can it be sent to the feds without involving Piper?" The one thing he didn't want to do was trigger a situation where she'd be sent to a safe house, especially now that Liam knew how sick her uncle was. Liam didn't want to be separated from her and if she went into a safe house, Piper wouldn't be able to see Romano.

His gaze shifted to the rearview mirror for an instant. Liam also didn't want Romano caught in the crossfire from Barone.

"Maybe. I can arrange an anonymous tip."

"Do it. The sooner, the better."

"I'll run this through the boss. He'll know who to pass the information to. Anything else I can help with?"

"Liam?"

He glanced over his shoulder at the older man. "Yes, sir?"

"The information in our possession would hold more weight if a witness came forward with it."

"If Piper takes the information to the feds, they'll put her into witness protection until Barone's trial. We're talking months, maybe years. In the meantime, Piper will be in seclusion without a life of her own."

"I wasn't talking about my niece. I was talking about me."

Piper twisted in her seat to stare at her uncle. "You can't. You're under a doctor's care. You don't have long to live, Uncle Gino. You should spend your final days in comfort with your friends close by, not sequestered in a safe house with US Marshals keeping watch over you."

"I want you safe. Matteo has a long memory and is a dangerous enemy to have. I don't have long to live anyway. It doesn't matter to me whether my old friend is trying to kill me or not."

"What do you think, Z?" Liam asked.

"Let me see if the anonymous tip will work first. If not, we'll talk again about our options." A pause, then, "Don't do anything foolish, Mr. Romano. This is not the time to rush. We don't want to tip our hand before we're ready. The result could be deadly for Piper and Liam."

"You speak with wisdom, young man."

"Not wisdom, sir. I speak from a wealth of experience. We care about Liam and Piper. We'll take care of all of you. Liam, I'll touch base with you later."

"Copy that."

Piper reached back and gripped her uncle's hand. "Thank you for offering to help."

"I want you to live life without constantly looking over your shoulder."

When they reached Romano's house, Piper's uncle paused at the front door. "Do you want to take the information?" he murmured to Liam.

"It's safer to do it here, Mr. Romano. Your security is compromised."

A scowl from the older man. "You need to do an evaluation of my system when this situation is resolved."

"I'll either take care of it myself or ask someone I trust to do it for me if I'm not able to."

"What would prevent you from completing the task yourself?"

"I won't let Piper face witness protection alone. If that's the best option to keep her alive, I'll marry her immediately and go with her."

He held out his hand to Liam. "Thank you for putting my niece first. She a lucky to have such devotion from her mate."

After a handshake, Liam slid his hand into his pocket. "I'm the one who's blessed, Mr. Romano. I don't deserve your niece. I give you my word that Piper will always be my top priority."

A slow nod. "Yes, I see that she will be. I regret that I won't have the opportunity to see your marriage flourish or hold my great niece or nephew."

He turned and kissed Piper's cheek. "I'm going to bed now. See you in the morning, my dear. Oh, I sent the list of candidates for your management team to your email. We'll talk about them tomorrow." With that, he turned and walked inside the house.

"Can we walk for a few minutes?" Piper asked Liam, voice soft. "I'm not ready to go inside yet."

He wrapped an arm around her shoulders and started them toward the garden at the back of the house. "Too many people at the Barone estate?"

"Wall-to-wall people made it hard to breathe in there. I'm also not ready to face the cameras and listening devices in this house. I'm not a good actress."

"It's hard to act normal under scrutiny." You couldn't relax, knowing a screwup would bring the enemy down on you with a weapon drawn. While Liam didn't think Gino Romano was spying on him and Piper, someone in his household was.

He led Piper to a garden bench and bent to retie his boot. While he dealt with the shoe lace, Liam slid the piece of paper Gino had given him into his boot. As he finished tying the lace, he scanned their surroundings, noting two people in the shadows at the edge of the property, watching them. Guards or someone else?

Not sure what they were dealing with, he pressed a button on his watch, alerting Zane that he might need assistance soon. If he didn't call off the alert within the next fifteen minutes, Z would notify Trent.

When he sat on the bench beside Piper, he gathered her against his side. "We have company."

She groaned. "I'm thinking about asking you to find a deserted island to take me to when we leave here."

Liam chuckled. Sounded like a great plan to him. Sun, sand, surf, and Piper. A perfect way to pass his leave time. "I'll see what I can find."

"Thanks for coming to Hartman with me, Liam."

He squeezed her shoulder. "I meant what I said before. I wouldn't be anywhere else."

Piper brushed his lips with hers. "I love you, Liam. I'm looking forward to being Mrs. Liam McCoy."

Before he could do more than tell her he loved her, heavy footsteps hurried up the path toward them. Recognizing one of the two security guards approaching, Liam stood and placed himself in front of Piper.

"You need to come with us," said the guard named Moe. "It's Mr. Romano."

Piper stood. "Is he all right?"

"I don't know, ma'am. I'm supposed to take you to him." He turned to Liam. "Just the lady. Mr. Romano said she'd be back in a few minutes."

Liam caught Piper around the waist and held her against his side. "That's not how this is going to work. Either I go with Piper or she doesn't go inside that house." And that was something Romano knew.

That knowledge plus the body language of the two men indicated they had a different agenda, one that didn't bode anything good for Piper.

He eased Piper behind him again. "What's going on here, Moe?"

The guard shook his head slowly, holding up an empty hand. "Look, I just know what I was told. The lady won't come to no harm." He and the other guard moved forward.

The second man lunged at Liam who shifted so the roundhouse punch thrown at his jaw missed, throwing the guard off balance.

Liam countered with a rabbit punch to the ribs. As his opponent dropped to the ground with a gasp, he caught movement from Moe in his peripheral vision. Liam turned to face off with the other guard when Moe pressed something against his side.

Liam heard the snap and knew he would be too late to escape. An electric current ripped through his body. He dropped hard when his muscles locked and refused to obey his mental command to move and protect Piper.

Moe pressed the trigger again and Liam's body jerked with the second jolt from the stun gun. As the darkness closed in, Liam felt Piper's arms around him and heard her begging the guard to stop.

CHAPTER THIRTY-FOUR

Piper cradled Liam against her as they rode in the back of a black van with no windows. She'd given up counting turns and trying to figure out where Moe and his buddy were taking them.

At first, she thought the guards were transporting them to Barone. Too many people were on the estate, though. Someone would see if they were carried into the house.

Maybe the oversized garage the crime boss had built. Although she couldn't see her watch, Piper sensed the ride had been longer than a drive to the other side of Hartman should take.

"Liam." She stroked his hair. "Please wake up."

How long had he been unconscious? Moe had scooped up Liam as soon as he was out and tossed him over one shoulder while his fellow thug grabbed Piper. Since they threatened to slit Liam's throat if she made a sound, Piper had kept silent as they walked to the estate's boundary and through the back entrance to the van parked beyond the gate.

Finally, the van stopped.

She drew in a deep breath. The clowns had taken her cell phone as well as Liam's and removed his weapons. Even if she found a way to escape, she refused to leave Liam in their hands. Live or die, they'd face it together.

The doors opened. Moe and his buddy peered inside. "Let's go, Piper."

"Why are you doing this? You've worked for my uncle for years. Hasn't Gino earned your loyalty?"

The big man shrugged. "Money talks. The boss says you won't be hurt if you give us Gavin's information."

Moe deluded himself if he believed Barone planned to release her and Liam. They knew too much. Didn't Moe have a sense of self-preservation? She and Liam could turn Moe and his fellow guard in to the cops.

What would Barone do when he learned he was too late to stop them from sending the information to the feds? Her stomach twisted into a knot.

Another thought occurred to her. Bravo or Texas had someone watching the house. Did something happen to Liam's backup? "Did Barone send you?"

He reached in and wrapped her wrist in a punishing grip. "Let's go. You don't want to fight me. I'd feel bad about it, but I'd hurt you if necessary. Can't say I'd show the same restraint for your boyfriend, though. Yeah, I'll be happy to take out my anger on your defenseless man." An ugly smile curved his lips as his grip tightened. "Thinks he's so much better than the rest of us. I'd love to teach him the meaning of pain and I will if you don't cooperate."

"No, please. Don't hurt him." She had to stall until Liam woke up. When he did, she wasn't sure how much time he needed to recover his ability to move. Didn't it take a while to throw off the aftereffect of an electric shock? No telling how long Liam would need to regain movement after two zaps from the stun gun.

Moe shoved her toward his buddy who wrenched her arm behind her back. Piper yelped.

"Shut up," he hissed and propelled her into motion.

She glanced back in time to see Moe haul Liam over his shoulder again with a grunt and stride after her and his buddy. Glancing around, Piper looked for clues to where the guards had taken them and frowned. Although there were no lights, she thought they were in a wide-open space because of the utter silence in the area. That couldn't be right, though. She saw the glow from a nearby city. Probably Hartman.

The second guard shoved Piper against a wall. "Try to escape and your boyfriend is dead." He rubbed his ribcage with a glare Liam's direction. "I owe him for that cheap shot to my side."

"Hurry up, Billy," Moe muttered. "This guy weighs a ton."

"Yeah, yeah." After another warning glare at Piper, Billy tapped a code into a sophisticated key pad. Piper committed the numbers to memory in case she and Liam needed them to escape the building without setting off an alarm.

A moment later, Billy opened a door and shoved Piper inside a building with a concrete floor. Every step they took echoed.

Billy steered her around a maze of wooden crates she could just make out in the dimly lit building. A warehouse. Piper frowned. Were they in Barone's oversized garage after all?

The guard dragged her toward the far end of the building and a darkened hallway. He opened a door and turned on a light. The interior room was empty except for one metal chair with sturdy-looking arms.

Piper glanced around the room, heart sinking. No windows for an easy escape once Liam regained consciousness. Why couldn't one problem in this whole situation have an easy solution?

Moe strode into the room. He dragged Liam off his shoulder and dumped him on the metal chair. Billy pushed Piper against the wall and pointed at her. "Stay put." He turned away and helped his buddy zip-tie Liam's arms and ankles to the chair. That done, they left the room, locking the door behind them.

Piper hurried toward Liam, glancing around the room and hoping a camera would be obvious. She didn't see anything but her skin crawled.

"Liam." Piper knelt beside the chair and cupped Liam's cheeks. "Sweetheart, please wake up."

He groaned, then fell silent again. No movement.

She patted his cheek. "Liam." He had to wake up. Although Liam might not be capable of defending himself, he had knowledge and experience to help her save them both.

He drew in a deep breath and his eyelids lifted to slits. "Piper."

"I'm right here."

"You okay?"

She bit her lip at his slurred speech. How bad had Moe hurt him? "I'm fine. Moe zapped you twice with a stun gun. You've been unconscious for at least half an hour."

A grunt. "Where?"

"I'm not sure where we are. Moe and Billy transported us from Uncle Gino's estate in a black van without windows. I know we're in a warehouse on the outskirts of a city. We're near Hartman since we weren't in the van that long."

"Push black button on watch."

"I don't know if we have a camera in here," she whispered.

"Hug me. Push button."

Piper leaned up, her gaze dropping to his wrist before she wrapped her arms around his middle. Laying her head on his shoulder, she used her body to block a camera's view of her hand.

She reached for his watch, found the right button, and pushed it in. "Got it," she murmured. "Now what?"

"Wait for help."

Several pairs of footsteps drew near.

Piper tightened her grip around Liam. "Someone's coming."

"Tell nothing."

"They'll hurt you." She knew whoever ordered them to be brought here would use Liam to force Piper to cooperate. She didn't know if she could watch Moe and Billy hurt him when she had the power to spare Liam pain. "Don't ask me to do that."

"If you talk, we're dead."

She sucked in a breath. Oh, man. "What should I do?"

"Hold out, no matter what happens. Help coming."

Yes, but would Bravo be fast enough to spare Liam's life?

CHAPTER THIRTY-FIVE

Liam prayed the pervasive weakness would leave his body fast. He knew from experience, however, it wouldn't be fast enough to spare himself or Piper from a lot of pain.

He dragged in a few deep breaths, forcing oxygen into his bloodstream. His head cleared a little more. Couldn't do that too often or he'd make himself dizzy. "If you get a chance, run."

Piper scowled. "I'm not leaving you here."

"I'll be okay." Maybe. "Need you safe."

"Tough. We go or stay together."

Liam hated being helpless, especially when Piper's life was in danger. He hoped his team was close. As soon as Piper sent the emergency signal to Fortress, Zane would have notified Bravo and Texas that he and Piper were in trouble and where they were located.

Even as he the thoughts surfaced in his mind, Liam felt the GPS tracker under his right shoulder blade radiate heat. Good. Trent and the others would come. All he and Piper had to do was hang on until help arrived or his muscles responded to commands for Liam to free himself and the woman he loved from the hands of their captors.

A key was shoved into the lock on the door. The knob turned and Moe walked inside the room, followed by the second guard. What did Piper call him? Oh, yeah. Billy.

The two traitors eyed Liam. Billy looked twitchy and had an ugly gleam in his eyes. Liam could guess which guard was going to volunteer first to work on Liam in an effort to force the secrets they wanted from Piper.

More footsteps, these lighter than those of the two guards.

Liam's gaze shifted toward the door again to see Brandy Strickland enter. His suspicions were right. Brandy was in this up to her pretty neck. His only question was whether she worked for Gino in this matter, herself, or Barone? If Barone called the shots, more thugs were at Brandy's disposal. At the moment, Liam couldn't defend himself or Piper against a kitten much less the two guards across the room. No way could he take on more of Barone's crew. Even if he freed himself, he'd end up in a heap on the ground. His fingers were starting to respond to commands. Not his legs, though.

Piper released Liam and stood, placing her body between him and the other three people in the room. Thankfully, she'd moved aside enough for him to see what was happening.

"Surprised to see me, Piper?" Brandy smiled, her eyes cold and hard. "You've always been gullible."

"Why did you kidnap us and bring us here, Brandy?"

"You know why."

"Spell it out for me."

Liam wiggled his fingers, mentally cheering as Piper stalled for more time. While Liam's teammates were minutes away, they still had to assess the situation and come up with a plan. Breaching a building without intel was beyond stupid. As much as Liam wanted Piper out of danger, he didn't want to cost a fellow operative his life.

Brandy's smile morphed into a frown. "Don't play dumb. I want the information Gavin left you."

"Why?"

A harsh laugh rang out in the empty room. "It's worth a boatload of money. That's why."

"You're selling the information to the highest bidder?"

"Don't be ridiculous. I'm giving it back to Gavin's father. Gavin stole the information. His father wants it back. I'm delivering it to him."

"Why would you do that? You're betraying Gavin's memory by returning information he gave his life for."

"It's worth everything to me."

"I thought you loved Gavin. How could you betray him for money?"

"He believed I loved him."

"But you didn't."

"He was weak with a wandering eye. When I found out what he'd been doing while you were dating, I knew I couldn't trust him."

"You stayed with him for three years after I left. Why do that if you didn't trust him?"

"He's not the real power in the Barone family. I stayed with Gavin until I could secure my place in his world."

"I don't understand."

"You wouldn't understand the way the real world works. You're short-sighted and naive, old friend."

"You want Barone," Liam said. His words came out clearer. Excellent. Another thirty minutes and he should be almost back to normal. Too bad he didn't think Billy and Moe would wait that long. Their mistress would demand answers soon. Impatience brewed in her gaze.

"Ding, ding, ding. Very good, Liam. Matteo is everything I've ever wanted. Money, power, fame, distinguished looks, generosity to those he loves."

"And you think he loves you?" Piper shook her head. "Gavin was the son of Barone's mistress. Father and son are exactly alike."

Fury lit Brandy's gaze. "Shut up, Piper. It's different with me. Matteo loves me."

"When did he tell you that?"

"Not long before you returned to Hartman."

"And you believed him? Come on, Brandy. He says he loves you yet he's still married to Gavin's mother. How does that make him different than his cheating son?"

Brandy crossed the few feet between them and slapped Piper. His woman stumbled back and partially fell against Liam.

Helpless rage filled him. He was trussed up like a turkey and he couldn't protect her. Distracting Barone's mistress was his only hope to prevent her from hurting Piper and give him a few more precious minutes to throw off the effects of the stun gun.

"What's your end game?" Liam asked her.

"Take over Galactic Games and use it to further Matteo's important activities. Soon, I'll take my place at his side as his wife. I'll help him run his empire." She laughed. "Brandy Strickland, the first lady of Hartman. What a kick that will be."

"You're already helping Barone, aren't you?" Piper asked. "That's why you wanted to be the CEO of Galactic Games. What are you hiding, Brandy?"

A shrug from the other woman. "I suppose it doesn't matter if you know the truth. Once you give me what I want, I won't have further use for you."

Moe's eyes widened as he stared at Brandy. Guess he hadn't expected to murder someone when he took on this job for her.

"One of the management team is sure to recommend you have the company's accounts audited. I can't allow that to happen."

Piper's hands fisted. "Because you're laundering money for Barone. You're the reason Uncle Gino is being watched by the feds."

"It's called creative financing," Brandy corrected. "Galactic Games wouldn't exist if not for Matteo's generosity. The company is his anyway." An ugly smile curved her mouth. "Galactic Games will be mine in the end. Matteo promised me the company. I'm not worried about the feds. Gino makes the perfect scapegoat. He's dying. If they prosecute him for laundering money, he won't live long enough for his case to go to trial. Besides, I have things lined up so the accountant takes the fall. Nothing will point to me. Now, you've stalled enough, Piper. It's time to give me what I want."

Piper straightened. "I can't do that."

"Wrong answer." Brandy glanced over her shoulder. "Moe." She inclined her head toward Piper.

Liam strained against the zip ties. Not recovering fast enough. "Don't, Moe. Don't hurt her."

The big guard gripped Piper's arms. "Sorry, man," he murmured and dragged Liam's woman across the room. She fought him every step of the way, kicking, punching, and scratching.

Billy's laughter filled the room as he watched the melee. "That one's a tigress."

"Billy." Brandy moved away from Liam and motioned to the remaining guard.

Satisfaction glinted in the other man's eyes as he approached Liam, flexing his hands.

"Brandy, no. Please, don't do this." Piper redoubled her efforts to get away from Moe.

The guard struck her with a backhand and knocked her to the floor. He rolled Piper to her stomach and cinched her wrists behind her back. That done, he flipped her over and hauled her to sit against the closest wall. When she scrambled to her feet, Moe slammed her against the flat surface, scowling. "Stay."

Billy's fist flew into Liam's jaw. A second blow landed in his gut followed by a third to his mouth.

Piper rammed into Moe, trying to move him enough to run to Liam.

The guard shoved her back and backhanded her a second time. The blow sent her crashing to the floor.

"Baby, stop," Liam managed to call out before Billy landed another blow, this one to his ribs. Yeah, pretty sure that one cracked a rib or two. No matter how painful his own wounds were, he couldn't let Piper be injured in her desperate fight to reach him. She couldn't help him right now and all she'd succeed in doing was place herself in the path of flying fists.

When her pleading gaze locked with his, Liam shook his head before another blow from Billy split his lip.

"Enough." Brandy held up her hand. "The pain stops if you give me what I want, Piper. When Billy grows tired of beating on your boyfriend, Moe will take over. Trust me. You don't want Moe to go to work on Liam. I can't guarantee he'd survive." A lazy shrug from the woman. "If he does, I have other men at my beck and call who will take over. Several love to hurt women. Maybe you don't love Liam as much as you pretend to. If you did, you wouldn't allow him to be beaten to pulp in front of you. What kind of woman are you to allow the man you love to suffer?"

Tears tracked down Piper's blood-stained face. Her gaze remained locked on Liam's, silently begging him to give her permission to tell Brandy what she wanted.

He couldn't do it. The only way to keep them alive was to remain silent. Liam shook his head again, then mouthed, "I love you."

More silent tears from his woman.

"What's it going to be, Piper? More pain for Liam or a reprieve?" Brandy folded her arms.

Piper kept her gaze locked with Liam's and refused to respond to Brandy's questions.

Smart woman. She'd figured out that her reactions incited their captors. The more she reacted, the greater harm they'd inflict with the intent to make her break and give them what they wanted.

A loud sigh. "Seriously? He's suffering needlessly, Piper. All you have to do is give me Gavin's information and Liam's pain stops." When Piper didn't respond, Brandy growled. "Fine. Since your boyfriend seems to be as tough as he looks, I guess we'll shift our persuasion techniques. Billy, take over for Moe. We need his special talents."

A resentful glare from Billy as he crossed the room and wrapped his hand around Piper's throat. "You fight me and I'll choke you until you pass out," he growled. "After that, I'll drag you out of here and find a nice, quiet room where no one will bother us. You need a real man to tame you and I'm just the one to do it." He tightened his grip around Piper's throat.

Billy the guard was a dead man as soon as Liam freed himself.

An abrupt movement by Moe caught Liam's attention. The guard brandished a four-inch fixed-blade knife. The steel gleamed in the light.

Moe lumbered forward, stopping in front of Liam, waiting for the go-ahead from his mistress. "You don't want to do this," Liam murmured. "Cut me free. We'll stop her together." He needed more time for his teammates to get here or to regain full control of his limbs.

"I don't have a choice," came the whispered response. "She threatened my kid."

"We can protect your family."

"What are you waiting for?" Brandy snapped. "You have your orders. Carry them out. If you don't, you know what will happen."

Moe swallowed hard. "Sorry, man." He plunged the knife into Liam's left shoulder.

Liam rode the waves of pain, keeping his expression blank as Piper watched him with anguish in her eyes.

"Again," Brandy demanded, her gaze riveted to the growing bloodstain on his shirt.

The knife blade penetrated the outside of his right thigh. Liam grunted at the flash of pain. At least Moe hadn't stabbed him in the inner thigh where he could have sliced Liam's femoral artery. So far, the wounds were painful but not mortal, the injuries designed to coerce Piper into talking.

The knife dripping with Liam's blood, Brandy smiled, her gaze shifting to Piper. "Still refuse to talk?"

Piper remained silent.

Liam had never loved her more than he did right at this moment. She was the strongest woman he'd ever met.

With a look of disgust, Brandy motioned for Moe to continue his work.

The guard circled the chair and came to a stop behind Liam. A moment later, the blade of the knife plunged into Liam's side.

Nausea roiled in his gut as the pain built. He didn't dare show reaction. Piper was suffering enough as it was. Another plunge of the knife, this time into his back above the liver.

Too much more of this and he'd pass out from blood loss. Weakness spread throughout his body and Liam's blood pooled under the chair.

A phone rang in the room. Brandy pulled out her phone and smiled. "My love is calling me. Moe, Billy, leave the two lovebirds and come with me. We'll come back to play with Piper and Liam in a few minutes. Maybe Liam will convince Piper to spill her guts before he bleeds out. If he doesn't, we'll turn your skills on her."

A moment later, the three of them were gone, locking the door behind themselves again.

Piper lurched across the room and knelt beside Liam. "Liam."

He dragged in a shallow breath. Man, breathing hurt. Definitely had at least one cracked rib. "I have knife in my right boot. Get it."

"What if they're watching on camera?"

"Move fast. We'll only get one chance."

She scurried to the other side of the chair. "Tell me where."

"Near the outside of my ankle."

Piper twisted to put her back to Liam and groped for his boot with her bound hands. She fumbled a moment, then grabbed the hilt of the knife and pulled the weapon free. "What now?"

"Hand it to me."

She maneuvered the knife until she gave him the weapon hilt first.

Liam fought off dizziness as he sawed at the zip tie restraining his right wrist. In seconds, the plastic gave way and he made quick work of the ties holding his other wrist and both ankles. "Hold your hands as far apart as you can." When Piper complied, he sliced through her restraint.

He rose from the chair and swayed, gritting his teeth to keep himself upright. Not good.

"The door is locked and Brandy and her merry band of thugs are on the other side of the door. I can hear them in the hallway." Piper steadied Liam with an arm around his waist.

"We do whatever is necessary to survive until help arrives." He nudged her toward the door. "Stand behind the door. I'll take down whoever comes into the room first. Slam the door in the face of whoever follows. Hopefully, we'll both be successful so we only have one of those clowns left to handle together." He didn't bother to tell

Piper he wasn't sure he would be mobile at that point. His goal was to keep her alive long enough for his teammates to arrive.

The voices in the hall grew louder. Brandy was wrapping up her phone call. Liam positioned Piper behind the door, shut off the light, and pressed his back against the wall on the other side of the door.

The door opened and Moe strode through first. "Hey, what happened to the light?"

Using Moe's momentum, Liam jerked the guard forward, throwing him off balance enough to fall to his hands and knees. Trusting Piper to give him a few seconds to handle Moe, Liam delivered a roundhouse kick to his head. The guard dropped to the floor and lay unmoving.

A rustle of movement at his back and a feminine scream had him pivoting to go to Piper's aid. She was on the ground, fighting with Brandy.

Before he could intervene, Billy tackled Liam with a roar of fury.

"I'm going to kill you, McCoy."

Liam didn't have enough breath to reply or strength to waste on taunting the security guard. He did, however, have the determination to stop Billy from hurting Piper.

He blocked two punches and landed an elbow strike to Billy's temple. The blow stunned the guard long enough for Liam to slam his fist in the man's throat and crush his windpipe. Billy's eyes widened and he grabbed his throat as he fell to the concrete, struggling in vain to breathe.

After making sure the other man didn't have weapons within reach, Liam turned toward Piper and staggered her direction just as his woman landed an uppercut to Brandy's jaw. Barone's mistress slumped to the floor and lay still.

Piper got to her feet and turned. "Liam."

He reached out and wrapped his arm around her shoulder. "We have to get out of here." Liam staggered to toward the door. One step, two. His legs gave out.

CHAPTER THIRTY-SIX

"Liam." Fear filled Piper's voice. His deadweight had taken both of them to the concrete floor. He had to get up. Piper couldn't carry him over her shoulder like one of his teammates could.

"Go," he whispered. "Run."

"I'm not leaving you."

"Moe and Brandy won't be out for long. Baby, please." He slumped to the floor.

No, no, no. "Liam." No response. Piper tapped his cheek. Nothing.

Oh, man. He needed medical attention. Where was his team?

Gunfire erupted outside the warehouse. Shouts of pain and anger permeated the walls. Bravo and Texas had to be out there.

There must be a bathroom with medical supplies close by. This was a warehouse, after all. Accidents happened. She wasn't a medic like Matt or Jesse, but she could find something to slow the bleeding.

Scrambling to her feet, she noticed Moe was stirring. She grabbed the chair and bashed the guard on the back of the head. He stopped moving.

Piper didn't know if she'd killed the man and right now, she didn't care. All the mattered was saving Liam's life. Concerned Brandy might wake up soon and pose a threat to Liam, Piper unlatched Brandy's belt, rolled her to her stomach, and restrained her hands. That ought to hold her until help arrived.

She stumbled into the hall and opened door after door until she found a bathroom. A quick search turned up a first-aid kit. Thank God. She ran back to the room where Liam lay.

Dropping to her knees, Piper opened the kit with shaking fingers. Rudimentary, at best, but the medical supplies would have to do. She grabbed gauze and a roll of bandages.

She wrapped his leg wound first, then turned her attention to his shoulder. Before she'd finished wrapping the wound, the gauze pad was soaked with blood.

Piper paused when she heard footsteps in the hallway. Friend or foe? She glanced around for the knife she'd pulled from Liam's boot. There, under Billy's foot.

She eyed the guard who had taken such pleasure in hurting Liam and threatening her. He hadn't moved. Was he dead? Didn't matter. She needed a weapon to protect Liam.

Piper grabbed the knife and positioned herself in front of Liam. She turned slightly so the knife was out of sight. A surprise attack was her only hope. Another guard would outweigh her and have some training.

A large figure dressed in black appeared in the threshold. "Piper, it's Matt."

"Liam's hurt. There's a light switch to your right."

A moment later, light flooded the room. Matt sucked in a breath when he saw Liam lying on the floor behind Piper. He touched the communication device as he hurried to

Liam's side. The medic dropped to his knees. "Trent, I found Liam and Piper. She looks a little beat up but Liam's in bad shape. We need transport out of here, fast."

"How can I help?" Piper knelt on the other side of Liam and set the knife to the side.

The medic opened his medical bag and handed her several white packets. "That's QuikClot. We'll pour the contents of the packets on his wounds. It will stop the bleeding until we can get him to the hospital."

He ripped off the bandages she'd placed on Liam's wounds. Blood flowed from each injury. He pivoted, the weapon in his hand aimed at the door when Jesse called out, "It's Jesse. I'm coming in soft." Matt didn't lower his gun until the other medic entered the room.

"What do we have?"

"At least four knife wounds. He'll bleed out if we don't stop the blood flow in the next couple minutes."

"They beat the crap out of him. He has to have internal injuries."

"We have to move him. The knife wound I'm most worried about is on his back. I think they nicked his liver."

Jesse growled. "Piper, open one of those packets. We're going to move fast. Matt and I will shift Liam's weight together to prevent additional injuries. Pour the contents of a packet on each wound."

She nodded and ripped open the first packet as Matt widened the rip in the cargo pants and spread the material away from the wound on Liam's thigh. Piper dumped the packet's contents on the wound, amazed to see the bleeding slow dramatically.

Jesse wrapped the wound with fast, efficient movements. "Shoulder next."

Matt tore Liam's shirt open and shoved the remnants away from his body. Piper poured the contents of another packet on this wound.

They repeated the process until all four knife wounds were treated and covered.

Matt checked Liam's pulse and growled. "Thready. He needs blood and an operating room." He activated his mic again. "Trent, how long?" He listened a moment, then said, "We'll need help getting him to the door, preferably someone with an O positive blood type."

"How long?" Jesse asked.

"Too long. They're still taking care of business out there. Barone sent reinforcements to protect his precious weapons stash."

"I have the right type of blood," Piper said. "Both of you might be needed to protect Liam. Let me donate blood."

"Lie down," Matt said. He reached into his bag for the equipment he needed. "If you're squeamish about needles, don't look."

No problem. She hated needles. When Matt reached for her arm, Piper averted her gaze. A swipe and a needle prick later, the deed was done.

"Breathe, Piper," Jesse murmured. He patted her shoulder. "You're doing great. You can brag to Liam about how you saved a big, bad Marine's life."

Matt gripped her other hand. "Tell me what happened while we wait for the signal to move Liam."

Piper summarized what happened from the time they walked into the garden until Matt had walked into the room.

He whistled. "Good grief, woman. You're one tough lady. You were going to attack me with Liam's boot knife, weren't you?"

"I didn't have anything else and he couldn't defend himself. The knife was my only option."

Another shoulder pat from Jesse. "He's a lucky man to have you by his side."

"Tell me the truth. Will he live?"

"Oh, yeah. A few scratches and bruises aren't going to take this guy down. He'll be fine once he has surgery."

Matt straightened and tapped his mic again. "Copy." He looked down at Piper. "Transport is parked at the side entrance. We'll have to carry you to the SUV."

Seconds later, Trent and Simon walked into the room. Both men scowled when they saw Liam's condition. "How do we do this, Matt?" Trent asked.

"We need to carry Liam and Piper to the SUV. His blood pressure was dropping so we couldn't wait for the hospital to give him a transfusion."

In less than a minute, Trent and Simon were carrying Liam toward the SUV while Matt walked beside them, carrying Piper in his arms. Jesse hurried ahead of the entourage to run interference in case of trouble.

Once they were situated in the SUV, Trent climbed behind the wheel while Simon rode in back with Jesse. Matt, Liam, and Piper were in the middle.

Matt glanced at Bravo's team leader. "Hurry, Trent."

Piper reached over and linked her hand to Liam's. "Hang on," she whispered in his ear. "Hold on me for, Liam. Your teammates and your family need you." She drew in a ragged breath. "I need you. Don't leave me."

He didn't respond.

CHAPTER THIRTY-SEVEN

Liam opened his eyes to utilitarian cream-colored walls and a television mounted in the corner. He frowned. Where was he? Slowly, noises began to register. Foot traffic, an elevator, muffled conversations, a public announcement system, laughter, carts passing in the corridor. The acrid tang of disinfectant clued him in to his location. He was in a hospital.

He frowned. Was he injured on an op? By degrees, the fog cleared from his brain enough for him to remember being in the garden with Piper, then waking up in a warehouse with Moe and Billy.

Pain from his injuries registered as Liam scanned the room. Simon slumped in a seat by his bedside. No Piper. Worry gnawed at his gut. Where was she? Was she all right? Had Moe or Brandy hurt Piper after Liam passed out?

He shifted on the hospital bed, intent on getting up to find Piper. Sharp pain spiked and a soft groan escaped. Man, Brandy and her buddies had worked him over good.

"Don't move." Simon climbed to his feet and leaned over him. "The doctor spent a lot of time patching you up. He won't be happy if you undo his work."

He blinked. "Sorensen?" His voice came out raspy.

A head shake. "You wouldn't have made it to Bayside. You're still in Hartman. Don't worry. We have you covered."

"Piper?"

"Matt took her to the cafeteria for a snack. Piper hasn't left your side in hours. She'll be back soon."

Liam gave a slight nod and felt the darkness begin to overtake him again. "Protect," he murmured.

"We'll protect her with our lives, Liam. Let go and rest."

The next time he surfaced, Liam turned his head and saw Piper. She'd fallen asleep with her hand wrapped around his, her head beside his arm.

The sight of her by his side eased his fear for her safety. Not that he could do much to protect Piper in his condition. He'd face plant if he stood at that moment.

Movement on the other side of the bed brought Matt into his field of vision.

"Hey. How do you feel?" the medic whispered.

"Like I've been hit by an eighteen-wheeler."

His friend grinned. "Not surprising considering what you've been through."

"Recovery time?"

"According to Sorensen, six to eight weeks."

"Are we in Texas?"

"Nope. Maddox flew the doc here to check on you and Piper."

His gaze settled on the woman he adored. "How is she?"

"A little bruised. Mostly she's worried about you. She saved your life, Liam."

That brought his attention back to the medic. "What do you mean?"

"Piper was prepared to fight off Barone's thugs with your boot knife when we arrived. Since that wasn't necessary, she donated blood to keep you alive. She gave more than she should have but Piper insisted the rest of us were necessary to protect you from further harm." Matt leaned closer. "Don't let this woman get away, buddy. She'll be the kind of wife you need to protect your family if we're deployed. Piper is a keeper."

He didn't have to be told that truth. He'd seen it for himself when Billy and Moe were working him over. "I don't intend to let her go."

At that moment, Piper stirred.

He squeezed her hand.

Her head popped up, eyes wide. "Liam, you're awake."

"And alive, thanks to you."

She sat on the edge of the bed as Matt left the room to give them some privacy. "I didn't do anything your teammates wouldn't have done." Piper cupped his cheek with her soft palm. "You scared me. Don't do it again." Tears sparkled in her eyes.

"I'm sorry, Sunshine. Are you okay? Did the goons hurt you?"

"I'm fine. A few bruises that will be gone in a few days."

"Matt says I have enforced vacation time coming."

"You're taking every day off that Dr. Sorensen recommends for your recovery."

"I'll take them if you promise me something."

"What?"

"Take two weeks off to spend with me at the beach."

"I still have a job, one I've neglected."

"We'll see if Delilah can handle more time without her partner." He'd pay someone to fill in for Piper if Delilah needed help. After the scare they'd had, he didn't want to be separated from her. If Sorensen held true to form, the doc would insist he spend a few days in the Bayside clinic to keep an eye on Liam's progress before Sorensen released him to convalesce somewhere else.

Liam didn't want Piper to go home to Otter Creek without him, not with Spencer waiting to pounce on the woman who owned Liam's heart.

"Spending two weeks enjoying the salt breeze sounds good."

He gave a slight nod and inched to the far side of the bed, his teeth gritted against the pain caused by moving.

"What are you doing?"

"I need to hold you."

"I'll hurt you."

"Worth it." He patted the empty space on the mattress. "We'll work it out."

She looked skeptical but climbed onto the mattress and settled gingerly beside him.

Liam eased his arm around her shoulders and her head settled against his chest. Perfect. Knowing his teammates were on watch in the hall, he allowed himself to fall asleep again, this time holding the woman with a lion's courage.

Sometime later, he woke when Matt stepped into the room.

"Maddox is here."

Liam's eyebrows rose. He must have been in a bad way if his boss flew down from Nashville to sit at his bedside.

"Liam, what's wrong?"

Piper's drowsy voice wrapped around his heart and made him long to rush the woman to the altar. He wouldn't, though. Right now, he wouldn't be rushing anywhere. Give him a few days and he'd be good as new. Okay, maybe a few weeks. "My boss is here."

When she started to slide from the bed, Liam held her in place. "Stay." He gave a chin lift to Matt.

A moment later, Brent Maddox walked to Liam's bedside. "How are you?"

"I'm okay, sir."

The blond SEAL grinned. "In other words, you feel lousy."

His lips curved.

"Barone's thugs did a number on you. I understand from Matt we're lucky you're still with us."

Liam blinked. He hadn't realized it was that close.

Maddox turned to Piper. "You must be Piper. I'm Brent Maddox, Liam's boss."

"It's nice to meet you in person."

"I'm glad to see you, sir, but why are you here?" Liam asked.

"Two reasons. One, I'm in talks with the ATF over the raid at Barone's warehouse last night. The feds aren't happy that we interfered with their operation."

Huh. The warehouse must have been storing illegal weapons if the ATF was involved. "When are they ever happy?"

A chuckle from Maddox. "True. The second reason I'm here is to escort you and Piper to Bayside, Texas so you can recuperate without worrying about your safety or Piper's."

"When are we leaving?"

"Tomorrow. Jesse will fly with us. The rest of his teammates will meet us at the clinic to provide security."

"What about Bravo?"

"I'll send them home to help set a trap for your old buddy Spencer."

"Details?"

"Later. We won't proceed until you're ready. Maybe next week. Depends on how fast you recover."

"You're going to draw him out."

"Can't leave him out there, Liam. Otherwise you won't be able to focus on your job when Bravo is deployed. We take care of this problem now."

Piper's breath caught. "You're using him as bait."

"Well-protected bait."

"I don't like this. Hasn't he suffered enough?"

"This is the fastest way to end the danger to both of you plus Bravo and Durango's wives and girlfriends." He folded his arms. "A woman who was prepared to fight hired thugs with nothing more than a small knife can handle a former Marine with a grudge against her man and a full team to back her up."

She smiled. "I suppose I can."

"That's settled, then. I'm making arrangement to spring you from this hospital, Liam. In the meantime, we'll follow standard procedure with one operative in the room with you at all times and one in the hallway. We'll leave early tomorrow morning while it's still dark. Anything I need to do in the meantime?"

"Check on Piper's uncle. Tell him what's going on. I'd like a team to evaluate his security at the estate. Piper and I also need our gear. Her bags are at Romano's house. Mine is in the back of my SUV. Romano needs a bodyguard he can trust until we're sure he's not in danger from Barone or his cronies."

"I'll take care of it. I'll have Texas do the security evaluation. Bravo has informed me they're providing your security while you're here."

"Are you surprised?" Matt said.

"I'd be surprised if you didn't." He turned back to Liam and Piper. "Rest as much as possible." After squeezing Liam's hand and nodding goodbye to Piper, he left.

"He's an interesting man," Piper said.

Matt snorted. "He's as tough as nails and would tear a strip off our hides if we did something stupid."

"Sounds like he cares about his people."

"He does." Liam kissed Piper's temple. "In our line of work, the consequences of carelessness can be deadly."

The day passed in a series of long naps for Liam and walks to the cafeteria for Piper with one of his teammates serving as her bodyguard. Although Barone had been arrested along with most of his criminal organization, a few of his employees might be out for revenge against the woman who brought down an empire with her stubborn refusal to run and hide.

Overnight, Liam slept lightly, aware this was the perfect time for someone to breach the room. When Simon arrived at midnight to take over the watch in the hall, he brought Liam a Sig. A little more tension eased from his muscles. At least he could protect Piper if the worst did happen. Thankfully, the night passed in relative quiet.

A few minutes after four, Jesse and Matt rolled in a wheelchair. Liam eyed the transportation with distaste.

"Don't argue." Matt patted the chair. "It's the only way you're getting out of this place. Let us do the work. If you pull stitches loose, you'll be stuck in here another few days."

"Yeah, yeah. Let's do this. I want Piper out of this town."

CHAPTER THIRTY-EIGHT

Liam scowled at a grinning Brody Weaver. He pointed at the Texas team's leader. "I won't be stuck in this bed forever. Continuing to flirt with my future wife is dangerous for your health, buddy."

"I'm not worried. Texas Rangers trump jar heads every time."

Piper rolled her eyes. "Knock it off, Brody. Antagonizing Liam won't score points with me."

Brody dropped to his knees, hand pressed to his heart, face a mask of mock misery. "Ah, sweet Piper. You wound me deeply."

Logan shook his head at his leader's antics.

Max pushed aside Brody and knelt on one knee in front of Piper. He reached into his sleeve and pulled out a silk flower and handed it to her. "Toss Brody and Liam to the female masses and run away with me. I'll treat you like a princess. You'll never have to work another day in your life. I'll bring you chocolate bonbons every day and flowers on Fridays."

Liam growled. The Texas team must not have a self-preservation gene in their bodies. He was going to kill every one of them.

"Sounds like a good deal to me," Logan said. "What do you say, Piper?"

"You aren't going to make your own pitch for my hand in marriage?"

A slow smile spread across his mouth. "Why should I? I'll be the last man standing after the rest of the team dies in mysterious explosions."

His teammates groaned. "Like you wouldn't be the first suspect," Brody said. "You're the explosives expert."

"I'm also experienced enough to make the accidents believable. Nope, sorry, guys. The girl will be mine in the end. If you're smart, you'll vacate the field of battle before you meet a painful death."

Jesse Phelps snorted. "You're all idiots. Liam doesn't have to be mobile to pull the trigger on his sniper rifle. From what I hear through the grapevine, he doesn't miss."

Liam shifted his glance to the medic. "Maybe I'll let you live. The others are doomed."

A brush of fabric against the hallway wall had all four men from the Texas team moving to form a wall between Liam and Piper and the unannounced visitor, weapons drawn and ready.

Sawyer Chapman peered into the room at Sorensen's clinic. "Jet's ready. We can leave as soon as Liam decides to quit lazing around and drags himself out of bed."

"Where's my rifle?" Liam asked. "I'll take out the lot of you now and save myself a bunch grief over the next two weeks."

The team and Piper laughed.

"We'll load the gear in the SUVs and come back for you and Piper." Brody narrowed his eyes at Liam. "Don't move, McCoy. We'll make you pull your own weight soon enough. For now, let us do the work."

REBECCA DEEL

Liam motioned for the team to go on.

Piper sat on the recovery room bed and entwined their fingers. "You know I would never cheat on you, right? They're teasing to get a rise out of you."

He cupped her nape and drew Piper forward to kiss her, pleased when the movement only cause a minor twinge of pain. Definite improvement over the past three days. "I know, Sunshine. These men are too honorable to make a move on a woman involved with a fellow operative. The needling is all in the spirit of fun."

She sighed. "Good. You never have to worry about that with me. I love you too much to hurt you that way."

Liam's thumb stroked lightly over her bruised jaw. "I adore you, Piper. You mean everything to me. I wouldn't jeopardize the gift of you by even looking at another woman that way."

Brody returned with Jesse at his heels. "Time to go."

When Piper moved out of the way, the men slowly raised Liam to a sitting position and held him steady while his equilibrium and stomach settled into place. Being this weak ticked him off and the last thing he wanted to do was barf in front of Piper.

"Okay now?" Jesse asked.

Not even close. "Let's go."

Sorensen pushed a wheelchair into the room. "Time for you to go, McCoy. You're grumpy enough that I'd say you're well on your way to a full recovery. Remember, no working for at least six weeks. If you think you're ready to go back before then, stop in and let me check you. Otherwise, I'll refuse to clear you. you'll be sent back to the beach."

Brody grunted. "Some hardship. Baking in the sun with a beautiful woman by his side."

Liam smiled and held out his hand to the Fortress doctor. "Thanks for everything, Doc. Don't worry about me returning to work without permission. Piper won't let me go back before my leave time is up."

"No way," she said. "I want every minute with you before I let Fortress have you for a month."

"Ah, but just think, Sunshine. I'll be able to romance you from a distance. You never know what will arrive in the mail to remind you of me."

"Hmm. In that case, let's get you well. You have my curiosity aroused."

He chuckled, then winced as his cracked ribs reminded him of the still-healing injury.

Brody and Jesse assisted Liam into the wheelchair for the trip to the SUV. Within an hour, Liam lay propped up on the bed at the back of the Fortress jet with Piper at his side.

Jesse patted his shoulder. "The pain meds I gave you should hold you until we land. When we reach the beach house, I'll give you more."

"Still hate taking them," he groused.

"Yeah, you and every other operative I've treated since I joined Fortress say exactly the same thing. You'll be glad you succumbed to my order by the time we land."

Jesse's assessment was spot on. By the time they landed in Florida, he was sore and hurting although he tried to hide his pain from Piper. At least she'd been able to rest while they were in the air. He couldn't get comfortable. The only thing that made the hours tolerable was holding Piper while she slept. He could so get used to that.

After the team loaded their gear into two SUVs Zane had rented for them, they drove to the isolated house with a large private beach front. The eight-bedroom yellow structure came complete with an elevator and a double kitchen.

"Do any of you clowns cook?" Liam eyed each member of the Texas team.

One by one, they shook their heads.

"I'm excellent at take-out," Logan said.

"Me, too." Sawyer smiled. "I also excel at shopping in the frozen food aisle in the grocery store. I make a mean frozen pizza."

"Lucky for you I can cook." Piper glanced around. "Find paper and a pen and I'll make a list. We'll test Sawyer's grocery shopping ability."

"I'm up for the task, sweet thing."

Liam narrowed his eyes. "You have a death wish, don't you?"

Laughter filled the sparkling, cheerful kitchen.

For the first week of his stay, Liam spent much of his time sleeping and eating the amazing meals Piper prepared.

At the beginning of the second week, Jesse cleared him to walk on the beach with Piper. Three or four times a day, they walked the flat portion of the beach with a couple operatives trailing in their wake, far enough to give them privacy but close enough to help if needed.

At the ten-day mark, Liam cornered Brody. "It's time to set the trap for Spencer. I'm more mobile and stronger. I can't take him on one-on-one but with you and your unit at my back, I don't have to."

Brody eyed him a moment, then nodded. "All right. Let's get to work."

Over the next two days, Liam and the Texas team planned and plotted, bounced ideas off each other, ragged on each other, and pointed out weaknesses in each option. On the third day, Liam insisted on walking the grounds to find the best places for line of sight and he rehashed the plan with the team until they finally outvoted him on the best option.

Liam shook his head. "I don't like it. Too many things could go wrong. It's too dangerous for Piper."

Piper cupped his jaw. "How can it be? You'll be right there."

"She's right." Brody folded his arms. "Think like a soldier, not a man in love."

Easier said than done. He wanted Piper more than his next breath. Liam couldn't live without her now. They were right, though. This was the best option. He gave a short nod. He still feared for Piper's safety.

However, he'd witnessed more than once over the past few weeks how strong his woman was. Piper could handle a disgruntled Marine just fine.

Right. So why didn't he believe that? Maybe because he knew how quickly an op could turn and go south. Him facing danger was one thing. For Piper to be at risk was something else entirely.

He sighed. "Make the call, Brody. Set the wheels in motion. I'm ready to end this thing with Spencer."

The Texas leader grabbed his cell phone. "Jesse, you're on watch. The rest of us will set up the perimeter."

The operatives scattered to carry out their assigned tasks while Jesse went to the next room to keep watch on the most likely access point to the house.

Piper kissed Liam. "Thank you for trusting me to handle this. I won't let you down."

"I'm the one who's worried about failing you. One misstep, Sunshine, and this will go bad in a heartbeat."

"It won't."

He prayed she was right.

Six hours later, his phone rang. Liam checked the screen and smiled. "How's Otter Creek, Trent?" he asked.

"Quiet. Wanted to give you a heads up. We've been dropping hints about you recuperating from serious injuries at a luxurious beach house in Florida all over town. Blackhawk's been in the woods around Otter Creek, searching for Spencer. He found his campsite. It's empty. According to the chief, the site hasn't been vacated long. I'd say Spencer is moving in your direction. Be ready, Liam.

I'll be ticked off if you come back to town with more holes in you."

"Copy that, sir."

When he ended the call with Trent minutes later, Liam wrapped his arms around Piper, praying he wasn't about to make a fatal mistake.

CHAPTER THIRTY-NINE

"We have movement in Quadrant 6."

Liam wrapped his hand around Piper's. "Confirmation of target?" He spoke in low tones to Brody over the comm system that he, Piper, and the other operatives wore.

"Hold."

"What do we do?" Piper whispered to Liam.

"Exactly what we're doing right now." He trailed the fingers of his free hand down her cheek. "Act as though we have nothing more important on our minds than enjoying a moonlit night, a tropical breeze, and each other's company."

Liam brushed her lips with his, pressure light, senses on high alert. "If this is Spencer, he has to walk in a quarter of a mile before he breaches the inner perimeter. We have time yet. The intruder might not be him."

"You could cover that distance in two minutes or less. Stands to reason Spencer could do the same."

"He could but he won't."

"Why not?"

"He's Marine Recon, like me. He'll expect a trap. If he runs in, he could miss one and end up injured or dead."

Piper frowned. "Do we have traps set up?"

"Yes, ma'am. If we make the trek in too easy, he'll know we set a trap and he'll pull back to wait until he controls the encounter instead of us."

"What if an innocent wandered into the trap?"

"Not likely, Sunshine. We chose the routes with the most cover, ones Spencer will choose. We don't like open spaces. No place to take cover. Most civilians, however, prefer open spaces. We also didn't activate the traps until nightfall."

"We've been watching to make sure a private citizen didn't stumble into the wrong area, Piper," Logan murmured.

Sawyer broke in. "Target confirmed. Spencer just passed the first perimeter. Heading toward the second."

"Copy." Liam pulled Piper to her feet. "You ready?"

She nodded.

"We have your back," Jesse whispered.

"Your friend is swearing a blue streak at the traps we set," Brody whispered. "Guess he doesn't appreciate all our hard work."

Liam grinned, threaded his fingers through Piper's, and led her from the deck to the hard-packed sand. He lingered at various places, pointing out a star or a shell to Piper as he gave his old teammate time to reach and observe them.

"Target approaching second perimeter," Max whispered.

"Copy," Liam responded. Two minutes, maybe less, before Spencer arrived. He exaggerated his limp and slowed his movements to give the appearance of a more limited range of motion. It wasn't far from the truth. He'd do whatever was necessary to protect Piper and deal with the physical aftermath if their plan backfired and he had to take on Spencer one-on-one.

He guided Piper toward the place he'd chosen for this standoff. He still didn't like the risk to her. In order to have the freedom to love her without fear of Spencer stalking them the rest of their lives, he'd deal.

He stopped and tucked Piper against his chest. Turning his back on an approaching enemy went against every ounce of his training but would entice Spencer from hiding. The Marine might suspect a trap, but he wouldn't be able to resist the chance to taunt Liam with his cleverness. Arrogance had always been the man's downfall.

"I love you," he murmured against Piper's ear. "After this is over, we're going home so I can buy you the biggest diamond I can find to warn off all the other men in Otter Creek."

"Remember the bonbons, sugar," Max murmured.

That comment made Piper laugh.

Perfect timing because the skin on the back of Liam's neck prickled.

"Target is 100 feet and closing," Brody said. "Status, Sawyer."

"Green light," came the reply.

Liam kissed Piper's temple. "I'm trusting you with her life," he whispered to the other sniper.

"I've got her."

"Liam," Piper whispered.

"We'll be fine. Follow the plan and remember how much I love you." He nuzzled her cheek, shifting to more fully protect her with his body.

"Fifty feet," Brody said. "Weapon in his hand. He's still on the move, checking for traps."

"Locked on target," Sawyer said.

"Thirty feet."

"I love you, Liam," Piper whispered.

Liam settled his mouth on hers for a quick, intense kiss before he pulled back far enough to look into her eyes.

"Show time," Brody murmured.

Liam cupped her face between his palms and waited for Spencer to make his move. He didn't have to wait long.

"Well, isn't this cozy," a raspy voice drawled. "The traitor and the fair maiden."

Liam stiffened. He slowly removed his hands from Piper's face and turned to his nemesis, careful to keep his body between Spencer and Piper.

"Jerome, what are you doing here?" Piper's voice conveyed the perfect amount of shock. "Do you live around here?"

A harsh laugh escaped as he lumbered a few feet closer. "Aren't you the sweet one? No, honey, I don't live around here. I followed you."

He stared at Spencer. Prison hadn't been kind to him. Yeah, he had bulked up, having nothing but time on his hands. Spencer must have skipped the stretching part of his regimen because his dexterity had suffered. Lack of sunlight had left his skin pasty. On top of that, his hair had thinned. He looked fifty instead of thirty-three.

"His name isn't Jerome, Sunshine. Jared Spencer was in my Marine unit." Liam scanned the man, noting at least two handguns, one in his right hand and one at his waist in a holster. A large knife was strapped to his thigh. Probably more weapons were hidden on his body. Jared had come prepared for a fight.

He should feel flattered at the indication of how dangerous Spencer thought Liam was despite his injuries.

Fury and hatred gleamed in the eyes of the man who had targeted Piper to draw Liam into a trap. To achieve his objective, Jared wouldn't have hesitated to hurt Piper. That was something Liam would never forget. "What are you doing here, Spencer?"

"What? No warm welcome? I just got out of prison, McCoy. A prison you put me in. You're the reason I lost five years of my life."

"Your choice to steal antiquities and profit from selling them to the highest bidder put you in that cell."

A slow nod. "I'll give you that. I did choose to profit from a few black market deals. You should have ignored the transactions. No one was hurt."

"You stole Afghani history. You hurt every citizen of that nation by stealing their heritage."

"They're nothing but a bunch of sand eaters. They don't know anything about heritage or loyalty." Spencer tilted his head. "Kind of like you, McCoy."

"What do you mean by that?"

"You forgot the Corp's heritage and loyalty. We watch each other's backs. We protect our brothers in arms. But what did you do? Stab me in the back and sell me out. You cost me everything, man. My job, my career, my freedom, and my woman." His gaze drilled into Liam. "I'll take all of that from you."

Liam's blood ran cold at the implication of Spencer's words.

Piper gasped. "You're crazy."

"Better hope I'm not, sweet Piper, or the rest of your life will be unpleasant."

"I don't understand."

"Simple. McCoy owes me. I'm collecting. You're the payment."

Liam's hands fisted. "You'll have to go through me to take her."

Spencer gave a harsh laugh. "I saw you walking. A good gust of wind would blow you down. Thought I'd have to be clever and fast to deal with you. You're a disappointment, old buddy. You've gone soft since you left the Corp. One punch and you'll be finished. Taking your woman will be a cinch."

"I won't go with you." Piper's hand rested on Liam's back as though she knew he was holding himself in control by a thread. "I'll die first."

"If you don't cooperate, I'll shoot your man. He looks like crap. How well do you think he'll recover from yet another wound? Yeah, I heard he was near death's door. I haven't had a chance to shoot a gun in years. I might hit something vital by accident, Piper. You want to chance it?"

"You wouldn't."

"Don't bet his life on that, honey. Either way, you'll be warming my bed instead of his for the rest of your life. Of course, I can't guarantee how long that will be. Depends on how much you please me."

"Hold steady, Liam," Brody murmured.

Hard to do when he wanted to wrap his hands around Spencer's throat and squeeze the life out of him. Still, he understood the game Spencer played. A man out of control reacted with emotion instead of logic. If Liam went into a fight that way, he'd die, plain and simple.

Spencer gestured at Liam with his weapon. "I know you're armed. Drop the weapons on the sand. Do it slow or I'll pull this trigger. Can't guarantee the bullet won't hit your woman, though."

Liam kept his face blank as he divested himself of his weapons. Two handguns, a knife, and two throwing stars. He held his arms away from his body and slowly turned so Spencer would see he was unarmed.

He faced his nemesis again.

"Now, Piper," Sawyer murmured.

Liam felt her small hand sliding the Sig she'd been hiding into his middle-of-the-back holster. "What now, Spencer?"

His expression was one of disgust. "You won't fight me to keep her? I thought you loved Piper."

"I'm crazy about her."

"You have a funny way of showing it, man. You don't deserve a woman as fine as she is. Get on your knees."

Liam stilled. No way. Piper was in the line of fire. Spencer could hit Piper by accident.

"Do it, Liam," Brody ordered through the ear piece. "Trust us."

Spencer's eyebrow rose. "You want to test me?"

"Liam, please," Piper whispered.

"Piper, shift to the right," Sawyer said. "Liam's concerned Spencer will shoot you by accident."

"I'm waiting, McCoy," Spencer snapped. "You have three seconds. After that, I'll shoot you and Piper can take her chances with the bullet."

Liam held up his hand. "All right." He slowly dropped to his knees, his grimace real as the injured muscle in his thigh protested the movement. Jesse had badgered Liam through rehab exercises for the past week to build his mobility for this confrontation. The medic had done an amazing job for the short time they'd had to work.

As Liam lowered himself to the sand, Piper moved to his right.

"Come here, Piper." Spencer's eyes glittered. "Unless you want to watch your man die."

"Don't hurt him."

"Move it, beautiful. I want my hands on you."

"You're doing great, Piper," Logan said softly. "Stick to the plan."

She trudged toward the ex-convict, her body trembling.

Liam gritted his teeth. Spencer would pay for scaring Piper. He shifted his body a fraction to the right to hide the movement of his hand toward the holster.

"You won't get away with this, Jared," Piper said as she neared the other man. "Do you think I'll let you touch me? I despise you. I'll escape the minute your back is turned. I won't give up until I succeed or die trying. By the time I'm gone, you'll wish you had never taken me from the man I love."

"Shut up and get over here." Spencer scowled at her. "Keep pushing me and I might decide you aren't worth the satisfaction of taking you from McCoy. The only thing keeping you alive right now is the knowledge of how much

McCoy will suffer knowing I have what he was too cowardly to fight for."

He grabbed Piper by the wrist and dragged her toward him.

"Now," Brody said.

Piper dropped to her knees. Spencer's weapon lowered a fraction as he shifted his weight to maintain his balance and keep his grip on Piper.

Liam freed his Sig, aimed, and pulled the trigger. The bullet slammed into Spencer's chest.

The man staggered back and sank to his knees, shock on his face. He slowly looked at his chest, then slumped to the sand as Piper scrambled away from him and ran toward Liam.

He stood and caught Piper against his chest. Liam kept his weapon trained on Spencer until Max raced from cover, his own weapon aimed at the man.

The operative stripped weapons from Spencer and tossed them away before checking the downed man's pulse. After a moment, he rose, caught Liam's eye, and shook his head.

Liam returned the Sig to his holster and wrapped his other arm around Piper, making sure she couldn't see Spencer's body. "It's over, Sunshine."

She shuddered. "Will we have to testify against him?"

He froze. Oh, man. He'd killed a man in front of her. Again. Yeah, Liam saved her life and his own. Still, he'd shot a man to death and didn't feel one ounce of remorse. She'd seen his work first-hand for the second time. Would she still want him? "No. Spencer is leaving this beach in a body bag."

"I'm not sorry he's dead but I hate that you had to pull the trigger to protect me."

"I'd do it again if it kept you safe."

She captured his mouth in an intense kiss. When she eased back, Piper smiled. "I hope someone has the cops on speed dial because I'm ready to go home."

CHAPTER FORTY

Piper checked her appearance in the mirror one last time before leaving her bedroom. She expected Liam to arrive any minute for another date.

Since they'd returned to Otter Creek four weeks earlier, Liam had ramped up his romance campaign. It wasn't necessary. She loved him and wanted to spend the rest of her life showing him how much. Piper had met his mother and sister the previous weekend and had bonded with them instantly.

When she protested that he should be recovering, not coming up with a new date idea each night, Liam had insisted that he wanted to cram as many dates in as possible before he was deployed again.

The dates had been fun. Sometimes they stayed in to watch movies. Other times, he drove her to a nearby town for a unique dining experience. One Saturday when the weather had cooperated, Liam drove her to a walking trail in the Smoky Mountains and shared a picnic lunch he'd packed.

She smiled. Liam McCoy, world-class sniper, was a closet romantic. She couldn't wait to see what he came up with for tonight. Although she'd begged him for a hint when he stopped by the shop to eat lunch with her, her stubborn future husband smiled and shook his head.

Her cell phone signaled an incoming call. She glanced at the screen. "How are you, Uncle Gino?"

"Holding my own for the moment. I've set a date for the first management team meeting and sent the information to the people you chose. The details are in your email."

"I'll look at it later tonight."

"How is Liam? Still recovering?"

"He's doing great. His rehab is right on schedule. If you didn't know he'd been injured six weeks ago, you wouldn't be able to tell. Frankly, I'm amazed at his quick recovery."

"Excellent. I'd like to see you both again before he deploys."

Her happiness dimmed. If Liam was sent on a long deployment, Gino could be gone by the time he returned. "I'll talk to him and see what we can work out."

"Good. I better go. I'm having dinner with friends tonight. I'll talk to you tomorrow, my dear."

"Love you, Uncle Gino."

"I love you, too, Piper."

A moment later, the doorbell rang. Piper hurried to the door, checked the peephole, and opened the door. She'd planned to greet him as she always did with a long, sizzling kiss until her gaze dropped to the gorgeous black and white dog sporting a red bandana tied around his neck, sitting beside Liam's foot.

She smiled. "Who is this handsome fur baby?"

"His name is Radar. He's a Texas Heeler."

Piper's brows knitted. "I've never heard of that breed."

"Radar is part Australian Shepherd and part Blue Heeler. Is it all right to bring him inside?"

"Sorry. Of course it is. I was surprised to see you with a dog. Are you dog sitting for a friend?"

Liam closed the door behind himself and Radar. "As of two o'clock this afternoon, he's mine. Well, he's our dog."

Piper sat on the couch and extended her hand to Radar and let him sniff. When he licked her fingers and nudged her hand with his head, she figured he'd decided she was a friend. "Where did you get him?"

"He's a shelter dog. We've talked about getting a dog soon and I saw his picture on the shelter's website. I went to see him after lunch and Radar bonded with me right off the bat. Texas Heelers are known as Velcro dogs. He'll be our shadow and he'll be great company for you when I'm deployed."

Piper rubbed his soft black ears. Man, this was one sweet dog. She glanced up at Liam and caught the worry in his gaze. "He's perfect, Liam. I love that he's a rescue dog."

He loosened his grip on Radar's leash. "I know we were going to search for a pet together, but I just couldn't leave him in that cage."

"I'm glad you didn't." She patted the cushion beside her and Radar leaped to the couch. He laid his head on her thigh and gave a great sigh.

Piper's heart squeezed as she leaned down to cuddle with him. She got a series of licks on the jaw for her effort.

With a laugh, she eased back and noticed something tied to the bandana. "What do you have tied to your scarf, Radar?"

She glanced at Liam and was surprised to see him getting on one knee. "Liam?"

He brought her hand to his lips and kissed the back of it. "I love you, Piper Reece. I never thought I would have you in my life. I know I don't deserve you, but I'll spend every day the rest of my life loving you."

Liam untied the small velvet bag from Radar's bandana. He pulled a diamond engagement ring from the pouch. "Will you marry me, Sunshine?"

Tears trickled down Piper's cheeks. "I would be honored to be your wife, Liam McCoy. I love you."

He slid the ring on her finger and leaned in to kiss her. A moment later, Radar licked both of them and tried to wriggle between them. Liam eased back with a chuckle. "We have to work on your timing, buddy."

His response was an enthusiastic bark.

Piper laughed, joy exploding inside her. "Come on. Let's take our fur baby for a walk. We have a wedding to plan."

Life with Liam McCoy would be an adventure. Love, laughter, a family, and friends. Walking through life with this honorable man was a dream come true.

REBECCA DEEL

RELENTLESS

ABOUT THE AUTHOR

Rebecca Deel is a preacher's kid with a black belt in karate. She teaches business classes at a private four-year college outside of Nashville, Tennessee. She plays the piano at church, writes freelance articles, and runs interference for the family dogs. She's been married to her amazing husband for more than 25 years and is the proud mom of two grown sons. She delivers occasional devotions to the women's group at her church and conducts seminars in personal safety, money management, and writing. Her articles have been published in *ONE Magazine*, *Contact*, and *Co-Laborer*, and she was profiled in the June 2010 Williamson edition of *Nashville__Christian Family* magazine. Rebecca completed her Doctor of Arts degree in Economics and wears her favorite Dallas Cowboys sweatshirt when life turns ugly.

For more information on Rebecca . . .

Sign up for Rebecca's newsletter: http://eepurl.com/_B6w9

Visit Rebecca's website: www.rebeccadeelbooks.com